A NOVEL BY
CAT WINTERS

IN THE SHADOW OF BLACKBIRDS

SCHOLASTIC INC.

PUBLISHER'S NOTE: This is a work of fiction. Names, characters, places,
and incidents are either the product of the author's imagination or are used fictitiously,
and any resemblance to actual persons, living or dead, business establishments, events,
or locales is entirely coincidental.

ISBN 978-0-545-70605-6

12 11 10 9 8 7 6 5 4 3 2 1   14 15 16 17 18 19/0

Printed in the U.S.A.   40

First Scholastic printing, January 2014

Book design by Maria T. Middleton

For Adam, Meggie, and Ethan,
who patiently share me with my characters

A YEAR THE DEVIL DESIGNED

· Portland, Oregon—October 16, 1918 ·

I STEPPED INSIDE THE RAILROAD CAR, AND THREE DOZEN pairs of eyes peered my way. Gauze masks concealed the passengers' mouths and noses. The train smelled of my own mask's cotton, boiling onions, and a whiff of something clammy and sour I took to be fear.

Keep moving, I told myself.

My legs shook and threatened to buckle, but I managed to clomp down the aisle in the brown Boy Scout boots I wore in case I ever needed to run at a moment's notice. The heavy tread drew unwanted glances and at least one raised eyebrow, but nobody uttered a word.

"Good morning," I said to a woman with a puff of black poodle curls crowning her head.

"Morning," the woman grunted into her gauze.

As I had hoped, all eyes soon lost interest in me and drifted back to their own concerns. I was merely a healthy-sounding sixteen-year-old girl in a navy-blue dress. I didn't talk like a foreign spy, and I wasn't sick with the flu. No harm there.

Coal-colored traveling suits paired with fresh cotton masks gave the compartment a surreal black-and-white appearance, blurred slightly by the onion scent snaking in from the dining car. I imagined the cooks dicing up the pungent bulbs in a mad scramble to keep the flu from overtaking the train, their eyes watering, their foreheads dripping with sweat. I blinked away the sting of the air and took the sole empty seat, beside a woman of middle age and stout build, with thick arms and thicker eyebrows. An anti-influenza pouch reeking of medicine dangled from her neck, overpowering even the onions.

"Hello." She rubbed the pouch and looked me over. "I'm Mrs. Peters."

"I'm . . ." I hoisted my black leather bag onto my lap and answered with a shortened version of my name: "Mary." The newspapers rustling around me more than likely carried an article about my father, and I envisioned a mention of me: *Also present at the house during the arrest last night was Mr. Black's daughter, Mary Shelley. The girl seems to have been named after the author of a certain horror novel with an extremely German-sounding title:* Frankenstein.

"Is that a doctor's bag?" asked Mrs. Peters.

"Yes." I squeezed the handles tighter. "It was my mother's."

"Your mother was a doctor?"

"The best one around."

"I'm sorry she's not on this train with us." Mrs. Peters eyeballed the other passengers. "I don't know what will happen if anyone collapses while we're en route. No one will be able to save us."

"If we get sick, we'll probably just get dumped off at the next stop."

She wrinkled her forehead and gasped. "What a highly unpleasant thing to say."

I shifted my knees away from her. "If you don't mind, I'd rather not talk about the flu."

Mrs. Peters gasped again. "How can you not talk about it? We're speaking through gauze masks, for heaven's sake. We're crammed together like helpless—"

"Ma'am, please—stop talking about it. I've got enough other worries."

She scooted an inch away. "I hope you aren't riddled with germs."

"I hope you aren't, either." I leaned back against the wood and tried to get comfortable, despite my surroundings and the nausea that had been haunting me ever since my father's arrest. Images of government officials punching Dad in the gut and calling him a traitor flickered though my head like grotesque scenes on a movie screen.

Steam hissed from all sides of the car. The floor vibrated against my boots. My hands and knees trembled, and my teeth chattered with the frantic intensity of a Morse code distress signal: *tap tap tap TAP TAP TAP tap tap tap.*

To escape, I undid my satchel's metal clasp and pulled out a bundle of letters six inches thick, bound together by a blue hair ribbon with fraying edges. I slid a crisp cream-colored envelope out from the top of the pile, opened the flap, and lost myself in the letter.

June 29, 1918

My Dearest Mary Shelley,

I arrived overseas four days ago. Our letters are censored, so I need to keep this message uneventful. The army will black out any phrases that indicate where I am, which makes me sound like an operative in a Sherlock Holmes novel. For example: I am in ▮▮▮▮▮▮▮▮▮▮ *and soon we'll be going to* ▮▮▮▮▮▮ ▮▮▮*. Mysterious, no?*

I received your letter, and as much as seeing your words on paper sent my heart racing, I hated reading that my package never reached you. It should have arrived at your house nearly two months ago. I blame my brother. But I'll write to my mother and see if she knows when and if it was sent.

I also received your photograph. Thank you so much, Shell. That picture means the world to me. I look at your face all the time and still find it hard to believe that little Mary Shelley Black, my funny childhood friend and devoted letter-writing companion, grew up to be such a beauty. I would give anything to travel back in time to your visit in April and still be with you. If I close my eyes, I can almost taste your lips and feel your long brown hair brushing against my skin. I want so badly to hold you close again.

Sometimes I can't help imagining what would have happened if I hadn't moved away at fourteen. What if my grandfather hadn't died and my parents hadn't rushed us down to live in his house on the island? Would you and I still be as close? Would we have grown more intimate . . . or drifted apart? Whatever the case, I feel robbed of your presence every day of my life.

Never worry about me, Shell. I chose to be here, so anything that happens to me is my own fault. You told me in your letter you wished you could have stopped me from leaving for the war when we were together in April. I was determined to go, and you know better than anyone else I can be as stubborn as you sometimes.

Write soon. Send me a book or two if you can.

I miss you.

Yours with all my love,
Stephen

A sneeze erupted in the seat in front of me.

My eyes flew wide open, and Stephen's letter fell to my lap. All heads whipped toward a skinny redheaded woman, who sneezed again. My lips parted to utter a taboo word—*gesund-heit*—but I quickly clamped them together.

"My wife has allergies!" said the woman's companion, a man with thick, mashed-potato swirls of white hair. He scooted closer to his wife and tightened her mask. "It's not the flu. Stop looking at her that way."

The watchful stares continued.

At that moment, the train jerked into motion, knocking us all off balance. The whistle's cry evaporated into the October mist. I tucked Stephen's letter into my bag and gazed at the brick buildings passing by, followed by bursts of red and amber trees that offered small reminders of what I'd miss most about Portland. Autumn had always been my favorite season, with the smells of burning leaves and mulling spices and the arrival of bright orange pumpkins in my father's grocery store.

Rain soon drummed against the window.

Everything outside turned to gray.

Beside me Mrs. Peters knitted her furry eyebrows at the lady who had sneezed. "We're all going to be dead by the time we get off this train, thanks to that woman."

I nearly replied that if we were dead, we wouldn't be getting off the train, would we? But, again, I clamped my jaw shut—something that had never been easy for me.

Everyone around me sat stone-still with straight backs, stinking of folk remedies. The stench of my neighbor's medicine pouch and someone's garlic-scented gum was strong enough for me to taste through the four-ply barrier of my mask. The wheels of the train *click-clacked, click-clacked, click-clacked* over the lack of conversation.

Was I dreaming? Could it all just be a terrible, terrible nightmare that would end if I pried my eyes open? I dug my nails into my palms with high hopes of stirring myself out of sleep, but pain and half-moon marks emerged. I was wide awake.

Surely, though, I must have stolen into the future and landed in an H. G. Wells–style world—a horrific, fantastical society in which people's faces contained only eyes, millions of healthy young adults and children dropped dead from the flu, boys got transported out of the country to be blown to bits, and the government arrested citizens for speaking the wrong words. Such a place couldn't be real. And it couldn't be the United States of America, "the land of the free and the home of the brave."

But it was.

I was on a train in my own country, in a year the devil designed.

1918.

ᴀᴜɴᴛ ᴇᴠᴀ
ᴀɴᴅ ᴛʜᴇ ꜱᴘɪʀɪᴛꜱ

· *San Diego, California—October 18, 1918* ·

AUNT EVA DIDN'T GREET ME ON THE RAILROAD PLATFORM when I arrived, which meant one of three things: she was running late, she hadn't received my telegram, or she had been stricken by the flu. The third possibility made me shake with both dread and loneliness, so I refused to dwell on it.

I slouched on a hard, uncomfortable bench in San Diego's Santa Fe Depot and stared up at the white plaster arches that spanned the ceiling like rainbows leeched of color. Great wagon wheels that held electric bulbs also loomed above me, so heavy they required a battalion of metal chains to keep them fastened to the arches. Sea air breezed through the open entryway—a mixture of salt and fish smells that made my empty stomach growl. My back ached and my brain longed for sleep after traveling more than a thousand miles. All I could do was sit and wait.

The posters hanging on the blue and gold mosaic walls had changed since my visit six months earlier. Back in April, signs in vivid red, white, and blue had screamed fear-inspiring slogans meant to rally us around the fight against the Germans:

BEAT BACK THE HUN WITH LIBERTY BONDS!
GIVE TILL IT HURTS—THEY GAVE TILL THEY DIED!
ARE YOU 100% AMERICAN? PROVE IT!
DON'T READ AMERICAN HISTORY—MAKE IT!

I remembered Aunt Eva grumbling about "questionable taste" when she steered me past an illustration of a slobbering German gorilla clutching a golden-haired maiden with bare breasts. DESTROY THIS MAD BRUTE. ENLIST. U.S. ARMY! barked that particular poster.

Aside from one navy recruitment notice, the propaganda signs were now gone, replaced by stark white warnings against coughing, sneezing, and spitting in public. The words INFLU-ENZA and EPIDEMIC watched over me from all directions in bold black letters—as if we all needed reminders we were living amid a plague.

A half hour after Aunt Eva was supposed to fetch me, a new train arrived, and it was full of U.S. Army recruits on their way to Camp Kearny, on the northern outskirts of San Diego. After a great deal of fuss and shouted orders, officers in olive-green tunics and flared-hip pants marched through the station, accompanied by a silent herd of young men outfitted in flu masks and Sunday-best clothing. The boys were young—most of them not much older than eighteen, now that the draft age had dropped from twenty-one. Some of them saw me, and their eyes lit up above their gauze, even though I must have looked like a sack of potatoes slumped there on the bench and wearing my ugly mask.

"Hello, dollface," said a burly one with light brown hair.

"Hey there, beautiful," cooed a scrawny one in black trousers too long for his legs. "Got a kiss for a soldier?"

Others whistled until the officers snapped at them and told them to remember they were respectable members of the U.S. Army.

I felt neither flattered nor offended by the boys' attention. Mainly, they reminded me of the way Stephen had looked the last time I saw him, with that strange mixture of bravery and terror in his brown eyes.

Through the windows, I watched the boys proceed to a line of green military trucks that waited, rumbling, alongside the curb. The recruits climbed one by one beneath the vehicles' canvas coverings with the precision of shiny bullets being loaded into a gun. The trucks would cart them off to their training camp, which was no doubt overrun with feverish, shivering flu victims. The boys who didn't fall ill would learn how to kill other young men who were probably arriving at a German train station in their Sunday-best clothing at that very moment.

Don't think like that, I scolded myself. *That's why they took Dad away. You can't afford to think like him.*

I curled up my legs on the bench and leaned my head against my mother's black bag. The depot grew empty and silent around me, save for the high-pitched wail of an ambulance screaming through the city streets.

I let myself doze.

A hazy dream about Dad cooking up a soup that smelled like San Diego tuna canneries flitted through my brain, and then I heard Aunt Eva call my name. I opened my eyes and saw a short youngish man in gray work clothes tromping across the tiles in grease-stained boots. No Aunt Eva. Her voice must have been part of my dream.

My eyes drifted shut, but again someone said, "Mary Shelley."

I propped myself up on my elbows and blinked away my grogginess. The short man approached me with steps that echoed across the empty depot. He wore a familiar pair of bottle-cap glasses above his flu mask. Short blond hair peeked out from beneath his cap.

I jumped to my feet. "Aunt Eva?"

"I'm sorry I'm so late. They wouldn't let me leave as early as I hoped." She stopped a few feet away from me and wiped her grubby hands on her trousers. "I'm not going to hug you, because I'm filthy. Plus you've been crammed together with all those people on the train. As soon as we get you home, we'll put you in a boiling bath to scrub any flu germs off you."

"What are you doing dressed like that?"

"What? Didn't I tell you I've been working in the shipyard since Wilfred died?"

"No. You didn't say a word about that in your letters. Holy smoke!" I burst out laughing. "Dainty Aunt Eva is building battleships."

"Don't laugh—it's good work. Clears your mind of troubles. The men all left for the war, so they rounded up us women to take over." She hoisted my iron-bottomed trunk with such ease that there must have been some mighty biceps inside those bony arms of hers. "I hope you're feeling fit enough to walk to my house. I'm avoiding the germy air on public transportation."

"Don't you breathe germy factory air?"

"I mainly work outside. Now come along. Pick up your other bag so we can leave this place and get home."

I grabbed my black bag of treasures. "I like your hair."

She growled through her gauze. "Don't mention the hair. I cut it short only because the other girls said it's easier for working. I haven't had a single man give me a second glance since I chopped it off." She walked ahead of me, lugging my trunk with her new brute strength.

I didn't have the heart to tell her the lack of male attention probably had more to do with her greasy boots and sweat stink than the short hair. I plodded after her in my own boots, knowing we made quite a pair—two young women, only ten years apart in age, whose femininity had become yet another casualty of war.

Hardly a soul lingered on the streets outside the station now that the recruits were gone, just a gray-haired man in a pinstripe suit shoving his luggage into the enclosed passenger section of a black taxi. The driver smoked a cigarette through a hole poked in his gauze mask, and wafts of the smoke intermingled with the sea salt and cannery odors in the breeze. Overhead, the spotless sky beamed in an innocent baby blue.

Aunt Eva led me northward. "They've closed down the city to try to keep the flu from spreading. They quarantined the soldiers sooner than the rest of us, but now it's the churches, theaters, moving-picture houses, bathhouses, and dance halls—all closed."

"Schools?" I asked with hope in my heart.

"Closed."

My shoulders fell. "Dad told me the flu wouldn't be as bad in San Diego because of the warmer weather. That's one of the reasons he wanted me here if anything happened to him."

"It's become catastrophic down here, too, I'm afraid. I'm sorry." She glanced my way. "I suppose it'll be boring for you, but it's better than being dead. Make sure you wear your mask at all times. They're strict here about keeping them on."

"I wonder if surgical gauze is really doing anything besides making us look like monsters from another planet. My science teacher, Mr. Wright, wore a mask, and he's just as dead as the people who didn't."

She didn't respond, so I trudged beside her with the words about my dead teacher echoing in my brain. Our boots marched in unison. We traded the trunk and the doctor's bag every two corners and broke the silence of the streets by huffing from the strain of my belongings. My nose and chin sweated beneath my mask. It was entirely too hot for October.

A few blocks north, we turned right on Beech Street. A horse *clip-clopped* behind us, and I smelled something so rotten I gagged.

"Don't look, Mary Shelley." Aunt Eva pulled a handkerchief out of a trouser pocket and pressed it over her mask. "Keep your eyes to the ground."

But, of course, Aunt Eva's words made me want to look at whatever horror she was trying to conceal. I peeked over my shoulder and saw a horse-drawn cart driven by a gaunt dark-skinned man who stared at the road with empty eyes. His sun-bleached wagon rattled closer, and in the back of the cart lay a pile of bodies covered in sheets. Five pairs of feet—a deep purplish black—dangled over the edge.

"I said don't look!" Aunt Eva thrust her handkerchief my way. "Breathe into this."

Instead, I pulled down my mask, bent over the gutter, and threw up the small snack I had eaten on the train.

Aunt Eva dropped the trunk. "Put your mask back on—quick."

"I need fresh air."

"There is no fresh air with this flu. Put your mask on *now*."

I yanked the gauze back over my nose and inhaled my own hot, sour breath.

We were quieter after the cart rolled by. We still switched turns carrying my trunk once my nausea passed, but our labored panting softened out of respect for the dead. In the distance, another ambulance shrieked.

Crepes in black, gray, and white marked flu fatalities on several front doors, just the way they did back home: a black piece of fabric for an adult, gray for an elderly person, and white for a child. The Brandywine twins down the street from my house in Portland had died three months shy of their eighteenth birthday, so their mother—unsure whether to call her girls children or grown-ups—had braided black and white crepes together. As we turned left and entered Aunt Eva's block of modest-sized clapboard homes, I worried about whether my aunt would one day need to hang a piece of cloth representing me on her front door. My stomach got queasy again.

"Somehow, we've managed to avoid the flu on this block." Aunt Eva navigated my trunk along her cement front path. "I don't know how, but I hope to God we stay immune."

She led me up the porch steps of her two-story Victorian, an oversized doll's house with scalloped yellow siding and wooden fixtures shaped like lace doilies above our heads. A tan card in the front window declared the household MEMBERS

OF THE UNITED STATES FOOD ADMINISTRATION and included the organization's official insignia—a red, white, and blue shield surrounded by heads of wheat. The pledge card ensured Aunt Eva would forgo meat, wheat, and sugar on the days the government requested, to save food for our soldiers and the starving in Europe. It also proved to her neighbors she wasn't a spy, a traitor, or a dangerous immigrant and should be left well enough alone.

I wondered what my life would have been like if my father had just gone along with Americanisms like that blasted pledge card and let the war progress around us.

Aunt Eva unlocked her door and led me inside the narrow front hall, which, once I tugged my mask down to my throat, smelled as pungent with onions as the train. A Swiss cuckoo clock announced the four o'clock hour from somewhere in the depths of her kitchen, in the back.

From around the corner, a childish voice murmured, "Who's there?"

Startled, I dropped my bag. "Who said that?"

"That's just Oberon." Aunt Eva plunked my suitcase onto the hall's scuffed floorboards. "He's a rescued yellow-billed magpie that belongs to my neighbor, a bachelor veterinarian off at the war. I'm taking care of the bird while he's gone."

I stepped inside her lavender living room, to the left, and encountered a beautiful black-and-white bird with tapered tail feathers twice as long as his body. He stood on a perch in a tall domed cage.

The bird lowered his dark head and studied me through the bronze wires. "Who's there?"

I smiled. "I'm Mary Shelley—your adopted cousin, I suppose. What else can you say?"

"He says his name and *Hello*, and he likes to whistle and squeak," Aunt Eva answered as she removed her work coat. "You can get to know him better later, but right now you should take your bath. Use water as hot as you can stand, so we can boil the germs off you. And wash your mask while you're at it."

"All right. He's a gorgeous bird. I love those white patches on his wings and belly." I went back out to the hall, picked up my trunk and black doctor's bag, and was just about to head upstairs when I caught sight of my own face staring at me from a pale purple wall across the living room.

The image was a photograph of me, taken in Stephen's older brother Julius's Spiritualism studio during my April visit to San Diego. I lowered my luggage back to the ground and crossed the room for a closer look.

"Mary Shelley?" asked my aunt from behind me.

My blue irises—almost hauntingly absent in the black-and-white photograph—stared back at me in a defiant gaze. I had been so skeptical about genuine spirits showing up in the developed photo and had done my best to look marvelously stubborn. A pair of silver-painted aviatrix goggles hung around my neck, even though Julius and Aunt Eva had wanted them off me, and I wore a breezy white blouse with a collar that dipped into a V.

Julius's words from the moment before he captured the image crept into my ears: *Stay still. Smile. And summon the dead.*

Beside me in the developed photograph knelt a hulking, transparent figure draped in a pale cloak that concealed every inch of its head and body. The creature clung to my chair and leaned its forehead against the armrest, as if it were either in immense pain or bowing to me in worship.

"What do you think of your photograph?" The floorboards behind me creaked from Aunt Eva's work boots. "We told you something amazing would emerge if you posed for him."

A shiver snaked down my spine. Instead of responding, I read the text below the photograph aloud: "'Miss Mary Shelley Black and an admiring spirit. Beauty resides within the sacred studio of Mr. Julius Embers, Spiritualist Photographer.'" I spun around to face my aunt. "Julius used me as an advertisement?"

"That advertisement has led a great deal of grieving individuals to solace in his studio. You look absolutely beautiful in that photograph. Look at the way he almost captured the chestnut hue of your hair."

"Who cares how I look? I'm sitting next to a fake spirit! That's probably a transposed image of Julius covered in a white sheet."

"That's not a fake, Mary Shelley. Julius thinks your visitor may be proof that you possess clairvoyance. I told him you always seem to be channeling your mother's scientific spirit."

"Channeling her spirit?" I said with a snort. "Are you out

of your head? My mother's love of science is probably in my blood, just like she gave me blue eyes and the shape of her mouth. Sir Francis Galton wrote papers on that very subject."

She heaved a sigh. "Did Sir Francis Gallon—"

"*Galton.*"

"Whatever his name is, did he write about sixteen-year-old girls—*sixteen-year-old girls!*—who invent improved versions of doorbells for their science fair projects?"

"He wrote about intelligence being inherited, and that's probably what happened with me. Why can't a girl be smart without it being explained away as a rare supernatural phenomenon?"

"I'm not saying you can't be smart. In fact, a scientific mind like yours should want to explore the communication between spirits and mortals. It's no different than the mystery behind telephone wires and electrical currents."

I turned back to the photograph and scrutinized the "ghost" through narrowed eyes.

Aunt Eva crept closer. "Julius Embers is a good man. He specializes in the spirits of fallen soldiers now. See?" She pointed to a neighboring picture frame that held an article from the *San Diego Evening Tribune.*

The article, dated September 22, included three photographs of dark-clothed people, probably parents and wives, behind whom posed transparent young men in U.S. Army uniforms. Ghostly hands rested on the peoples' shoulders. The supposed spirit faces disappeared into blurry mists.

"Do you still visit Julius?" I asked.

"I didn't at first." A chill iced her voice. "I was too humiliated after what happened between you and Stephen that day."

I flinched.

"But then Wilfred died," she continued before I could say a word. "Julius's photography helped me with my grief." She nodded toward a small photograph of herself and a hazy man with a slim build, who could have been my uncle if you looked at the image cross-eyed. "I felt guilty for not loving Wilfred enough when he suffered so deeply from his illness." She straightened the photograph with her thumb. "But Julius and his mother always welcomed me into their home with warm smiles. He's photographed Wilfred and me a few times now."

"For a large fee, of course," I muttered.

"Stop criticizing Julius. Here—look closely at the last paragraph in this *Tribune* article." She tapped the glass framing the story with a fingernail caked in shipyard grime. "There's a local photography expert, a man named Aloysius Darning, who exposes fake Spiritualist photographers across the country. He sent two men to jail up in Los Angeles, but he can't find a single trace of fraud in Julius's work. He attends my church, when it's not shut down for the quarantine, and I've heard him discuss Julius's spirits."

I leaned toward the article and silently read the line about the fraud catcher:

Mr. Aloysius P. Darning, renowned for his ability to catch crooks in the act of falsifying spirit images, still cannot find one shred of proof that Mr. Embers is a fraud—much to Mr. Darning's chagrin.

"It's still impossible to believe." I shook my head. "Stephen told me this is all the work of a drug addict and a cheat."

"Julius isn't an addict."

"Stephen mentioned opium."

"Maybe Stephen was the one who was lying. Did you ever think of that?" She plopped onto her sofa's flowery cushions and untied her boots, which unleashed the foul odor of her feet. "Stephen was always jealous of his brother's success."

My stomach lurched. "What do you mean *was?*"

"I mean . . . Stephen's battalion headed to France over the summer."

"I know. We still write to each other."

Her face blanched. "Oh, Mary Shelley." She uncrossed her legs. "You shouldn't be in contact with him. Does your father know?"

"He's seen me receive Stephen's letters."

"No," she said, "does he know what happened between the two of you when you were last down here?"

"He doesn't know the made-up version you heard from Julius."

"Why would Julius lie about what he saw?"

"I told you back in April, he and Stephen were having a fight."

She pulled off her right boot without looking me in the eye.

I sank into the rocking chair across from her. "What has Julius said about Stephen's whereabouts? Has their mother received any letters?"

"Only one since Stephen arrived overseas."

"When was that?"

"June or July, I think."

"My last letter from him was dated June twenty-ninth, right after he made it to France. Then he stopped writing." I clutched my stomach. "Why hasn't he written anyone since then? Does his family think he's all right?"

She yanked off her other boot with a grunt. "As far as I know."

"Why hasn't his brother gone to war?"

"The draft board turned Julius down. He suffers from flat feet."

"Oh, poor Julius." I rolled my eyes. "I'm sure he's suffering deeply because of those feet."

"I was sincerely hoping you would have calmed down about Julius Embers during these past six months. He invited you over for another free photograph tomorrow. And he has something for you from Stephen."

"The package?"

"You know about it?"

"Stephen kept saying he asked his mother to send me a

parcel right before he left, but it never arrived. Why didn't she ever mail it?"

Aunt Eva avoided my question by rubbing the sole of her foot. I could see a gaping hole in her black stocking. Oberon let out an angry squawk, no doubt to break the tension gripping the room.

"Why didn't she mail it, Aunt Eva?"

My aunt's face flushed pink. "Mrs. Embers probably felt the relationship wouldn't be good for either of you. You were both too young and too unmarried for that sort of intimacy, Mary Shelley. You should have never gone into that room alone with Stephen."

"We didn't—"

"It took me two months before I could show my face to the family, and it's only because Mrs. Embers reached out to me after she read Wilfred's obituary."

I shot out of the rocking chair with the intention of grabbing my belongings and escaping upstairs.

"Mary Shelley—"

"My dad never even let me near Stephen's brother when I was growing up." I picked up my bags. "But you act like Julius is a saint. He told a terrible tale about his brother and me, but you worship him."

"Stop. Please stop." She kept on massaging her smelly old foot. "I know you're upset about Stephen and your father, and I know I'm only ten years older than you—"

"I just want you to understand that what happened that

day was a thousand times more innocent than what Julius told you. Will you please start believing your own flesh and blood instead of this *friend* who's striking it rich off war deaths?"

She lowered her head.

"Please, Aunt Eva."

"Julius has been so good to me," she said. "You don't understand how hard it is to be alone when the world's unraveling around you."

"Yes, I do. I understand completely."

She met my eyes, and her expression softened. She dropped her foot and exhaled a sigh that told me she was dead tired of everything, including our conversation.

I took a calming breath. "Despite this problem with Julius, I am extremely grateful you and I can be together right now. And I appreciate you letting me live here without once mentioning the danger Dad has posed to the family members still up in Oregon."

She jutted her chin into the air with typical Aunt Eva pride. "Thank you. I've been worried about my brothers ever since we saw those people beat on that German man during your last trip. A Swiss German surname like Boschert doesn't sit well with some people these days."

"I know. The inability to see the truth about a person is a terrible thing."

She returned to fussing over her foot, choosing to ignore the fact that I was still talking about Julius. "Go change out of those clothes, Mary Shelley," she said without any fight left in her, which made me feel guilty. "I'll start running your bathwater. Look on the bedside table while you're up there. I've left you something that belonged to Wilfred."

"Thank you." I cleared my throat. "I'll go look for it." I climbed the stairs with my traveling trunk thumping against the wood.

The gift she had left for me in my room was Uncle Wilfred's weighted brass nautical compass, inherited from his seafaring grandfather and mounted in a mahogany case the size of a large jewelry box. A gorgeous device.

While my bathwater roared through the downstairs pipes, I wandered around my new room with the compass, checking to see whether the walls behind the gilded paper contained any metal strong enough to move the needle. And for a short while, the lure of scientific discovery blotted out the sea of masked faces on the train ride south, the purplish-black feet rattling in the back of that cart, my father getting punched in the gut in front of my eyes, and the first boy I'd ever loved fighting for his life in a trench in France.

3

MR. MUSE

I TWISTED AND TURNED, TRYING TO GET COMFORTABLE IN my new bed. The mattress springs whined with every restless movement I made. Ambulance sirens screamed in the distance. I couldn't sleep. I ached to see and touch Stephen again. The briny air I'd smelled all afternoon reminded me that we were last together only a few miles from Aunt Eva's house—before the flu, before my father's arrest, when Stephen still lived in his home across the bay.

I reached down to the black doctor's bag on the floor and fetched Stephen's second-to-last letter, dated May 30, 1918. The picture he had included fell out of the envelope—a portrait taken at a studio where all the Camp Kearny recruits had gone to get photographed in their army uniforms. He wore a tight-fitting tunic that buttoned up to his throat, narrow trousers that disappeared inside knee-high boots, and a ranger-style Montana peak hat that hid his short brown hair. I could tell from the stiff way he held his jaw that he was attempting to look serious and bold for the picture, but mainly he resembled a Boy Scout ready for camp.

His lovely handwriting on the letter shone in my oil lamp's steady light.

Dear Mary Shelley,

They're shipping us overseas soon, even though I've barely been in training. We're needed in Europe something desperate, I guess. I'll be on a train to the East Coast in the coming weeks and then boarding a ship to cross the Atlantic.

I've been wondering why you haven't responded to the package I prepared for you the morning I left. At first I worried that I somehow offended you with the gift . . . or that I offended you by kissing you. But if you were offended, you would have told me so directly, wouldn't you? You have never been shy or evasive. So I choose to believe the package never reached you.

If you aren't mad at me, I would love to hear how you are doing and to receive a recent picture of you. I'm including an Army Post Office address where you can write to me at any point, even when I'm overseas. The only photographs I have of you are from your days of mammoth hair bows—those giant loops of ribbon that looked like they would start flapping and fly off the top of your head. I'm trying so hard to remember the grown-up version of you, with your bewitching smile and those haunting blue eyes that seemed to understand exactly what I was feeling.

If you would rather not attach yourself to someone heading off to war, I understand. After your aunt hurried you out of my house that day, after Julius told his vicious version of what happened, my mother yelled at me and called me cruel. She reminded me you have your whole life ahead of you and said the last thing an intelligent girl like you needs is to ruin her life for a boy heading off to war.

You don't need to wait for me, Shell. I'm aware you need to live your life without worrying about me. If you do want to write, however, if you do think of me, I would love to receive your letters. I miss you so much.

Yours affectionately,
Stephen

P.S. I wish I had those goggles of yours that supposedly let you see the future. I could really use them right now.

I smiled at his last line and leaned over to my black bag again. Down in the cloth-lined depths of one of the side compartments were the coarse leather straps of my aviatrix goggles—a gift from Aunt Eva, purchased to blot out the memory of the crowd beating on the German man at the Liberty Loan drive during my last visit. We had come across the chaos just as the police were dragging the victim away in handcuffs, his right eye swelling, his nose and mouth a mess of bright red blood. Men with angry blue veins bulging from their foreheads had shouted words like *Kraut bastard* and *goddamned Hun*, even with ladies and children present.

I shoved aside the memory of the violence, fastened the goggles over my face, and lay back against the cool sheets to stare through the bug-eyed lenses at the empty white ceiling. Stephen's letter rested against my stomach—an invisible weight, but there just the same. My mind opened to the possibility that the goggle salesman's promises of enchantment had been true, as preposterous as the idea was. I would see the fate of the world through the glass lenses.

Yet the future refused to emerge.

Only the past.

I saw myself getting off the train on April 26 to celebrate my sixteenth birthday in Stephen's new city . . . and to distract Aunt Eva from life with a husband wasting away in a home for tuberculosis patients. She and Uncle Wilfred had moved to San Diego for the healthier air, and I jumped at the opportunity to visit her—and perhaps see my old friend again. Faces didn't yet hide behind gauze masks. Soldiers and sailors arriving for training smiled up at the Southern California sunshine and smacked one another on the back as if they were on vacation, and the air rang out with laughter and war talk and the boisterous melody of a brass band playing "Over There."

Aunt Eva had met me on the train platform in a lacy white dress that fell halfway between her knees and ankles. Her hair, still long enough to reach her waist, was pinned to the back of her head in shimmering blond loops of girly curls.

As soon as we had escaped the bustle of recruits and music in the depot, I asked her, "Have you seen my friend Stephen Embers's family since you moved here?"

"Actually, yes." Her leg bumped into my swinging suitcase, which she did not offer to carry. "Julius now runs the family photography studio. He's a spirit photographer—he captures images of the dead who've returned to visit loved ones."

"I know." I squinted into the burning sunlight. "Stephen mentioned that in one of his letters. He didn't sound pleased about his brother's work. And I've only received one letter from him since their father passed away in January. I'm really worried about Stephen."

"I've posed for Julius."

"You have?"

"A couple of times." The sun glinted off her round spectacles, but I could see a funny little gleam dancing in her hazel eyes. "I recognized his name in the newspaper when he presented an exhibit of his work in February, and I was absolutely flabbergasted when I saw his photos. He's trying to summon your mother and Grandma Ernestine for me."

I stopped in my tracks. "My mother and Grandma Ernestine have shown up . . . in spirit photographs?"

"I think so." She glanced at me out of the corner of her eye. "On three separate occasions, Julius captured the images of two glowing figures hovering behind me, but their faces haven't yet fully materialized for us. I told him you're very much like your mother. I explained she named you after Mary Shelley because of her love of electricity and science, and he thinks you may be able to lure her into making a full spirit manifestation."

"What? No!" I slammed my suitcase to the ground. "Dad would hate it if I posed for Julius Embers. Julius always got caught drinking and smoking at school and wound up in all sorts of fights and trouble."

Aunt Eva sniffed. "He's straightened his ways. He's quite the gentleman now—so tall and handsome, with his dashing black hair. Barely twenty-two years old and already a gifted Spiritualist photographer."

I gaped at her. "You sound like you're in love with him."

"Don't say that, Mary Shelley. I'm a married woman with a deathly ill husband. I simply admire the man's work."

"You're blushing."

"Stop it." She swatted my shoulder with her white-gloved hand. "I scheduled a sitting for you at Julius's in-home studio in two days, and if you behave yourself, I'm sure you could see his brother directly afterward."

I rubbed my shoulder and felt an uncomfortable twinge course through my stomach at the thought of posing for wild Julius Embers in close quarters.

However . . . I possessed a ticket to Stephen's house— a ticket to Stephen himself—which was exactly what I had wanted when I stepped off that train.

Two mornings later, Aunt Eva whisked me across San Diego Bay to the Emberses' home on Coronado Island. In Portland, Stephen's family had lived in a neighborhood exactly like ours, with homes so squished together that if houses could breathe, their sides would knock against one another when they inhaled.

This new residence, though—Stephen's grandparents' summerhouse, which the family had inherited in 1914—was an enormous seaside cottage covered in vast windows and thousands of cocoa-brown shingles. The neighboring house, a towering brick monstrosity, could have been Thornfield Hall from *Jane Eyre*, or any other grand estate that ruled over the English moors. I felt like an insignificant speck of Stephen's former life entering this luxurious new world.

Julius greeted us and made jokes about how tiny and serious I used to look. He took my photograph in his chilly studio in the family's living room, and, afterward, Mrs. Embers—a robust woman with ink-black hair rolled into two thick sausages at the nape of her neck—served my aunt and me tea in a dining room awash in springtime sunlight. Through the open windows we could hear the crashing of waves from the Pacific Ocean. Thirteen different photographs of Coronado beaches dotted the dark paneled walls.

"Where's Stephen?" I asked, unable to take a single bite of Mrs. Embers's lemon cake. The anticipation of finally seeing him again had stolen my appetite.

"I was just wondering the same thing." Mrs. Embers leaned

back with a squeak of her chair and called toward the dining room's entrance. "Stephen? Come down and visit your friend, please. Stephen?"

I strained my ears but heard nothing. Sweat broke out across my neck. *Stephen is avoiding me,* I realized. *He hasn't been writing me since his father's death because he's tired of me.*

Mrs. Embers sighed and went back to stirring her Earl Grey. "He's probably upstairs, packing."

"Packing for what?" I asked.

"Didn't he tell you in one of his letters?"

"Tell me what?"

"He's leaving for the army tomorrow."

It felt as though someone had just socked me in the chest. I clutched the edge of the table.

Aunt Eva grabbed my arm. "Are you all right, Mary Shelley?"

I stared into the depths of my teacup and struggled to catch my breath while Mrs. Embers's sentence replayed over and over in my head.

He's leaving for the army tomorrow.

Back in Portland, one of my classmate's uncles had just lost half his body to a massive shell explosion on a battlefield in France. Only a week earlier, an eighteen-year-old neighbor from back home—Ben Langley—died of pneumonia at his Northern California training camp.

"Mary Shelley?"

I cleared my throat to find my voice. "I didn't know Stephen had enlisted. He won't even turn eighteen until June. What is he doing going over there?"

"About a month ago he started insisting he wanted to get out of this house." Mrs. Embers blotted a drop of tea before it could stain the tablecloth. "He'll be training at Camp Kearny, just up north, but he says he doesn't even want to come back home to visit if he gets a weekend pass. His father's death hit him hard."

"That's very sad to hear," said my aunt. "Hasn't Julius ever helped Stephen through his grief? Perhaps if their father's spirit showed up in a photograph—"

"No, that's never going to happen." Mrs. Embers smiled, but her brown eyes moistened. "My two boys couldn't be any more different from each other. They're like a volcanic eruption whenever they're together."

I couldn't keep my legs still. I had to hunt down Stephen. "May I use your washroom, Mrs. Embers?"

"Certainly. Go past the bottom of the staircase. It'll be the first door on your right before the study."

"Take those silly goggles off your neck first," said Aunt Eva, with a tug at my leather straps.

Mrs. Embers chuckled. "I was wondering about those goggles. It seems like you were always wearing some sort of new contraption whenever I saw you in the old days, Mary Shelley."

"I bought them for her yesterday at the Liberty Loan drive." Aunt Eva shook her head at me. "Some salesman with

ale teeth tried to convince her they'd let her see the
and I think she half believes him."

m hoping they'll be my good-luck charm." I rose with
as much grace as a person defending quasi-magical goggles
could muster. "You know I've always admired aviatrixes."

"But you don't need to wear them all the time." My aunt
sighed. "Boys were giving her the oddest looks when she
walked around Horton Plaza Park with those things over her
eyes. You should have seen their faces."

"I wasn't trying to impress boys at a Liberty Loan drive." I
gripped the back of my chair. "I was desperate to see if there's
anything in my future besides a war. Thank you for the tea,
Mrs. Embers."

"You're welcome, dear."

As I made my way to the heart of the house, I overheard
Aunt Eva explaining my obsession with aviatrixes, electricity,
anatomy, and machinery, as though I were some sort of bizarre species—the rare *Female scientificus, North American*. "I
don't know if you remember, but my older sister, her mother,
was a physician," she said in a voice she probably assumed I
couldn't hear. "Mary Shelley seems to be channeling Amelia's
love of exploration and technology. That girl has always been
passionate and headstrong about everything."

Dark, knotty wood lined every wall, ceiling, and floor in the
Emberses' entry hall—an immense space that reminded me
of the belly of a ship. A brass lantern hung overhead. I almost
expected the floor to roll with the swell of a wave.

The soles of my shoes pattered across the floorboards to the rhythm of a beast of a grandfather clock that rose to the ceiling at the opposite end of the hall. I slowed my pace, placed my goggles over my eyes, and approached the clock with interest. The minute hand ticked its shadowy finger toward the twelve on a face painted to look like the moon, with eyes and a mouth and pockmark craters. The metallic gears spun and clicked deep inside, all those shiny pieces fitting into just the precise positions to make the contraption work. The pendulum swung back and forth, back and forth, hypnotizing with its gleaming brass.

"The boys who gave you odd looks don't appreciate originality."

I jumped backward a foot at the unexpected voice.

Through my lenses, I viewed a stunning boy who looked to be an older version of the Stephen I remembered, with hair a rich brown and deep, dark eyes that watched me with interest. He sat toward the bottom of the staircase, a book in hand, with one of his long legs stretched down to the floor. A black band of mourning encircled his white shirtsleeve. A gray silken tie hung down to his stomach and made him look so grown up, so distinguished, compared to my Portland childhood friend.

I caught my breath. "The Stephen Embers I knew wasn't an eavesdropper."

"Did a man really try to convince you those goggles would let you see the future?" he asked.

"Yes."

"And what do you see?"

"Only a person who lurks in the backs of houses instead of coming to see his long-lost friend."

He grinned and revealed a dimple I'd long forgotten.

I smiled and pulled the goggles down below my chin. "You're not as gentlemanly as you used to be, Stephen. I remember you used to jump to your feet whenever a lady entered the room."

"I'm far too stunned by the fact that you are a lady now." He scanned me down to my toes. "You used to be so small and scrawny."

"And you used to wear short pants that showed off your knobby knees and drooping socks. Plus you always had that scuffed-up old camera satchel hanging off your shoulder."

He laughed. "I still have that satchel."

"Well, I'm glad to hear not everything's changed." I stepped closer to him, my heart beating at twice its normal rate. My skin burned as if with fever. "Why are you hiding back here instead of coming out to see me?"

"Because . . ." His dimple faded. "I got the impression you came to see my brother instead of me."

"That's a silly thing to assume. The only way my aunt would let me come over here was if I sat for a photograph. She's madly in love with your brother's work."

Stephen closed his book—Jules Verne's *The Mysterious Island*. "Julius is a fraud, Shell. He'll scam you out of your money faster than that goggles salesman. Did you let him take your picture?"

"I think he's working on developing it right now."

"Then you're hooked." He glanced over his shoulder, through the balusters of the stair rail, and then returned his attention to me. "Why'd you let him do that? I thought you of all people wouldn't be gullible."

"I didn't say I believed in his photos."

"You shouldn't."

"What makes you so certain he's a fraud?"

He sat up straighter. "My father told me how Julius is creating his ghosts—doctoring the plates, creating double exposures, damaging his brain with too much opium until he convinces himself the mistakes he makes while developing the plates are spirit images."

"Julius is an opium fiend?"

"Are you really that surprised?"

"Well . . ." I had heard tales of artists and depraved gentle-men who frequented dark opium dens, smoking the drug from long pipes until they hallucinated and passed out. But never in my life had I known anyone who tried it. I closed my gaping mouth. "I suppose your brother would enjoy something like that."

Stephen stretched out his other leg. "He also runs a fan over ice blocks in between sittings to cool the air in there. He tries to make everyone feel like phantoms are hovering around the studio."

"Really?"

"Yes, really. I've caught him doing it. And he leaves the windows open all night to capture the chill from the sea. He locks the doors to the studio to keep me from getting in, but I've crawled through the windows and closed the panes to save the equipment. He's contemplating installing bars to keep me out."

A lump of disappointment settled in my stomach, even though I had started off so skeptical about the spirit images. "My poor aunt. She's convinced Julius will find my mother and grandmother for her."

"Tell her the truth. I hate seeing people so desperate for proof of the afterlife they'll sacrifice just about anything to communicate with the dead." Stephen pursed his lips and rubbed his thumb across *The Mysterious Island*'s leather cover. "I hear them crying when they receive their finished photographs. It's heartbreaking. They react to Julius's photos like rummies chasing bottles."

I thought I heard a moan in a floorboard down the hall. My eyes darted toward the sunbeam-hazy front entrance to make sure no one was listening.

Aunt Eva and Mrs. Embers tittered over some shared anecdote in the dining room.

Nothing else stirred.

I turned back to Stephen and asked in a lowered voice, "Why is Julius doing this to people? I didn't think he ever wanted to have anything to do with photography."

"He didn't, but an odd, ghostly image appeared in one of Dad's photographs last Christmas, and Julius showed it around the hangouts of rich tourists. He claimed he was saving Dad's business by finally bringing some solid money to it. Dad hated having his studio turned into a theatrical exhibit. It could be one of the reasons his heart failed."

"I'm so sorry." I wrapped my arm around the slick newel post at the end of the stair rail, so close to Stephen that the citrus and spices of his bay rum aftershave filled my nose. "I know you were close to your dad."

He turned his head so I could see only the side of his face. His eyelashes fluttered like mad, and I could tell he was fighting off tears. "You always told me . . ." His voice cracked with emotion. "You always said you feel like a piece of you is permanently missing."

I bit my lip and nodded. I'd often told him part of me was missing because my mother died the day I was born. "Yes."

"Now I know what that feels like." He cleared his throat and regained control of his breathing. "It's agonizing."

"It'll get better over time. You'll always feel that missing piece, but it will get easier."

His eyes, now bloodshot, traveled back to mine. He took hold of the baluster closest to my hand. "It's really good seeing you again, Shell. I've missed you."

"I've missed you, too." A lump caught in my throat. "You know, you're still the only boy who hasn't ever made fun of my science experiments and machinery obsessions."

"I'm sure that's changed, now that you're looking"—a grin awakened in the corners of his mouth—"older."

I shook my head and felt my cheeks warm. "It's only gotten worse. They still call me names, like Monster Brain and Frankenstein, but now they also make obscene jokes about me and some lecherous old professor who lives near the high school. The girls can be terrible, too."

"I'm sure everyone's just intimidated by you. They're probably afraid of sounding stupid when they talk to you."

"That never stopped you from talking to me."

"What?" His mouth fell open. "Hey!" He chuckled, a new, deep laugh I didn't recognize, and nudged my arm.

I giggled and nudged him back, though what I wanted so badly was to wrap my arms around him and hold him close.

"Stephen?" called his mother from the dining room. "Are you back there? Did you find Mary Shelley?"

"Show me some of your new photographs before we have to go sit with the ladies," I whispered.

"They're going to wonder what's taking you so long."

"I don't care."

"All right." He put *The Mysterious Island* aside on the stairs and stood to his full height, about five inches taller than me but probably six inches shorter than his giant of a brother. I noticed his sturdy arms and lean stomach beneath his white shirt and found my blood burning fiery hot in my veins. I debated placing my goggles back over my eyes in an attempt to conceal my physical reaction to him.

He led me into a back sitting room wallpapered in peacock green. Chairs and a sofa upholstered in a pinkish hue that reminded me of the inside of a seashell formed a circle around the room's center. Vases of dried lavender sweetened the air. Framed photographs—nature scenes, family members, still lifes—formed a patchwork quilt of glossy sepia across the walls.

Stephen headed toward the corner behind the largest armchair, lifted one of the photos off its nail, and brought it to me. It was the image of a monarch butterfly drinking nectar from a rose. Even though the photograph was printed in brown and white, the clarity of the insect's shading made me feel as though I were looking at wings a vivid orange, a flower the softest whisper of yellow.

"This is one of my favorites," he said.

"It's gorgeous. How did you manage to catch a butterfly in a photo? They fly away so quickly."

"My father taught me how to stay extremely still and keep a camera pointed in the right direction. I had to sit in our backyard for an hour before I caught it."

"You're the most patient person I've ever known, Stephen. I wish some of that quality had rubbed off on me."

"You're patient when you work on a project you love."

"Not the way you are." I reached out and touched the frame, a couple of inches below his fingers. "What did you write down here at the bottom?" I squinted at two words in the lower right-hand corner. "*Mr. Muse?*"

"That's a fake title. Julius makes fun of the names I give my pictures, so I turn the real ones into anagrams to keep him from figuring them out."

"I wonder . . . let's see . . . *Mr. Muse* . . ." I examined the words, letting their letters unscramble and fit back together like puzzle pieces in my brain. "Ruse . . . rum . . . sum . . . *Summer*?"

"Cripes." He grinned. "You've gotten faster than when you were little."

"You taught me well."

"I'm going off to war, Shell." His words just flew out there, smacking me in the face like a stinging bucket of ice water.

"I know." I shrank back. "Your mother told me. Why on earth did you enlist when you're so close to finishing school? I thought you were going to college."

His eyes shifted toward the window to his right. "I need to get out of this house. Everyone on this island ends up spoiled or corrupt. There's so much wealth and pampering and selfishness. I'm tired of being part of it."

"Are you running away?"

"I don't know." His fingers inched closer to mine on the frame. "Maybe."

"Be careful over there, Stephen."

He turned his attention to the floor.

"I've grown up looking at my father's Spanish-American War scar," I said. "Remember that pink line running down his left cheek?"

Stephen nodded. "I remember."

"He says it gives his face character, but it's always made me terrified of war."

"I'll be fine." He looked directly into my eyes with an expression that made me think he wasn't necessarily sure he would be all right. He held my gaze, and I almost felt he was about to lean forward and kiss me, even though we had never once kissed when we were younger. We stood close enough that I could smell spearmint on his breath, even over the aftershave.

I slid my fingers up the frame until I touched his hand. "Please stay safe. It's not everyone who has the patience to photograph a butterfly."

He gave me a smile that seemed both grateful and sad.

I swallowed, and he continued to search my eyes with his own, as if he were trying to say something he couldn't articulate with words. The space between us shrank. Our breathing accelerated until it became the only sound in the house. My heart pounded like I was about to leap off a cliff a hundred feet high.

Before I could say anything awkward to break the spell, he pulled my face toward his and kissed me. I lost my balance at first, but then I closed my eyes and held his smooth neck and enjoyed the warmth and hunger of his mouth. His hand moved to the small of my back and brought me closer. Our stomachs touched. Our chests pinned the photograph between us. He wrapped his arms around me and held me tight against him, as though he were kissing life itself good-bye.

A deafening *bong* rang out in the hallway. Our lips parted, and the grandfather clock chimed eleven times. Neither of us said a word—we simply panted and remained together, entangled, tipsy, our mouths hovering a few teasing inches apart. His hairline above his neck felt both soft and bristly against my fingertips, which intrigued me.

The clock fell silent.

"Stephen?" called his mother.

A palpable sense of urgency passed between us. Stephen took my hand, hurried me across the sitting room, and closed the door, sealing us inside. He kissed me again and knocked us both off balance until I found myself bumping against one of the peacock-green walls.

His mouth left mine and kissed its way down to my neck. "Your goggles are in the way," he whispered.

I snickered and struggled to yank the lenses over my chin, but they wouldn't budge. He helped me pull the straps to the top of my head and then dove back to my awaiting throat, where his lips sent delicious chills spilling down to the tips of my toes. I closed my eyes again and sighed in a way I never had before, losing myself in his dizzying scent, the pressure of his hands around my hips, the pulse-quickening intimacy of his mouth against my bare skin.

The door opened.

"Jesus, Stephen. Control yourself."

Stephen and I both jumped.

The spell shattered.

Julius clutched the brass doorknob with his paw of a hand and smirked at our entwined bodies and flushed faces. His hair was darker and wavier than Stephen's, his features more rugged. His six-and-a-half-foot form filled the doorway. "Is that what you used to do to her back when you were little kids? Back when I thought you'd grow up to be a fruit?"

"Leave us alone." Stephen drew me closer. "Give us five more minutes."

Julius snorted. "You think I'm going to close this door and let you ruin Eva Ottinger's niece when she's sitting right out there in the other room? Have you ever met Eva Ottinger?"

"For Christ's sake, Julius, I haven't seen Mary Shelley in four years. We might not ever see each other again. Give us five more minutes."

Julius pondered the request while running his tongue along the inside of his cheek. He cocked his head and parted his lips, and for a moment I thought he was about to give us one small, precious gift of time.

Instead, he pushed the door farther open with the tips of his fingers. "Mary Shelley, the ladies are waiting for you."

My heart sank.

Julius waved for me to leave. "Let her go, Stephen."

"You're an ass, Julius," said Stephen. "I'll never forgive you for this."

"Let her go. Don't tease the poor girl before you run clear across the world."

Stephen swallowed loud enough to hear. He cupped my cheek and studied my face as though he were creating a photograph of me in his mind. I followed his lead and memorized every single one of his features—his dark eyes and brows, the soft shade of his lips, the faded freckles on his cheeks from summer days when he forgot to wear his cap—sick with fear that he was right: this would be the last time I'd ever see him.

He gave me one last kiss. A small, tender one fit to be seen by a brother. "Keep *Mr. Muse*, Shell."

"Keep it?" I felt the picture frame dangling from my fingers against his back. "No—I couldn't."

"It's just going to disappear off the wall. Julius has destroyed my work before."

"Why?"

"Who knows?"

I glanced at Julius and saw his jaw tense. "But he's your brother."

"Half brother," Stephen reminded me. "Only half. We had different fathers."

"But still—"

"His father was a drunk who treated my mother terribly before she left him. And violent, thieving drunks often breed violent, thieving children."

Julius tugged Stephen away from me, straight out of my arms, and hurled him against the sharp wooden ridge running across the top of the sofa. The impact knocked the sofa askew, and Stephen landed on the floor with an awful thud.

"Why did you say that to her?" asked Julius with genuine hurt in his voice.

"Obviously, I'm not lying," Stephen said from the ground. "You just proved my point."

"Mary Shelley, go back out to the ladies."

I didn't budge.

Julius's eyes pierced me. "I said go back."

"What are you going to do to him?"

"Now!" Julius stormed toward me with enough anger and humiliation in his eyes to send me scrambling out of the room. I ran away, foolish coward that I was. I ran away and left Stephen on the floor, twisted in pain.

The door shut. Something slammed against the wall in there—once, twice. I could hear all those picture frames rattling from the force.

Silence followed.

The door opened, and Julius exited, alone.

Sincerely Yours
Will Thomas

THE MYSTERIOUS ISLAND

· *October 19, 1918* ·

FOOTSTEPS WOKE ME AT SUNRISE.

I blinked my eyes and tried to reorient myself in the foreign landscape of my new bedroom, but the lingering shadows of night crouched in the corners and crept across the unfamiliar furniture. My traveling trunk and Boy Scout boots huddled together in a disheveled heap next to a pine wardrobe.

It was October, no longer spring. I now lived in Aunt Eva's house as a refugee in the middle of a pandemic. Stephen was long gone.

My aunt couldn't afford electricity, so her face and flu mask glowed in the flickering light of a candle next to my bed. "Why are you wearing your goggles?" she asked.

I pulled off the straps and felt indentations from where the rubber had pressed against my skin. "I must have fallen asleep with them on."

"Are you feeling all right?"

"Yes, why?" I lifted my head. "Do I look sick?"

"No. I just worried all night you'd wake up with the flu from the train."

"I feel fine." I rubbed my dry eyes.

"We need to leave for Julius's studio in two hours. Get dressed soon so we can eat breakfast. We also need to make sacks of camphor balls to wear around our necks so the stink can fight off germs on the ferry."

On that repulsive-sounding note, she left the room.

I curled beneath my covers and watched the sun rise behind the lace curtains of my new window. Portland felt impossibly far away. I wondered when my father would go to trial. After the authorities had locked his wrists in handcuffs and punched him in the gut, I grabbed my bags, headed out the back door, and ran to telegraph Aunt Eva from the Portland Union Depot, as Dad had instructed me to do. I spent the night on a bench at the station until the morning train took me away. No one came looking for Mr. Robert Black's sixteen-year-old daughter. There were too many other concerns in the world for anyone to bother with an accused traitor's grown child.

I shut my eyes and pushed back the memory, finding breathing painful.

My thoughts turned to Aunt Eva's troubles and poor, dead Uncle Wilfred. He had died in June in the tuberculosis home, but I wondered if his spirit had found its way back to his own house. Despite my skepticism of Julius's spirit photography, and of ghosts in general, the possibility of life after death never seemed entirely foolish when I lay in bed all alone, my imagination whirring. I actually convinced myself I heard Uncle Wilfred cough in the room next door, which sent me flying out from under my blankets to get dressed.

I lifted the lid of my traveling trunk and grimaced.

"Cripes. What a morbid wardrobe."

My dresses and skirts were either black or a navy blue so dark it was almost black. The lack of German dyes in the country drained every ounce of color from our clothing, ensuring we all looked as grim as the world around us. I pulled out a navy dress with a calf-length hem, a sailor-style collar, and a loose tie the same shade as the rest of the garment. In an attempt to brighten my appearance, I opened the wide mouth of my mother's leather bag, slid my fingers inside the same slippery pocket that had held my goggles, and pulled out a necklace my father had made me from a clockmaker friend's spare brass gear.

Even the gleaming metal looked dull against my drab, dark wool.

"You're not going to see Stephen at his house," I reminded my reflection in the mirror. "You can look dour. Who's going to care?"

I gathered my long hair in a white ribbon at the base of my neck and tucked my gauze mask into the sash around my waist for later. Fumes from Aunt Eva's onion omelets bombarded my nostrils.

"Are you almost ready for breakfast, Mary Shelley?" my aunt called from downstairs.

"Who's there?" squawked Oberon.

"I'm coming," I said.

I looked at another of my treasures nestled inside my mother's black bag—Stephen's butterfly photograph, *Mr. Muse*—before facing the rest of the day.

WE TRAVELED TO CORONADO ON THE SAME FERRY WE'D taken back in April—the *Ramona*—and leaned against the polished rails of the vessel's bow while the cool winds of San Diego Bay whipped through our hair. During the trip in April, the breeze had carried the sharp scent of tar from the slips where the ferries docked, but this time around I could only smell my own onion breath stinking up my mask, as well as the menthol-like pungency of the camphor pouches hanging around our necks. Steam whistled into the clear sky from the ferry's two black smokestacks. Side paddle wheels churned the waters into a salty white spray that flicked against my hands.

"Before our last trip, I always pictured the Emberses living on the Swiss Family Robinson's island," I admitted to Aunt Eva as we cruised toward the populated stretch of land no more than a half mile across the bay. A biplane from the Naval Air Station on North Coronado buzzed into the cloudless sky. "Stephen always wrote about living on an island, so I envisioned him swinging on vines and eating his dinner out of coconut shells. But it's not even an island, is it? It's a peninsula."

"No one calls it that," said Aunt Eva.

"Stephen said there's a narrow road connecting the island to the mainland for people who don't mind driving around the bay."

"I wonder if this is a terrible idea." My aunt picked at the rail with one of her freshly scrubbed fingernails.

"If what is a terrible idea? Sitting for another spirit photograph?"

"No, taking you back over there. Letting you have that package."

"What do you think is going to happen if I get that package? Stephen will magically appear and ravish me right there in his brother's studio?"

"Shh! Mind your mouth, Mary Shelley. Good heavens." Aunt Eva eyed two children eight feet away from us—two little girls with big blue eyes half hidden beneath their flu masks. They stretched their chubby arms over the rails and called out to seagulls circling over the water, "Come here. Come here, silly birds."

My aunt lowered her voice so I could scarcely hear. "You used to be as pure as those little girls."

"Let's not have this conversation again."

"At your age, you shouldn't even know what men and women do behind closed doors." She shook her head with a pained sigh. "You're sixteen years old, for pity's sake. I didn't know about those sorts of things until my wedding night."

"You should have read Gray's *Anatomy*, then."

"Well, there you have it." She held up her hand as if she had just solved the deepest mysteries of the universe. "You read too many books that encourage the loss of innocence."

"I lost my innocence on April sixth, 1917. And it had nothing to do with Gray's *Anatomy*."

"What?"

"The day this country declared war against Germany," I reminded her. "The day spying on neighbors became patriotic and boys turned into rifle targets. That's enough to take the sweetness out of a girl."

"Shh." She furrowed her brow. "Mary Shelley Black! Don't you dare publicly announce such things about the war."

"Don't publicly announce such things about me losing my innocence." I kicked the toe of my boot against the rail and felt the vibration shinny up to my fingers.

Ten minutes later, we arrived at the island that wasn't an island and disembarked.

A double-decker electric streetcar that looked like one railroad car had been squished on top of another transported us down Coronado's main road, Orange Avenue. We clacked down the tracks, past plaster bungalows and traditional clapboard houses that loomed larger than the average American home. Buicks and Cadillacs rumbled by the streetcar, belching clouds of exhaust that smelled of city life and wealth. No signs of poverty existed anywhere on the island, but still, black and white crepes marked the Spanish influenza's lethal path just the same.

For half the journey, a motorized hearse drove by our side, its cargo—a shiny mahogany casket topped with calla lilies—on full display through open scarlet drapes. I ground my teeth and clenched my fists and felt as though Death himself were riding along next to us, taunting us. He was a nasty schoolyard thug, bullying us with a killer flu when we were already worrying about a war, flaunting the fact that we couldn't do a thing about the disease.

Just go, I thought. *Leave us alone.*

I turned my eyes to the passing palm and magnolia trees, and like everyone else on the streetcar, I tried to pretend the hearse wasn't there.

After reaching a stretch of shops and a pharmacy, Aunt Eva and I climbed off the streetcar, walked two blocks southwest, and arrived at the familiar row of houses that ran alongside the beach, separated from the white sands by Ocean Boulevard and a seawall of boulders. Waves crashed against the shore with a roar, echoed by the cry of seagulls combing the sand for food at the water's edge.

"You're going to see a noticeable change in the Emberses' front yard," said Aunt Eva when we neared our destination.

"What?"

"Look."

The brick chimney and brown shingles of the Emberses' home rose into view, as well as a serpentine line of black-clad men, women, and children that wound from the side of the house to the wall of privets along the property's front edge. As on the train from Oregon, I saw only desperate eyes and ugly white patches of gauze where mouths and noses used to be.

I sucked in my breath. "What are all those people doing there?"

"I told you, Julius specializes in photos of fallen servicemen now. People have been traveling across the country to benefit from his work, and the flu has tripled demand." Aunt Eva quickened her pace and led me across the Emberses' front lawn, past the waiting customers.

"There's a line, lady," barked a short woman with squinting eyes.

"I know the family, thank you very much." Aunt Eva adjusted the wide-brimmed hat she wore to conceal her boyish hair and, with an air of pride, bypassed the crowd.

I gulped at all the glares shooting our way over the masks and slouched with embarrassment.

We made our way to a side entrance that led directly into the studio. In April a simple wooden sign bearing the words EMBERS PHOTO STUDIO had greeted us, but now a large oval plaque made of polished brass announced in bold-faced letters:

MR. JULIUS EMBERS
SPIRITUALIST PHOTOGRAPHER

"Excuse me." Aunt Eva hiked up the hem of her dress and climbed past a small group on the cement steps. "I know the family."

A heavyset woman shoved her back to the ground. "Then use the main entrance."

"Mr. Embers told me not to."

"Then you must not know the family well."

The side door opened, and out poked the masked face of a thickset girl no older than eighteen, with a nest of chaotic brown hair pinned to the back of her head. Her white blouse bunched at the waist of her wrinkled gray skirt, and she had the overall appearance of a melting ice-cream cone. "Please make room for the exiting customers," she said in a voice as frazzled as her hair.

A family of four—two malnourished-looking parents and a small boy and girl—filed out of the studio with wreaths of garlic strung around their necks, as if they were warding off vampires instead of the flu. Behind them blared John Philip Sousa's "Stars and Stripes Forever."

"Good afternoon, Gracie." Aunt Eva elbowed her way back up the steps to reach the girl at the door. "Tell Mr. Embers I've brought Mary Shelley Black for him."

A hush fell over the crowd when my aunt spoke my name. All masked faces turned my way.

"Mary Shelley Black?" Gracie sized me up with eyes as large as golf balls. "Oh, my—it is you. Come in." She grabbed my hand with cold fingers, yanked me and Aunt Eva inside, and shut the door on the crowd with a *thwack*.

A wall of frigid air hit my skin the moment we entered. I shivered and adjusted my eyes to the dimness of the long rectangular room. Meager shafts of natural light came through three windows shaped like portholes on the western wall. Candles burned on all sides of the room.

"I'm so happy to finally meet you," shouted Gracie over the patriotic music trumpeting out of a phonograph's black-horned speaker. "I'm Julius's cousin. My brother and I have been helping out as his assistants ever since the flu took our mother last month."

"Oh . . . I'm so sorry to hear about your loss." I squeezed her hand. "It's nice to meet you, too. Stephen mentioned you in his—" I froze, for on the wall to my right, from floor to ceiling just inside the doorway, hung a poster featuring an artist's rendition of my photograph with the kneeling, white-draped ghost. My own painted eyes stared me down, as if in challenge.

"Hello, Mary Shelley." Julius Embers stepped out of the shadows of his studio wearing a black suit, an emerald-green vest, and a smile that almost looked hesitant. No flu mask concealed his mouth and nose, as if he were unafraid of Death striking him down. "It's good to see you again."

"What do you mean *again*?" I dropped my hand from Gracie's. "It looks like you see me every second of the day on your wall over here."

"That's true." His smile broadened to his usual overconfidence, any hint of uncertainty banished.

I straightened my posture to feel taller around him. "Did you use me in this advertisement to make your brother mad?"

"Not at all. I used your image because of the impressive spirit you lured into the photograph. My customers enjoy how regal you look with your proud expression and your ethereal visitor kneeling by your side. You bring everyone comfort." He stopped directly in front of me. "I want to capture you again—see what else you can give me."

I studied his face and caught a similarity between his and Stephen's eyes that I hadn't ever noticed before. He was four years older and at least a half foot taller than his brother, but his eyes were the same shape and shade—the deep, inviting brown of dark, liquid chocolate. I glanced away from him, unsettled by the resemblance. The words he had used to describe the way he found Stephen and me the last time I was in that house burned in my brain:

I found them on the sofa. He had her skirts pulled up to her waist and was on her like an animal.

"It's really good to see you, Julius," said Aunt Eva with a tender squeeze of his arm. "You look like you're holding up well, considering all the work you're doing."

"I'd look even better if I hadn't just endured a difficult morning with Aloysius Darning."

"Oh no."

"Oh yes." Julius sighed and took his arm away from Aunt Eva's clutches. "That nincompoop is so determined to prove me a fraud that he hovered over my sittings from eight o'clock to nine thirty. He made some of my customers nervous with all his poking and prodding of my equipment."

"I'm sure he didn't find anything amiss, though," said my aunt.

"Of course not. Because nothing was amiss."

I lifted my eyes back to Julius's. "Aunt Eva said you're finally going to give me Stephen's package."

"Yes." He took my hand and pressed it between his hot palms. "My mother only just told me about it when we heard you were coming to San Diego. I'd also be happy to lend you some of his novels if you'd like."

"Isn't that nice of him, Mary Shelley?" Aunt Eva slipped my hand out of his. "I told him you'd be bored with no school and nothing to read but the dull old dictionary."

"Thank you," I said to Julius. "I'd like to borrow them."

The music stopped. The phonograph's needle traveled to the center of the record with the crackling hiss of static. Julius whipped his head toward the sound. "Gracie, stop gawking at Mary Shelley and attend to the music, please."

"I'm sorry, Julius." Gracie hustled to the phonograph. "I was just so excited to meet her. Stephen always talked about her letters, and I've seen her face so often on your wall there, I almost feel like I'm meeting someone from Hollywood—"

An odd banging erupted from the floor above us.

Gracie's forehead turned as white as her mask. She peered toward the ceiling with an expression of such horror, I half believed something sinister was thumping against the wall upstairs. My heartbeat quickened. I found myself gazing at the ceiling as well, while the painting of the white-cloaked phantom lingered in the corner of my eye.

"Gracie—the phonograph!" said Julius.

Gracie fumbled to replace "Stars and Stripes Forever" with a new record. She turned the crank on the phonograph, and "The Battle Hymn of the Republic" started up at full volume.

"Why are you blasting the room with patriotic music?" I asked Julius over the commotion.

"The spirits of fallen war heroes appreciate it. It makes them feel they didn't die in vain." He steered me by my shoulders, away from my aunt and toward his growing collection of spirit photographs. What must have been a hundred sample photos hung on the longest interior wall, their frames wedged against one another in a fight for space on the walnut panels. The majority of the faceless spirits wore military uniforms and stood behind mortal sitters. Some of the ghosts rested their hands on their loved ones' shoulders.

I heard breathing near the back of my neck and turned my head with a start. Aunt Eva had followed us like a shadow.

"Eva, please have a seat in the chair back there." Julius nodded to a chair in the corner by the door—the pesky relative seat, or so it seemed.

"Do you need me to help with Mary Shelley's hair or—"

"Please have a seat." Julius gave another nod. "The spirits won't want a crowd."

With a wounded look, Aunt Eva retreated, and Julius pressed his fingers around mine again, guiding me across the room. "Let's take off your mask and get you seated."

"I'm not taking off my mask," I said.

"I want to see your whole face in the photograph."

"Are you off your rocker?" I tensed my legs in a solid stance and shook him off me. "I've seen how many people come into this musty, dark room. I'm not risking my life for a photograph."

"All right, all right." He took my hand again and chuckled as though he found my fear entertaining. "Good God, I'd forgotten what a stubborn old mule you are."

"I also have two provisions before I sit for you."

He lifted his eyebrows and laughed again. "And they are?"

I untangled my fingers from his. "First of all, you need to tell Aunt Eva you lied about the way you found Stephen and me the last time I was here."

"Mary Shelley, our host is giving you free photographs," said my aunt from her corner. "Please just sit down for him and stop embarrassing yourself."

"I won't sit down until he tells the truth." I stared at Julius until he could no longer meet my eyes. Over by the phonograph, Gracie scratched at her arm and glanced down at her shoes.

"I may have exaggerated a little." Julius peered straight at me again. "I'm sorry."

"We weren't on the sofa, were we?" I asked.

"No, but you were—" He bit his lip. "My brother said some things to me of a personal, sensitive nature, and—as brothers sometimes fight—I might have added some details about what I saw." He studied my face for a reaction.

I turned toward my aunt. "Did you hear that, Aunt Eva?"

"The entire island of Coronado heard that, Mary Shelley. Please just put this subject to rest and sit down." She rubbed her flushed neck and looked like she wanted to disappear inside the walls.

I returned my attention to Julius. "I'd also like to see Stephen's parcel before I sit."

"Of course. Gracie, pull out the package Stephen prepared for our guest. It's in the top drawer of the desk."

His cousin scuttled over to a small desk topped with three glowing candles, and the flames twitched and danced as she approached. The flickering light made the faces in the nearby photos seem to move.

Gracie squeaked open a drawer and held up a rectangular item wrapped in brown paper. "Is this the one?"

"Yes," said Julius. "Will you assure Miss Black it's Stephen's handwriting on the front?"

"Oh yes, it's his." Gracie beamed at the words on the paper. "His penmanship was always so much better than mine."

That *was* of hers made my blood run cold.

"All right." I gave Julius a nod. "Those were my conditions. As long as you understand I'm only doing this for my aunt's sake and not because I believe in your ghosts, I'll sit for one quick picture."

He gestured toward a high-backed chair with a plum-colored cushion, positioned in front of a black background curtain. "Please have a seat."

I walked over to the chair and lowered myself to the cushion with a shiver. The room felt like a northern basement at the peak of winter, musty odor included. Stephen's words from my last visit entered my mind: *He also runs a fan over ice blocks in between sittings to cool the air in there. He tries to make everyone feel like phantoms are hovering around the studio.*

Julius knelt to position me as he desired and guided my knees to the left in a way that tickled, but I clamped my teeth together to keep from flinching or laughing. He tilted my gauze-covered chin to the right.

"How badly did you injure him that day?" I asked in a voice too quiet for Aunt Eva to hear.

"What are you talking about?"

"You know what I mean. My aunt dragged me out of here so quickly, I never got to ask if those thuds were the sounds of you slamming his head against the wall."

He kept my chin in his hand. "Brothers fight when we upset each other. That's just how we are."

"Is everything all right?" asked Aunt Eva. Uneasiness tinged her voice.

"Everything's fine." Julius got to his feet.

I swallowed. "Has Stephen written? Do you know if—"

An airplane growled overhead and drowned out the music and my question. The thunder of its engine shook the photos on the walls and vibrated in the pit of my stomach.

More thumps and bangs emerged from the floor above. Julius and I both looked at the ceiling.

"What's happening up there?" I asked.

Julius tore his eyes away from the beams overhead. "My studio causes everyone's imaginations to mistake normal house sounds for mischievous ghosts." He strode over to his stepfather's beautiful black camera and ducked his head under a dark cloth behind it. "It's probably just my mother cleaning. She's become a little obsessive. Keeps her from worrying about Stephen."

My eyes drifted back up to the ceiling while he brought me into focus and finished the camera's preparations. I would have felt much better if I could have seen Mrs. Embers myself.

"All right." His head reemerged from beneath the cloth. "Let's get started. Stay still now, and keep looking this way." He leaned his lips toward the camera's outstretched leather bellows and whispered something to the machinery—a ritual I'd seen him perform the last time I posed for him. From the few words I could hear, I gathered he was making some sort of plea to the other side. He then straightened his posture and cried out, "Spirits, we summon you. I bring you Mary Shelley

Black, named after an author of dark tales who believed in the mysterious powers of electrical currents—"

Something dropped to the floor upstairs. Julius flinched and raised his voice: "She's drawn hundreds of mourners to me with her angelic image. Send us another spirit to stand beside her. Bring her a loved one she wants to see." He held up his tray of flash powder. "Mary Shelley Black—summon the dead!"

He opened the cap of a round lens that gaped like the eye of a Cyclops.

The flash exploded with a blinding burst of flames and smoke.

Inside the camera, a chemically treated plate was imprinted with a miniature version of my body.

"There." Julius coughed on a dense white cloud that drifted around his head. "It's done." He screwed the lens cap back into place and inserted the glass plate's protective dark slide inside the rear of the camera.

My eyes watered so much from the scorching air that I had to wipe them with my sleeve. The blast made me remember the Christmas when Stephen's father burned off his eyebrows with a particularly volatile flash explosion.

"Shall I give the package to her now, Julius?" asked Gracie.

"Yes."

Another thump from above caused dust from the ceiling's beams to shower upon us. Footsteps pounded throughout the house, far louder than the phonograph's music. I blinked through the smoke and saw Julius's face go as pale as his cousin's.

The pocket doors to the front hall crashed open. Mrs. Embers stumbled into the studio, strands of dark hair falling across her eyes. "I need your help, Julius. I'm hurt." She clutched her stomach.

"Christ!" Julius put down the flashlamp. "Get them out of here, Gracie." He charged across the room and grabbed his mother by the arm to escort her away.

"You need to go immediately." Gracie handed me Stephen's parcel and pushed on my back to get me to move faster.

I looked over my shoulder. "What happened to Mrs. Embers?"

"Please, just go."

"When should we come back for the photograph?" asked Aunt Eva.

"I don't know. Monday morning, maybe." Gracie opened the door and gave me another shove. "A family emergency has arisen," she called to the line of customers, which now spilled over onto the front sidewalk. "The spirits are letting us know they need their rest. Come back another day." She propelled Aunt Eva outside behind me and slammed the door closed on all of us.

Cries of unrest came from the black-clothed grievers.

"What did you do in there, you little hussy?" asked the same heavyset woman who had pushed Aunt Eva off the steps. "Why'd you ruin it for the rest of us?"

"That's Mary Shelley Black," said a young brunette behind her. "You can't talk to her like that."

"I don't care if she's Mary, Queen of Scots. I've been waiting four hours to get a picture taken with my poor Harold, and she just ruined it all."

"I didn't ruin anything—"

Aunt Eva grabbed my hand. "Let's run."

"That'll only make us look guilty," I said.

"Run!"

Two hefty men from the back of the line were now headed our way with murder in their eyes, so I did as she said—I used my Boy Scout boots' double soles of reinforced solid oak leather and bolted across the grass and down the coastal neighborhood's sidewalks, until Ocean Boulevard disappeared behind us.

We didn't stop running until we jumped onto the streetcar, and even then my heart kept racing. I sat beside my aunt on the wooden seat and clutched Stephen's parcel to my chest.

"What was all of that about?" I asked while trying to catch my breath. "What happened to Mrs. Embers upstairs?"

Aunt Eva gasped for air and rubbed a stitch in her side. "I don't know. But I'm sure meeting mourners on a constant basis . . . and worrying about a loved one overseas . . . can destroy one's nerves."

"Poor cousin Gracie seemed as anxious as a frightened mouse."

"Poor cousin Gracie is a flu survivor. Her hair went white

and fell out from the fever. That's why she wears a wig."

"That was a wig?"

My aunt nodded.

I gulped. "It almost seemed to me, with all the spirit activity in that house, the family believes they're being haunted."

Aunt Eva fidgeted in her seat, but she didn't admit the Emberses' house disturbed her. It certainly disturbed me. I could almost understand why Stephen was in such a hurry to get out of there.

I lowered the package to my lap and trailed my fingers over my own name, penned in handwriting I adored—handwriting that mirrored the writer's artistic nature. The *S* in *Shelley* resembled a treble clef. The *B* in *Black* could have been called voluptuous. My odd, dark name always transformed into something lyrical and beautiful through Stephen's pen.

I noticed the string tying the parcel paper together hung loose on one end, as though someone had already slid the string aside to inspect the contents of the package. A small tear also marred the paper. "I think someone's already opened this. Do you suppose Julius—?"

"Mary Shelley." My name passed over my aunt's lips as a tired groan.

I peeled back the tampered end of the paper and slid out a framed photograph. My labored breath caught in my throat. Warmth flushed throughout my face and chest and spread to the tips of my fingers and toes. The strings of my mask tightened with a grin the size of Alaska.

As his last gift to me before leaving for the war, Stephen—fully aware of my love of electricity—had given me a photograph of a jagged lightning bolt striking a sepia nighttime sea.

A TRANSPARENT FIGURE

I HADN'T PLANNED TO HANG ANY DECORATIONS ON THE walls of my bedroom in Aunt Eva's house. Doing so would have been an admission that San Diego was to become my home for a long while.

However, on Sunday, the day after we visited the Emberses, I couldn't help but mount Stephen's lightning bolt on a strip of gilded wallpaper just beyond the foot of my bed. I asked Aunt Eva's permission to pound two nails into her wall and hung both of his photographs side by side, the butterfly and the electricity. I never found any note in his parcel and was certain Julius had taken it. But the picture had finally reached my hands.

I discovered Stephen had crossed out some words in the

lower right-hand corner, perhaps a rejected title, and between gold and white ripples in the ocean, he had written one of his anagrams:

I DO LOSE INK

I squinted and pulled other words out of the letters. *Sink. Die. Nod. Skid. Oiled. Link.* But none of the phrases I deciphered struck me as being the name of a photograph of a powerful storm over the Pacific.

Aunt Eva knocked on my open door and breezed into my room. "I think I'll go pick up Julius's picture of you early tomorrow morning before work. I can catch the first ferry. I'll just wear a skirt over my work trousers."

I stepped away from the images on the wall. "Will the studio be open that early?"

"I assume so. Julius is a hard worker."

"I'll go with you."

"That's not a good idea. You shouldn't be out in public air any more than you have to be."

"I didn't *have* to go to his house yesterday, but you let me. It's mainly clean ocean air we'll be breathing."

"I'll think about it." She spied the mounted photographs. "Are you sure you want those hanging on your wall?"

"Why wouldn't I? They're beautiful."

"Oh, Mary Shelley . . ." She tutted and took my hand. "Come here. Sit down with me for a moment so we can talk about something important." She sat me on my bed and perched beside me on Grandma Ernestine's old blue and white quilt that served as a bedspread. "I know you've never had a mother in your life to teach you the ways of the heart—"

"Don't bring up that morning I kissed Stephen."

"I'm not. I just want to say I know you think you're deeply in love with that boy, but you need to keep in mind you're still so very young. And . . . he might never come home."

"I already know that." I pulled my hand away from her. "Why would you remind me of such a thing?"

"Because every time his name comes up in conversation, your eyes brighten like he's about to walk into the room. And now you're hanging his photos on the wall and further surrounding yourself with him. Did he even ask you to wait for him?"

"He said I didn't have to wait unless I wanted to. He doesn't want me to waste my life worrying about him."

"Oh." She sounded surprised. "Well . . . that was kind of him."

"He's a kind person."

She took my hand again and cradled it in her calloused palm. "If he urged you to be free, then let him go. Don't waste your youth wondering if a boy from your past will ever return to you."

My throat itched with the threat of tears. "I don't think you fully comprehend how much Stephen and I mean to each other."

"Mary—"

"Did I ever tell you how we became friends?"

Her hazel eyes softened behind her glasses. "No, I don't think you did."

"I was eight at the time, and he wasn't yet ten. I'd seen him at school before, but he was always just a nice, quiet boy with an interesting last name, and I mainly played with girls. This one day, though, he brought this little Brownie pocket camera to school." I used my hands to demonstrate the camera's width, about eight inches. "It was just a small one with a beautiful deep-red bellows and an imitation leather covering. I was walking home with my friend Nell and two other girls, and I saw him in the distance, taking pictures of a tabby cat lying on the steps of an old church. Well"—my shoulders tensed at the ensuing memory—"these older boys swaggered up to him and teased him about being Julius's sissy brother. They grabbed his camera and threw it onto the sidewalk. I heard a terrible crack and watched pieces scatter across the cement. And then those boys shoved him in the shoulder and walked away."

Aunt Eva cringed. "I'm sure their father was furious that a camera got broken."

"That's what Stephen shouted after them. He said, 'My father's going to call the cops on all of you,' and then he added some colorful curse words I'd never heard come out of a nice boy's mouth before. I told my friends to go on home, and then I joined him to help find all the lost pieces. Some screws had come loose, and part of the wood casing had split apart beneath the fake leather. Stephen said I wouldn't be able to help him because I was a girl, but I sat right down on the steps of that church and screwed everything back in place with a little spectacle repair kit Dad had given me. I also pulled my ribbon out of my hair and wrapped up the cracked body to avoid any further damage before he could glue the wood back together at home."

"Ah, yes." Aunt Eva nodded. "Wasn't that around the time Uncle Lars decided to buy you a larger tool kit?"

"I think so."

A smile lit her face. "I'd forgotten all about that."

"So there I was," I continued, "piecing Stephen's camera together like a puzzle, fastening the nickel lens board back in place, chatting about the book poking out of his satchel— Jack London's *White Fang*. And all the while Stephen stared at me as if I were something magical. Not the ugly way other people sometimes stare at me, like I'm a circus freak. But with respect and recognition, like he was meeting someone in a foreign country who spoke his language when no one else could. That's how it's been between us ever since. We understand each other, even when we astound each other."

Her eyes dampened. "I just don't want you to get hurt. I hope you'll be able to move on and find other things in life that make you happy."

"Just let me keep hope in my heart for him for now, all right? Let me leave his photographs hanging on my wall to remind me that something beautiful once happened in the middle of all the year's horrors."

She pulled me against her side and sniffed back tears. "All right. But keep your heart guarded. I know what it's like to have love turn agonizing. There's nothing more painful in the world."

NO ONE ANSWERED THE STUDIO DOOR AT DAWN. WE stood outside the Emberses' house in a fog so thick we couldn't see the Pacific across the street.

I tugged my coat around me. "Should we knock on the front door?"

"I don't know." Aunt Eva waddled down the side staircase and peered through the mist toward the main entrance. She wore a blue plaid skirt over her work trousers to disguise her uniform, and the pants beneath produced so much bulk that she looked like a giant handbell—skinny torso, bulbous hips. "I don't want to disturb his mother. She seemed ill the other day."

"You can't be late for work, though."

"I'm not sure what to do." She trekked back up the stairs and knocked again.

The sound of an automobile motor sped our way. We both craned our necks to see the approaching vehicle through the fog: a plain black Model T. The car careened around the corner, clipped the curb with its carriage-sized wheels, and squealed to a jerking stop on the side street next to the house.

A man with uncombed black hair spilled out of the passenger seat.

Aunt Eva rubbed her throat and asked in a whisper, "Is that Julius?"

I squinted through the fog. "I think so."

"You going to be OK, Julius?" asked the driver, a solid-looking, bespectacled fellow who appeared to be closer to my age than Julius's. "You sure you don't want me running the studio instead of closing it for the day?"

Julius ignored the driver and stumbled up to the house, his shirt untucked, his chin dark with whiskers. His face resembled Uncle Wilfred's in the throes of tuberculosis: gray, clammy, sunken. His red-rimmed eyes caught sight of us standing on the steps. "Why are you here?" He didn't sound pleased.

"We came for Mary Shelley's photograph. Are you unwell, Julius?"

He blustered past us, smelling of cologne and something sweet, even though he looked like he could use a bath. "Come in and take it quickly. Then please go. I'm not feeling well."

Aunt Eva jumped out of the way. "It's not the flu, is it?"

"No, it's not the damn flu." He fumbled to open the door and reached around to a switch that lit a quartet of electric wall lamps. "Wait here. I'll get it." He went in.

Behind us, the Model T rumbled away.

I stepped a foot inside the studio and watched Julius disappear through a doorway next to the dark background curtain.

I'd always assumed the door led to a closet, but it appeared to be the entrance to an office in which photographs hung on a string to dry like laundry on a clothesline.

"What's wrong with him?" I asked.

Aunt Eva still massaged her throat. "I have no idea. I've never seen him like this."

"Is it the opium?"

"Mary Shelley!"

Julius walked back into the studio with a brown folder. "Here, take it." He held out the concealed picture in the tips of his fingers.

I approached and took it from him, feeling my stomach dip with nervousness as I did so.

His red eyes watered. "Now go. Please."

"I'd like to see the photograph first."

"Go."

I held my breath and flipped the folder open. There I was, in black and white, seated on the velvet-cushioned chair with my camphor pouch and clock-gear necklace strung around my neck. My pale eyes peered at the camera above my flu mask.

A transparent figure stood behind me—a handsome brown-haired boy in a dress shirt and tie.

Stephen.

Stephen was the ghost in my photograph.

Aunt Eva took the folder from my hand. "Oh no, Julius. Is that your brother?"

The words cut deep. I realized what they implied.

"Is he . . ." Aunt Eva's lips failed to shape the word.

Julius cleared his throat. "We just learned he died in battle. The telegram said it was a ferocious fight at the beginning of October. He went heroically."

All the oxygen left that room. I held my stomach and heard the warning signs of unconsciousness buzz inside my eardrums. My vision dimmed. My legs started to give way.

Aunt Eva took hold of my arm to steady me. "Mary Shelley, are you all right?"

Julius turned his back on me. "Take her outside."

A scream from upstairs jolted me to my senses. We all peered toward the ceiling.

"Stephen!" cried Mrs. Embers, as if someone were tearing her heart to shreds. "Stephen!"

Julius grabbed my arms and turned me around. "I said take her out of here. Both of you, get outside. Go far, far away. My brother's childhood sweetheart is the last person we need to see right now."

My feet tripped from the reckless way he steered me across the floor. Before I could regain my balance, Aunt Eva and I were back outside in the fog. The door slammed behind us. We could still hear Mrs. Embers's screams beyond the walls, even over the thunder of the waves.

"Let's go." My aunt took my hand and guided me down the steps. "We need to let them mourn. What a terrible, terrible thing to lose a loved one clear across the world."

My body felt out of control. I couldn't walk or breathe right. Pain squeezed my lungs so hard that Aunt Eva had to shoulder my weight to help me move.

"I warned you not to long for him." She put her hand around my waist to better support me. "I knew he'd break your heart."

"I want—" I choked and sputtered as if I were crying, but no tears wet my eyes. "I want you to throw that photograph in the bay when we're on the ferry. Stephen . . . he would have hated seeing it."

"I don't think that's a good idea with the way you're acting. I'll keep it for you in case you change your mind."

"No."

"You may want it in the future."

"No."

"Shh. Just concentrate on walking. You'll feel better when you get back home."

"My home's in Portland. I'll never get back there. I'll never feel better."

We continued to hear Mrs. Embers's screams, even as we made our way past the house next door, before the crash of waves swallowed up her cries.

6

THE BUZZ OF ELECTRICITY

WE PARTED AT THE FERRY LANDING ON THE SAN DIEGO side of the harbor. I could tell from Aunt Eva's pinched eyebrows she regretted sending me off alone, but she had to go to work. I staggered away without looking back at her. The photograph floated somewhere halfway across the bay, ripped from its protective folder and thrown in the corrosive salt water.

The quarantine had silenced the heart of downtown. A stray newspaper page scuttled down the sidewalk on the wings of a southerly wind. Overhead a pair of seagulls cried to each other as they soared toward the ocean, eager to escape civilization. I didn't blame them. A handful of men and women departed a yellow electric streetcar near Marston's Department Store at Fifth and C. Like me, they were all dressed in dark clothing and masks, heads bent down with the weight of the world, eyes on the watch for death.

We all looked like bad luck.

The word CLOSED hung from every other shop door, and the stores that did stay open lacked customers. I passed a barbershop in which the barber stooped in front of his mirror and trimmed his own hair, probably out of boredom. The tobacco shop next door displayed a poster with a bloody German handprint. THE HUN—HIS MARK, it said. BLOT IT OUT WITH LIBERTY BONDS.

The Hun—Stephen's Killer, was all I could think.

"No, he's not dead," I murmured. "He's not dead. He's supposed to come home. He's supposed to send me another letter."

A man in a derby hat with a sandwich board slung over his shoulders crossed the street on the other side of the intersection. "Sin is the root of all evil in the world," he yelled to no one in particular. "God is punishing us with pestilence, war, famine, and death." The sign around his neck read THE FOUR HORSEMEN OF THE APOCALYPSE HAVE ARRIVED! YE WHO HAVE SINNED SHALL BE STRICKEN DOWN.

I watched him with horror and realized, *We're all simply waiting to be killed. All that's left is blinding sorrow and a painful death by drowning in our own fluids. What's the point of being alive?*

I couldn't breathe. I turned to face a sandstone wall, removed my mask, and gasped for air. I gulped and gulped until I swallowed as much of the tuna-scented breeze as possible, even though the odor made me sick. Everything made me sick. Why wasn't I the one to get killed by germs or bombs? Why was I standing alone in the middle of a deserted city? Why did a bright and talented boy have to go and do a stupid thing like enlist?

Unable to divine any answers from my empty street corner, I trudged on like a sleepwalker, my feet as thick as sandbags. My erratic breathing mutated into hiccups that stabbed my sides.

In the residential district I spied—and smelled—from across the street an undertaker's clapboard house with a grisly scene in the front yard: stacks of pine caskets, piled two to three high. Even worse, four little boys climbed over the coffins as if they were playing in a wooden fortress. They chanted a rhyme I'd heard at the beginning of the school year, when the flu first raised its monstrous head:

I had a little bird,
Its name was Enza,
I opened the window,
And in-flu-enza.

"Hey, get off there!" I yelled at the children. "You're climbing over dead bodies. Can't you see the flies? You're going to get sick."

The leader of the group—a brown-haired boy in knee pants—balanced his feet on the teetering wood and called out, "It's the Germans, boys. Shoot 'em!"

The other chubby-cheeked kids leaned over the caskets and fired rounds at me from invisible rifles.

"Where are your parents?" I asked.

"Keep firing, men. Show the filthy Boche what you've got."

They continued to attack me with pretend ammunition, with no sign of leaving their disgusting playground. A rumble of thunder in the purpling sky to the west set off a series of delighted *oobs* and *wows* from the boys.

"That's the blast of our cannon, Boche," said the leader. "You're going to die."

"You're going die if you keep playing there, you stupid kids. Get out of there." I marched up the low slope of the yard, into the thick of the stench and the flies, and grabbed the brown-haired boy by the arms. "I said get out of here."

"Let go of me."

"No." I gripped him with viselike strength and dragged his flailing body off the undertaker's property.

"Let me go!"

"Go back home to your mother." I pushed him away down the sidewalk. "I don't want to hear about any more dead boys."

"You're crazy, you know that?" He glared at me over his shoulder and wandered away. His friends fell into place behind him, snickering.

Before I could get to the end of the block, the brown-haired boy shouted from down the street, "For your information, my mother's lying in the hospital with the flu. I *can't* go home to her."

I rubbed away tears with the back of my hand and kept walking.

Three blocks later I arrived at Aunt Eva's yellow house and discovered someone had parked a bicycle next to her roses. A lanky boy no more than twelve, in an official-looking cap and black tie, waited on the front porch with an envelope and a clipboard. He saw me making my way up the path and came toward me at a brisk gait. I braced for more bad news.

"Hello, miss." The boy's voice sounded muffled inside his mask, which looked as if it were tied tight enough to hurt. "Are you Mrs. Wilfred Ottinger or Miss Mary Shelley Black?"

"I'm Miss Black."

"Please sign here."

The words he directed my way on the clipboard blurred together in my tired eyes. All I could make out was WESTERN UNION at the top. Someone had sent us a telegram.

"Oh no." I shoved the clipboard back at him. "I can't take another death today. Don't give it to me. Don't tell me my father's dead."

"I don't read the messages, miss." He pushed the board my way. "Please sign it. I can't leave without delivering the telegram if someone's home."

I wobbled and had to clutch the boy's arm to avoid passing out.

"Please, miss. It'll be all right."

He steadied me, and with shaking fingers I scratched a sloppy version of my signature. I took the tan envelope, tore it open, and read a short message from Uncle Lars in Portland:

```
THEY'RE HOLDING HIM WITHOUT BAIL.
    TRIAL SET FOR DECEMBER.
  POSSIBLE 20-YEAR SENTENCE.
     KEEP M.S. WITH YOU.


            L.
```

Twenty years.

If a jury decided that fate for my father, he'd be sixty-five at his release. I'd be thirty-six. And all because Dad hated war.

The message fluttered out of my fingers to the sidewalk. I marched a dirty footprint across the paper on my way into the house and slammed the door behind me with enough force to rattle windows. Oberon squawked from his cage. That Western Union boy probably jumped out of his skin and pedaled away as fast as his bony legs could take him.

I thumped upstairs to my room and yanked off my mask. Stephen's photographs still hung on the gilded wallpaper, teasing me with memories of a time when he was alive and my father wasn't rotting away in jail. I paced the floor and pulled at my hair until my scalp ached. "Get me out of here. *Get me out of here!*"

A low boom echoed in the distance. My eyes shot to the window. I held my breath. Ten seconds later, the menacing clouds to the west flashed with light, followed by another crash of thunder.

A lightning storm.

I pulled up the window's sash and felt the tiny hairs on my arms bristle with static. Lightning ignited the air, and I wanted its bolts to shock me out of my nightmare world and send me back into my old reality.

I scrounged around my room and found the makings of a kite—the parcel paper from Stephen's package for the body, wire coat hangers for the frame, and a rope of hair ribbons for string. My clock-gear necklace would act as my conductor. I slipped my aviatrix goggles out of my leather doctor's bag, fitted them over my face, and hurried downstairs with my creation.

The claps of thunder now followed the lightning by two seconds. The wind whipped my hair across my face, while fresh-smelling rain streaked my lenses and soaked the string of ribbons, rendering them useless. How stupid to have thought the fabric wouldn't get drenched and heavy. The parcel paper would never soar. My name written in Stephen's handwriting bled into black smudges, gone forever.

Lightning shot across the sky in an erratic streak more blinding than Julius's flashlamp. Thunder reverberated against the soles of my boots a mere second later. The storm gathered overhead. My blood craved the buzz of electricity to replace the poison of the world. I wanted to touch it. I *had* to touch it.

I grabbed the clock gear and held it in the air with my bare fingers.

Another streak of light illuminated the front yard. A roll of thunder clapped overhead, and a slight shock of static zapped the tips of my fingers.

But that was all.

"Come on!" I yelled. "Give me something I can feel."

Someone shrieked from across the street, distracting me enough that I turned my head, but then the world went yellow and crashed against my ears. Electricity burned my hand, threw me backward to the ground.

And killed me.

DEATH

THE SCIENTIFIC METHOD HELPED ME COMPREHEND THAT I was no longer alive.

First you formulate a question: *Am I dead?* Then a hypothesis: *If I'm sitting up here in Aunt Eva's eucalyptus tree, looking down at my own body sprawled across the grass in the rain, then I must be dead.* The test: *A redheaded woman in an apron runs across the street, sees my smoking clothing and my lifeless eyes staring through my goggles, and tries to shake my limp body back to life—to no avail. "Oh, dear God, she's dead," she yells to another woman sprinting across the lawn. "The lightning struck this poor girl dead."* The conclusion: *Mary Shelley Black is indeed no longer alive.*

Oh, God, I thought. *What did I just do?*

I looked up: a black cumulonimbus cloud bellowed around the eucalyptus like a seething beast. A siren cried out from somewhere nearby. Neighbors in flu masks gathered below me.

"What did I do?" I called down to the people, although no one seemed to hear. The version of me that sat in the tree looked solid and mortal, in my opinion, but I feared I was little more than a mirage up there. "This doesn't feel right. What am I supposed to do?"

A black police ambulance drove into view. The neighbors waved it down with frantic arms. Men in uniforms jumped out of the vehicle and grabbed a stretcher. I could still see my prone, empty body, with its singed fingers and gray face, and no one, not even the men from the ambulance, could revive me. One of the men pushed my goggles to my forehead and pulled my eyes shut, and my skin looked cold and hostile and ugly. The idea of dropping back into that lifeless flesh sickened me, and I guessed the landing would be excruciating. But sitting in a tree above myself wasn't right, either. This wasn't at all the way death was supposed to be. There were no angels, harps, or pearly gates—just me staring down at my corpse, not knowing what to do.

Go back, I told myself when the officers lifted my body onto the stretcher. *It's clearly not your time. Quick! Before it's too late.*

I pushed myself off the eucalyptus branch, and down I plunged into that unappealing shell of a girl with the torturous sensation of falling into a pool of arctic water. Every square inch of me stung. I gasped for air like a dying fish and heard a pair of doors slam shut near my feet.

My arms and legs sank deep into a canvas bed in the back of a dark compartment. I had entered the too-small skin and bones of a freezing-cold girl made of lead, whose skull throbbed and right fingers burned with a pain more intense than anything I'd ever experienced. Beside me, a person gurgled and wheezed, sounding like he was drowning. The automobile's motor vibrated against my vertebrae.

A few minutes later, we careened around a corner with a squeal of tires, and the wheezing person and I slid to the right, where my knee and elbow hit a metal wall.

A pothole threw me into the air and slammed me down again. The brakes screeched to a stop and I skidded toward the front of the compartment. More metal banged against me. Doors slammed shut. Footsteps scrambled around the vehicle.

A gangly man in an olive-green police uniform opened a set of doors just beyond my feet, blinding my eyes with the glare of the sunlight that must have followed the storm.

"Holy—" The policeman's round eyes widened above his mask. "She's alive!"

"What?" A plumper male face popped up beside him.

"The girl with no pulse. She's alive."

"But—"

"Look at her."

They stared at me as if they were witnessing a foul and bloated corpse rising from the grave.

The gurgling person beside me gasped once more and then fell silent. A whisper of a breeze shivered across my skin, drifted to the top of the ambulance, and passed through the roof, where it disappeared in a flood of yellow warmth.

"The person beside me just died," I found myself saying.

TWO MASKED NURSES IN HATS LIKE GIANT ASPIRIN TABlets wheeled me on a gurney through the hallways of a stark white hospital. Cots crowded both sides of the passageways—temporary beds for shivering flu victims who curled on their sides and coughed up blood. I saw cheekbones covered in mahogany spots and entire faces an unnatural reddish purple, which, like black feet, signified the end. The scent of antiseptic cleaning solutions burned my nostrils.

The stockier, white-haired nurse peeked over her mask. "Put your head down. You're lucky to be alive, young lady. Let's keep you that way." Fatigue rolled off her body, exhausting me. "We're in the middle of a plague, sweetheart, and you better heal up quick before this hospital kills you."

They maneuvered me into one of the examination rooms, but a beady-eyed man in a white coat flailed his arms and shouted, "We're out of room. She needs to go in the hall."

"She got hit by lightning," said the stocky nurse. "It's not the flu."

"There's no room. Put her in the hall."

The nurses swiveled me out the door and around the corner, and I gripped the sides of the gurney to make sure I didn't slide and bruise like during my ambulance ride. More flu victims trembled on all sides of me. A rotten flavor lined my mouth. We seemed to travel down those writhing, wheezing, rancid corridors for a good five minutes.

Finally the nurses shoved me in a dark corner. I could see a black foot with a toe tag on a neighboring gurney, but the lack of light kept me from making out the rest of the body.

I grabbed a nurse's cold hand. "Is my aunt here?"

"I don't know, dear."

"Please find her. Her name is Eva Ottinger. She works in the shipyard."

"I'll make sure we contact her. Stay here and rest. The doctor will see you soon."

The nurses pattered away in their soft shoes, leaving me alone with the toe-tagged foot, the darkness, and the macabre chorus of drowning flu victims echoing off the walls.

"WHERE'S MY NIECE? MARY SHELLEY! MARY SHELLEY Black!"

I blinked my eyes open and saw Aunt Eva storming toward me in her greasy work clothes, blond hair flying, glasses shoved up on her nose, flu mask swelling and deflating from violent breaths. Anger radiated from her in pulsating waves, and strangely enough, I could taste her rage—hot, metallic, like a fork that's been heated in an oven.

She gripped the side of my gurney. "My sister didn't die bringing you into the world just so you could take yourself out of it. How dare you spit on your mother's memory?"

"I'm sorry—"

"I've spent day and night worrying about you dying from the flu, and then you go and stick yourself in the middle of a lightning storm."

"Stop shouting."

"I will *not* stop shouting. They told me you died for several minutes. Someone at the front desk just showed me your blackened clock-gear necklace and those stupid goggles—"

"Please. Sick people are trying to sleep." I grabbed her hand with my undamaged one.

The effect my touch had on her was immediate.

The metallic taste faded and transformed into a flavor sweet and light and airy, like whipped cream when it's reached its point of perfection. Her shoulders lowered. She studied my fingers surrounding her flesh. I could see her hazel eyes watching my hand through her spectacles.

"What is it?" I asked. "Why are you looking at my hand that way? That's not the one wrapped in bandages."

"It's nothing. I . . ." Her eyelids closed, and a blissful sigh escaped her lips beneath her mask, as if I'd given her a sedative. "I just don't want you to die."

I chewed my dry and cracking lip and tried to figure out how to tell her what had happened when I *did* briefly die.

"Is the library still open during the quarantine?" I asked.

Her eyes opened. "Why on earth are you asking about books? All you should be thinking about is healing."

"I wonder if there are any books that discuss returning from the dead."

"You shouldn't read horror novels at a time like this."

"No, not a novel, a textbook that discusses what typically happens when people die for a short while like I did. I'm curious if what happened to me is normal."

She lifted her eyebrows. "What do you mean?"

"I need to tell you something, Aunt Eva, but you have to swear you won't bring up Julius's spirits."

She nodded as if she wanted me to continue. "Go on."

"Do you swear you won't mention his name?"

"I swear."

I swallowed, which made my parched throat ache. "I left my body and sat on the branch of your eucalyptus tree for a bit. I saw myself down there, with my clothes smoking and the neighbors gathering around me. It didn't feel right, like I was stuck between life and death, and I wasn't sure where to go."

"You mean . . . you were a spirit?"

"I'm still not saying I believe in all that."

"Was Wilfred there? Or your mother?"

"I didn't see anyone. An ambulance showed up, and I decided to push myself back into my flesh, which hurt like mad."

She squirmed with excitement. "We should tell him."

"Don't say his name. Don't you dare compare what happened to me to those photographs."

"He should know you've been to the other side. Oh, Mary Shelley, can you imagine what he'd photograph now if you posed for him? Do you realize how much serenity your body is emanating? I can feel it in your touch. It's like you're partially still in the spirit realm."

"Don't say that." I snatched my hand away from hers. "I've had a hard enough time fitting into this world without thinking I'm only halfway here."

"That's what it feels like."

"Stop."

"Oh, Mary Shelley." She clutched my arm. "What an opportunity you've been given. You've gone somewhere the rest of us have only dared to imagine, and you've brought a portion of its wonders back with you." She removed her glasses and wiped her watery eyes with the back of her wrist. "This is going to change everything. I just know it."

I studied the hand that had soothed her and tried to figure out if I looked or felt any different than before. My trembling fingers still seemed to be made of flesh and bone. No heavenly glow surrounded my body. Spirits didn't huddle around my bed and try to make their presence known.

But she was right. Something had changed.

THE EXPERT

THE HOSPITAL RELEASED ME AS SOON AS I COULD STAND up on my own. I wasn't gasping for my last breath; therefore, they didn't have any spare time for me. Nurses were tying toe tags around flu patients who hadn't died yet, so I made no complaint about vacating my dark corner.

My head still throbbed, as did my fingers wrapped in bandages, and my back was sore from being thrown to the ground by the force of the shock—not to mention the bruises sustained during that ambulance ride. Aunt Eva hired a taxi to take us home so I wouldn't have to walk.

I stared at the back of the driver's black cap and balding head through the window of the enclosed passenger area.

"My father goes on trial in December," I told my aunt. "Uncle Lars sent a telegram."

"He did?"

"I dropped it on your front lawn. I don't know if it's still there."

"It's on my front lawn?" Aunt Eva clutched her handbag to her stomach. "It doesn't mention the word *treason*, does it?"

"No. But Uncle Lars said Dad could be sentenced to twenty years."

"Twenty years?"

I tried to nod, but the movement hurt my head. "He shouldn't even be in jail."

"Do you know what he did up there, Mary Shelley? Do you know his crimes?"

I wrapped my arms around my middle. "I believe he helped men avoid the draft."

"That's right. Uncle Lars said your father was running some sort of group out of the back of his grocery store. Do you know how much trouble the rest of us could be in if anyone learns we're related to a traitor?"

"Don't call him a traitor. He's a good man."

"Then why are you a thousand miles from home, sticking yourself in lightning storms, winding up half-dead in a hospital? If he was so good, why didn't he worry more about keeping his own daughter safe?"

I leaned back against the padded taxi seat and clenched my jaw, unable to come up with an answer.

BACK AT HER HOUSE, AUNT EVA TUCKED ME INTO BED and told me to push aside all the unpleasantness that had coaxed me out into that lightning storm.

"Your job right now is to heal," she said as she pulled the warm sheet up to my chin. "Don't use your brain to do anything else."

So heal I did.

I lay there in bed with my skull splitting in two and my fingers burning and itching inside my bandages, but I refused to take any medicine to kill the pain. I wanted to be able to think without any substances blurring my mind. While Oberon chattered downstairs and Aunt Eva divided her time between the shipyard and me, my body repaired itself. All the tiny cells, nerves, and tissues worked like an efficient machine below the surface of my skin, and I longed to learn more about anatomy and physics and lightning and to listen to music that would challenge the recovering synapses of my brain. But the schools remained closed, and my body continued to stay stuck in a bed with springs that sounded like an accordion, my head and arms surrounded by bags of garlic-scented gum. Aunt Eva insisted the bags would chase away the hospital's flu germs. She also made me wear a goose-grease poultice on my neck and stuffed salt up my nose. I felt like she was preparing me as the main course for a dinner party instead of protecting me from an illness.

Stephen's photographs watched over me from beyond the foot of the bed the entire time, their presence a source of both comfort and anguish. Sometimes, when I let my body relax and my mind go numb, I almost believed I saw him standing there, directly in front of his photos. I almost believed the lightning had indeed brought me in touch with the spirit world.

And sometimes, when I was feeling strong enough to lift my head, I investigated another odd new phenomenon I'd discovered shortly after Aunt Eva first put me into that bed. It involved Uncle Wilfred's brass compass in the wooden case, which I kept on my bedside table.

The needle no longer pointed north.

It pointed to me, even if I moved the compass around. It followed me.

"Holy smoke," I whispered every single time I saw the needle swing my way.

I was now magnetic.

ONE WEEK INTO MY CONVALESCENCE, WHEN I WAS ABLE to sit upright without feeling like someone was whacking my spine with a sledgehammer, Aunt Eva came into my room with a forced smile on her face. "I've sewn a covering for Oberon's cage to keep him quieter during the day while you recover." She carried a long beige cloth as well as a white envelope.

I tilted my head for a better look at the envelope. "What's that?"

She drew in her breath. "It's from your father."

"My father?"

"I forgot to look at yesterday's mail. I just found this below the bills." She gave me the letter. "I'll let you read it in peace, but try not to get agitated by whatever he has to say. Let me know if you need me to come back."

I nodded, and murmured, "Thank you."

She left me alone to stare at the top line of the return address—the name of my father's new home:

PORTLAND CITY JAIL

Those three brutal words churned up all the hurt and rage from the night he left me—the night before I climbed aboard that train crammed with paranoid passengers bound for San Diego.

I remembered the two of us huddled around the kitchen table, finishing a bland meal of rice and beans and dry bread made of cornstarch instead of wheat. Dad ran his fingers through his whitening brown hair and told me, "Mary Shelley, if anything happens to me—"

"You're not going to die from a measly flu germ, Dad," I said.

"I don't necessarily mean dying. If something—"

"What? What's going to happen to you?"

"Shh. Let me speak." He wrapped his sturdy fingers around my hand. "If something happens, I would like you to go straight to Aunt Eva's. The weather's not so cold there. You'd be more likely to survive the flu with open windows and sunshine. And we'd keep the Oregon side of the family out of trouble."

"What type of trouble?"

He avoided my questioning stare.

"Tell me, Dad."

He cleared his throat. "Trouble that comes from doing the right thing, even if it's not safe. That's all I'm going to say about it, because I don't want anyone pressing you for information." He swallowed down a sip of coffee. "Eva's been living all alone in that house ever since Wilfred succumbed to his illness. I'm sure she'd be grateful for the company. Pack your bags after supper, just in case."

I glared at him, my nostrils flaring.

"Mary, please don't ask any questions. I'm not going to give you answers."

He only dropped the second part of my name when he was deadly serious.

I jabbed at my food with my fork until the tongs screeched against the porcelain and made him wince, but I didn't ask anything else. There was no point. If he didn't want to elaborate, he wouldn't. He was as bullheaded as I.

And here I was, more than a thousand miles away, all alone except for a jittery aunt, a chattering magpie, a broken heart, and an envelope with the words PORTLAND CITY JAIL.

I inhaled a calming breath and ripped open the paper.

October 20, 1918

Dear Mary Shelley,

I hope you are safe. I hope you are healthy. I hope you can forgive me for what I have forced you to endure. You may not be able to understand the reasoning behind my sacrifices, but one day when you're older and your anger at me has diminished, perhaps you will see the two of us are alike. We have a great deal of fight inside us, and sometimes our strength of spirit forces us to choose truth and integrity over comfort and security.

I know the world seems terrifying right now and the future seems bleak. Just remember human beings have always managed to find the greatest strength within themselves during the darkest hours. When faced with the worst horrors the world has to offer, a person either cracks and succumbs to the ugliness, or they salvage the inner core of who they are and fight to right wrongs.

Never let hatred, fear, and ignorance get the best of you. Keep bettering yourself so you can make the world around you better, for nothing can ever improve without the brightest, bravest, kindest, and most imaginative individuals rising above the chaos.

I am healthy and, for the most part, doing well. No need to worry about me or the store. I'm letting the bank take possession of the business so we don't have to trouble your uncles. Take care of yourself. Please write me soon so I know you are still alive.

Your loving father

I gritted my teeth and breathed through silent tears that plunked wet stains upon the paper.

"Oh, Dad," I said to his tidy loops of black handwriting. "Why should I bother making the world better when some of my favorite parts about it are gone?" I wiped my eyes. "You're locked away and Stephen's dead, and I don't feel like one of the brightest, bravest, and kindest individuals without you."

THE FOLLOWING EVENING, AFTER AUNT EVA RETURNED from work, a familiar baritone voice drifted up to my bedroom from the entryway.

My father's voice.

I swear up and down—I heard my dad.

I hurled myself out of bed in my nightgown and bolted to the staircase, wondering if the telegram and the letter were mistakes—or mere dreams. Dad wasn't going to be sentenced after all. He had come to fetch me.

"Dad!" My bare feet scrambled halfway down the steps and slipped out from under me. My backside slammed against wood.

"Don't break your neck, Mary Shelley!" said Aunt Eva from down in the entryway. "Why are you running?"

I regained my balance and pulled myself upright. "I heard—" My fingers went limp around the banister when I got a good look down below. My aunt stood by the front door with a slender stranger in a brown suit. Not my father.

"Oh." I stooped with disappointment. "I didn't know you had a visitor."

The gentleman's face, aside from his blue-green eyes, was hidden beneath a flu mask. He removed his derby hat and said, "Good evening, Miss Black," and I saw receding hair the glistening golden red of copper wire.

I lifted my chin. "Do I know you?"

"No," said Aunt Eva, "but you've heard of him. This is Mr. Darning."

"Mr. Aloysius Darning?" I took a single step downward. "The photography expert who's been investigating Julius?"

He nodded. "The one and the same. I was just across the bay at Mr. Embers's house, paying my respects for his brother, and he told me the young model from his handbill had experienced a recent taste of death."

"I told you not to tell Julius what happened to me," I snapped at my aunt.

"Don't get huffy in front of our guest, Mary Shelley. I simply telephoned Julius to let him know you'd been badly injured."

"He seemed concerned about you," said Mr. Darning. "And once I learned your name, I realized I knew your aunt."

"Mr. Darning attends my church." Aunt Eva rubbed the

back of her neck in a nervous manner. "While I don't care for the fact that he questions Julius's photography, he is a kind man."

Mr. Darning's eyes smiled above his gauze. "I appreciate that, Mrs. Ottinger. I know supporters of Julius Embers often view me as the villain."

"I want you to know," I said, traveling two more steps, "I had no idea Julius Embers used me in that advertisement until I arrived in San Diego over a week ago."

"Oh . . . really?" He lifted his copper eyebrows. "He didn't obtain your permission?"

"No, and I wouldn't have given it to him, either. Stephen told me all the ways Julius doctors his images. Double exposures, alterations in the developing process—"

"Believe me, I know all about the tricks of the trade, Miss Black. I've investigated all those possibilities with Julius Embers numerous times, but I'm afraid the man is either outsmarting me or genuinely photographing spirits."

"But Stephen was so insistent it's all a hoax," I said.

"I know, I know—I understand Stephen's concerns entirely. An amateur photographer who becomes a false celebrity is just about the worst thing a real photographer can encounter. But I can't find one shred of evidence that Julius is a fake."

I squeezed the handrail. "Isn't there anything else you can do?"

"Mary Shelley." Aunt Eva shook her head at me. "Please don't tire yourself out with subjects that upset you. Go back to bed." She turned to our guest and grabbed the doorknob. "Thank you so much for stopping by to see how she's faring, Mr. Darning."

"If there's anything I can do to help with your investigation," I said before Aunt Eva could shut the door on the man, "please let me know."

"Thank you," said Mr. Darning. "I'll keep that in mind." He took a parchment-colored business card out of the breast pocket of his brown coat. "And when you're feeling better, I invite you and your aunt to come to my studio for a complimentary sitting. I'd love nothing more than to show Julius Embers I can create a superior print of one of his prized subjects—even without a spirit involved." He handed my aunt the card, placed his derby back on his copper hair, and bid us a cordial good-bye in that gentle baritone voice that made me ache for home.

Aunt Eva shut the door and looked my way, her eyebrows raised. "Why were you calling for your father when you came down?"

"His voice sounded like Dad's."

"Oh." She averted her eyes from mine and hugged her arms around herself. "I know how that feels. There's a man at church who sounds like Wilfred."

"May I have Mr. Darning's business card?"

"Why?"

"Just to have it."

"No." She tucked the card into her apron pocket. "I don't

want you trying to get Julius in trouble when he's grieving for his brother."

"I wouldn't. If Mr. Darning is interested in debunking frauds, I'm guessing he enjoys science. I'd like to write to him and ask him some questions—to give me something to do."

"You don't need to be corresponding with a grown man you barely know. I'll put his card in my file in the kitchen, and we can consider the complimentary photograph in the future." She pointed upstairs. "Now go back to bed before I make supper and draw your bath. You're still paler than a ghost."

"Have they buried Stephen yet?"

She lowered her arm. "What?"

"Have they held his funeral while I've been recovering?"

"No. Not yet." She cast her eyes away from me again. "They've been waiting for his body to come home."

A sharp pain pierced my stomach. "Let me know when they do, all right?"

She nodded. "I will."

I retreated back up to my room on unsteady legs.

To chase away images of Stephen's body coming home in a casket, I forced myself to imagine him crawling through the porthole windows of his family's studio to save the photography equipment from the salty air, as he told me he did. He probably had to somehow scale the outside walls just to reach the high openings and risked breaking an ankle to jump down to the studio's floor. My lips turned in a small grin at the thought of Stephen's acrobatic feats of heroism. But I had to wonder what was happening to the camera's precious metal and glass now that he was no longer there to protect it.

I pulled a box of matches from the top drawer of my bedside table, lit the pearl-hued oil lamp, and checked in with Uncle Wilfred's compass before climbing back into bed. My legs found their way under the sheets, and I was about to sink my head into the pillow when my brain registered something my eyes had just seen. I sat upright and looked again at the compass. My mouth fell open. A shivery chill breezed down my spine.

The needle had stopped following me. For twenty-two more seconds, the little metal arrow directed itself with steadfast attention toward two objects across the room—two objects related to the person who had just dominated my thoughts.

The needle pointed to Stephen's photographs.

9

BLUE SMOKE AND WHISPERS

· *October 29, 1918* ·

AUNT EVA WOKE ME UP THE FOLLOWING MORNING BY exhaling a loud sigh next to my bed.

I held my breath and opened one eyelid. "What's the bad news?"

She held her mask in her hand, so I was able to see her pursed, whitened lips. "Julius telephoned me last night. They're burying Stephen this morning. I'll be working an extra shift later so I can take some time off work to go to the funeral. The Emberses were so kind to me when Wilfred died."

"I want to go, too."

"No, you need to heal."

"I want to be there. Please don't make me miss saying good-bye to him."

She sighed again. "All right, but I'm bringing you home the moment you seem too unwell to be there. I'll feed you onion hash this morning to make sure you stay safe, and I'm putting us in another taxi so we don't have to ride on the streetcars."

"OK." I closed my eyes, for they had started to sting.

Aunt Eva patted my arm. "Pick out your nicest dress. We need to leave in an hour."

EVERYTHING I PUT ON MY BODY THAT MORNING—FROM A big blue hair bow to my black silk taffeta dress—felt like iron weights bearing down on my bones. My healing lightning burn itched worse than a poison oak rash beneath my bandages. Even my mouth hurt, probably because Aunt Eva made me eat enough onion hash to disintegrate my taste buds. I felt like a broken, clumsy version of myself as I made my way back into the briny outside air for the first time in more than a week.

The funeral rooms of Barrett & Bloom, Undertakers, were located on a hill east of downtown, inside a white colonial-style house with black shutters and two front doors that seemed three feet taller than a normal entryway. If caskets of flu victims had flooded the premises like at the undertaker's house where I'd seen the children playing, then Mr. Barrett and Mr. Bloom must have kept them well hidden. All I saw on the lawn were trim hedges a vibrant shade of green and magenta bougainvillea that climbed the wall, twisting toward the second-story windows.

We entered a white foyer, and I stiffened at a disturbing sight: a glowing purplish-blue haze that drifted across the floorboards and rose to the ceiling like a restless band of traveling phantoms. The smell of freshly lit matches permeated my mask.

I inched backward. "What is this?"

"They've sprinkled sulfur over hot coals to fight the flu." Aunt Eva nodded toward a metal bucket half hidden by the ghostly plumes. "They tried that same technique at church before the quarantine closed it down. The smoke burns blue."

"That's because it's sulfur dioxide." But knowing the scientific reason for the eerie blue smoke didn't make me feel any better. "I don't like it in here."

"It's to keep us safe." She hooked her arm around mine. "Come on. I'll be by your side."

We followed the sound of voices and organ music through a doorway and found ourselves in a room about thirty feet long, wallpapered in a pale yellow. More buckets of smoking coal bathed the masked mourners in that noxious blue haze and made my eyes smart. If we hadn't been wearing the gauze, none of us would have been able to breathe.

At the far end of the room, a bronze electric chandelier illuminated a closed, flag-draped casket shrouded in smoke, on display in front of amber curtains. My knees went weak, but I forced myself to stay upright, even though the luminous blue clouds billowing around the coffin made it look like the undertakers had placed Stephen in the middle of a giant laboratory experiment. A photograph of Stephen in his army uniform—the same portrait he had mailed to me—sat propped on a white pillar.

Aunt Eva squeezed my arm to give me strength and led me farther inside the sulfuric room.

Two dozen or so masked mourners milled about in the smoke or sat in the spindle-back chairs facing the coffin. A handful of girls my age, perhaps slightly older, dabbed their eyes with handkerchiefs, and I wondered, with a sting of jealousy, if any of them had ever been Stephen's sweetheart. We had never discussed an interest in other people in our letters.

I tore my eyes away from the girls and met Mr. Darning's gaze across the room. He was busy conversing with a few professional-looking men, so he merely gave me a polite nod of recognition. I was tempted to walk over to him just so I could hear that comforting voice of his.

Stephen's cousin Gracie wandered by Aunt Eva and me, looking lost. Her stringy wig slid down the left side of her head, revealing a bald patch above her ear. Her flu mask—poorly tied—hung off her chin like a deflated balloon.

Aunt Eva touched the girl's broad shoulder. "Gracie, how are you?"

Gracie turned our way with pale brown eyes that didn't seem to focus on us. "I don't know. Stephen's mother couldn't come. Nothing's going well at all."

"I'm so sorry." Aunt Eva embraced the girl in a firm hug. "You've been through so much lately, what with Stephen . . . your mother . . . your own fight with the flu." She helped Gracie pull her wig back into place to hide the ravages of the illness.

I tried not to stare. "Where's Stephen's mother?"

"She's away for a while." Gracie lowered her head. "She hasn't been the same since Stephen . . ." She swallowed, and a peculiar emotion rose off her like a vapor—I could taste it over the sulfur, the same way I had tasted Aunt Eva's metallic rage in the hospital. A sour, rotten flavor, like curdled milk.

Julius, wearing a mask for the first time that I'd seen, came our way. At his side strolled the bespectacled young man with the solid build who had driven him home the morning I learned of Stephen's death.

"Go sit down, Gracie—you don't look well." Julius turned our way. "Thank you for coming, Eva. Mary Shelley, I was sorry to hear about your lightning accident. Are you better?"

"Yes. Thank you."

Aunt Eva touched his arm. "How are you doing, Julius?"

"Not well. Um . . . There was something . . ." He rubbed his swollen eyes. "Uh . . . What was I just going to say? Oh— have you met my other cousin? This is Gracie's twin, Grant."

I gave Grant a polite nod. "It's nice to meet you."

"Nice to meet you, too," said Grant. "I've seen your picture enough times, even though I can barely recognize you in that mask. Girls look ludicrous in that gauze."

I opened my mouth to retort that he probably looked better *with* the gauze than without, but I pressed my lips shut out of respect for Stephen.

Aunt Eva kept hold of Julius's arm. "Gracie told us your mother's not well."

"No, she's not," he said. "She's in a terrible condition. Everyone in this miserable family is either dying or cracking to pieces. It's getting hard to take." He slipped his arm away from my aunt's and pulled a handkerchief from his coat pocket. Plump tears leaked from his eyes—a sight I hadn't expected. He seemed too masculine to cry, even at a funeral for his own brother, but I tasted the genuine bitterness of his grief.

Everyone's emotions seemed to come alive upon my tongue.

"So strange," I whispered, to which Julius lifted his red eyes.

"What's strange?" he asked.

"Just the way I'm feeling."

I looked toward Stephen's coffin again and had the urge to walk over and touch the surface. Aunt Eva guided Gracie to a chair. Julius wiped his eyes and mumbled something about spirits, but I excused myself and made my way toward the front of the room. Stephen's dark eyes in the photograph watched me through the incandescent blue fog.

Two boys near his age stood by the casket for about a minute before I could approach, and I heard them saying something about "rotten luck" and "the damned Krauts." They patted the lid like they were giving a reassuring touch to Stephen's shoulder and departed with bowed heads.

I stepped toward the casket, my lungs wheezing and my legs rubbery. It was just the two of us up there: Stephen and me. I laid my nonbandaged hand on the flag covering the wood and tried to envision the way he'd looked when he watched me from his staircase—the interest in his brown eyes, the dimpled grin blooming across his face, the Verne novel lying open in his lap. The funeral room closed around us, becoming as intimate as the Emberses' peacock-green sitting room, where we had dared to inch closer to one another.

"Stephen," I whispered, "I've hung both of your photographs on my bedroom wall. I know we've never believed much in ghosts, but I have to wonder, were you in my room yesterday? Were you visiting your photos? Or me?" I closed my eyes and blocked out the hum of conversations behind me. "Do you know who I am, Stephen?"

Nothing happened that indicated he had heard me.

My lips shook beneath my mask. "It's Shell, Stephen. Mary Shelley. I'm here for you, all right? I've been unwell, but I'd never miss saying—" I gulped down a lump as sharp as a razor blade. "I even wore one of my gigantic hair bows for you because I thought it would entertain you. Like when we were kids. I'd give anything to hear you—"

I stopped, for a heavy weight, thick and poisonous, had settled across my shoulders. My mouth filled with the same hot-metal flavor of rage as when Aunt Eva had yelled at me in the hospital. The fabric below my hand prickled with static, which made my heart pound.

"Stephen?" My voice rose an octave. I ran my fingers along the flag and shut my eyes again. "Are you all right?"

The flavor in my mouth grew more intense, and the flag beneath my hand sparked and crackled. Everything else in the room slipped away.

"Is something wrong, Stephen?" I asked again, feeling in my bones I'd hear an answer.

Three heartbeats passed. A whisper brushed against my ear.

"Very wrong."

My eyes flew open. I peered over my shoulder to see if anyone stood nearby, but there was no one within ten feet of me. I dropped to my knees, pulled down my mask, and bent my bare lips closer to the coffin. "Did you just say *very wrong*? Oh, my God, did you just speak to me?"

"Mary Shelley?" called Aunt Eva from behind me.

"Stephen, talk to me again. What's wrong? Why aren't you all right?"

Another word burned in my ear. *"Blackbirds."*

"What are you doing?" Aunt Eva grabbed my shoulders. "Stand up and put on your mask."

"He's whispering to me. I hear him. He's talking."

"Don't say that."

"Please be quiet—I need to hear him. He's not all right. Something's wrong."

Two pairs of strong male hands pulled me backward.

"Wait." I fought to break free. "He's whispering. He's talking to me."

The soles of my dress shoes skidded across the floorboards. Everything else had gone silent: the organ music, the mourners. Stunned eyes looked at me through the smoke over white patches of gauze. The flag-draped casket disappeared from my view.

"Don't take me away!" I kicked and flailed and arched my back. "I heard him in there. He said something about birds. Don't take me away from him. He's talking to me. He's talking to me!"

My captors steered me toward the lobby, out of view of the horrified mourners. One of the men—Julius—turned me around and clutched my arms so hard it hurt. "What's going on?"

"He was whispering to me. I heard him. He said something's wrong."

"Mary Shelley, stop," said Aunt Eva behind me. "Stop it right now."

The Emberses' cousin Grant stood beside Julius with his hands on his hips and his brow furrowed.

Julius studied me with eyes that so resembled his brother's, and I gripped the cuffs of his black coat sleeves. "Open the casket, Julius. What if he's stuck in there?"

"We can't open it."

"Please—open it. I swear I heard him talk."

"We can't open the casket, Mary Shelley." Julius's eyes went bloodshot again. "His head is too damaged."

His words tore into me with a bite a hundred times more vicious than the pain of the lightning bolt. My lips turned cold and sore with the realization that there would never, *ever* be another kiss. I'd never again feel the pressure of Stephen's hand against the small of my back. I'd never receive another letter from him.

His head is too damaged.

A sob shook my shoulders. I hung my head and bawled like I'd never cried in my life.

Julius hugged me against his chest and allowed my tears to drench his coat's black wool. I wept and choked on the blue sulfur smoke, while Aunt Eva struggled to situate my flu mask back over my mouth and nose.

Julius stroked my hair. "Take her back home, Eva. She shouldn't have come."

"That's a good idea." My aunt took my elbow and pulled me away from Stephen's brother. "Come on, Mary Shelley."

"I know I heard him."

"Don't talk about that right now." She guided me to the door. "I know you're hurting, but you need to let Stephen go."

But I couldn't.

Stephen wasn't completely gone.

THE BUTTERFLY AND THE LIGHTNING BOLT

MY AUNT AND I RODE HOME IN THE BACK OF ANOTHER taxi without exchanging a word. All I wanted was to be alone. I was relieved when we returned to the house and she almost immediately flew out the front door, headed for work in the shipyard.

The need to write to Stephen hit me after she left.

During the past four and a half years, whenever something upset me or intrigued me more than I could bear, my first response was to spill my thoughts across a blank sheet of paper for him. I'd slip the letter in a mailbox and imagine it bundled in a brown postal bag, traveling down to Coronado by rail, jostling amid all the other letter writers' stamped parcels for friends and relatives. And I'd picture Stephen reading my words with a smile on his lips and his own pen at the ready.

Fetching two sheets of stationery and a fountain pen from my bedside table might make everything feel normal.

But what's normal anymore, Shell? I pictured Stephen asking as I headed up the staircase. *Normal ended a long time ago.*

"I just need to write," I said out loud to the empty air.

I grabbed the writing utensils and went back downstairs to a weathered wooden table in the backyard. It sat under the sagging branches of sweet-scented orange trees. Breathing in fresh California air without my mask, I penned a message I knew I would never be able to mail.

October 29, 1918

My Dearest Stephen,

Do you want to hear something odd? I attended your funeral today.

Yes, you read that grim sentence correctly. Now I have to ask you something, and I want you to answer me truthfully: Did you speak to me when I was leaning over your casket? Do you see me writing this letter right now? Was your brother right all along about spirits hovering around us, waiting to be captured in photographs, or has something changed in me? My sense of smell has become extraordinarily acute—as if I can smell and taste emotions. Then there's the compass needle, and your voice at the funeral—I'm not who I was before being struck by lightning.

You whispered to me that something is wrong—something about birds. I don't care how many times I've skeptically laughed at the talk of ghosts, I heard you, Stephen. You sounded like you were in trouble.

And if something has happened, does that mean you're unable to rest in peace?

Answer me, please—in any way that you can. Tell me what happened. Let me know if you are suffering. I want to help you, even if it means looking at life and death in strange new ways that make me shudder with fear and awe. If you're stuck and afraid, I'll do my best to help you figure out what's wrong.

If you can still be with me again, then come.

Yours,
Mary Shelley

WHEN DAYLIGHT WANED AND THE AIR COOLED TOO MUCH for me to linger outside, I tucked my letter to Stephen in the dictionary I'd been reading all afternoon and opened a cabinet outside the kitchen door to switch on the main gas valve. Then I dragged myself into the house, grabbed a matchbox, and poked flames in the wall lamps' glass globes to ignite the delicate honeycomb mantles hidden inside. The matches smelled of sulfur dioxide—a scent I knew I'd forever associate with Stephen's casket—and the odor made me want to retch. It took me twice as long as it should have to bring the lamps to their full brightness.

Aunt Eva planned to work late to cover her missed morning shift. Five hours to go before she would come home. Five hours of dwelling by myself after dark.

Supper was the furthest thought from my mind, but I knew Aunt Eva and I would both need to eat. I stirred up a bland pot of canned vegetable soup over her coal-burning, nickel-trimmed cookstove and ate in silence, wishing she could have afforded electricity. Not only did I enjoy the soothing hum of incandescent lightbulbs, but the gaslights emitted an eerie white glow far too similar to the blue haze in the funeral room. My shadow rising and falling across the pea-soup-green wallpaper made me jump and peek over my shoulder every few minutes.

When my bowl was halfway empty, a voice called out from another part of the house, "Hello."

I froze. The hairs on my arms and neck stood on end.

The voice then asked, "Who's there?"—a horrible, squeaky sound that resembled a child speaking on a phonograph record.

I braced myself for more words or movements from the other room and eyed the window as a means of escape. Was it a robber? Stephen? Another side effect of the lightning?

A squawk blasted through the silence.

Oberon.

"Oh . . . of course." I sighed. It was just that silly bird talking, not Stephen or an intruder. Just a trained magpie saying what he always asked when someone entered the room.

I returned to my soup, swallowing down limp beans and

carrots that tasted like rocks, when a thought struck me: Why did Oberon ask the question he always asked when someone entered the room *if no one had entered the room?*

I leapt out of my chair and charged into the living room, convinced I'd find Stephen standing by the bronze cage.

Oberon was alone, but he fluffed up his black-and-white feathers, lowered his raven-dark head, and screamed bloody murder at the empty lavender room.

"What's wrong, Oberon?" I approached the bird with cautious footsteps. "Did something scare you?"

"Who's there?" he screeched again.

I spun around and scanned the living room, not liking the atmosphere. I swore I heard one of Aunt Eva's picture frames tapping against the wall.

"Everything's OK, Oberon," I said in a voice meant to soothe the both of us. "Everything's fine."

"Who's there?"

"Please stop saying that."

"Who's there?"

"I said stop!" I tossed the beige cover over his cage.

"Who's there?" Oberon rustled his wings beneath the cloth. "Who's there? Hello. Hello. Who's there? Who's—"

"Stop!"

"Who's there?"

"Shut up, you stupid bird. No one's there. Absolutely no one's there."

I kicked the sofa instead of succumbing to an urge to

knock over his cage, and limped back to the kitchen, where I huddled in my chair with my hands clamped over my ears until the bird stopped yelling.

AUNT EVA TRUDGED THROUGH THE FRONT DOOR SOME-time after her whistling cuckoo announced ten o'clock. She slouched at the kitchen table as though her back ached, and her eyelids drooped, so I served her leftover soup and sat with her for five minutes, never mentioning the bird or the uneasy feeling that had settled over her living room.

"Are you all right, Mary Shelley?" she asked in a voice beaten down by fatigue.

"As right as I can be."

"Go up to bed. Put today behind you."

I nodded and pushed myself up from the chair.

Pots clattered in the sink from her cleaning up in the kitchen while I wandered down the hall and up the groaning staircase.

I stepped across the threshold into my bedroom. The air didn't feel right at all.

The first objects that drew my attention were Stephen's photographs, and I remembered something I had once read: according to everything from Christian lore to Slavic legend, butterflies symbolized the flight of the soul from the body. I felt I was looking at pictures representing him and me—the butterfly and the lightning bolt. The lost soul and the girl who toyed with electricity.

A movement in the corner of my eye distracted me.

Uncle Wilfred's compass.

I crept closer to my bedside table and lit the oil lamp's wick with a match. The compass's needle spun in every direction.

"I'm going to turn off the gas after I change into my night-clothes," said Aunt Eva, giving me a start as she padded across the hall behind me to her bedroom. "Good night."

I blew out the match. "Good night."

I stared at the compass for ten more minutes. It never settled down.

Close to eleven o'clock, I changed into my nightgown and crawled under my blankets, keeping the oil lamp lit beside me. The pine dresser and wardrobe looked calm and homey, but still the strange energy hummed around me. The flames of my lamp grew restless, casting shifting shadows that leapt across the wall. I held my breath in anticipation and fear, re-minding myself to breathe when I felt dizzy, and it must have been well past midnight before I finally fell asleep.

I awoke, curled on my side and facing the wall, as the downstairs cuckoo announced three o'clock. The muted glow of the oil lamp still illuminated my golden wallpaper, but the blackness of night crowded around me as if it were a living creature. The scent of burning fireworks scorched my nostrils. A coppery taste lined my tongue and caused the fillings in my teeth to ache, while my heartbeat echoed inside the mattress, pounding like a second heart.

Someone was with me.

I'd experienced that sensation before, in the dark, fresh out of a nightmare—the belief that something was staring at me from across the room in the shadows of my furniture. In the past, the stranger always ended up being a doll or a chair reflecting moonlight. But this time I was positive someone would be there if I checked.

Just turn around and look, I told myself. My breaths came out as shallow flutters of air against my pillowcase, and I could have sworn I heard that needle spinning around in the compass.

Just look.

I inhaled as quietly as possible, not wanting to disturb the room. I squeezed my eyes shut and counted silently to three.

One.

Two.

Three.

I flipped myself over. Opened my eyes. And found Stephen next to my bed.

11
PHANTOM

BEFORE I HAD TIME TO FIGURE OUT HOW I SHOULD RE-spond to his presence, he was gone. He jerked back, as if someone had yanked him by the collar of the white undershirt he wore, and disappeared.

The buzzing energy in the room died down. The compass began following my movements again. Stephen's photographs remained on the wall—motionless, untouched.

I trembled under my sheets, overwhelmed by a barrage of emotions—terror, shock, amazement, concern, elation, love—and unsure what I should do next. My lips tried to form Stephen's name, but they shook too much to function. My arms and legs couldn't move. Black and gold spots buzzed in front of my eyes. I panted until I must have passed out, for I didn't remember a single other thing about the night besides a dream.

A nightmare about a bloodstained sky.

A MASKED FACE SHONE IN THE LIGHT OF A CANDLE IN MY doorway.

I gasped and sat upright.

"What's wrong?" Aunt Eva, not a spirit, came toward me. "What is it?"

"Nothing's wrong."

"Are you sick?"

"No." I looked around the room for signs of Stephen in the weak light.

"What is it, Mary Shelley?" She brought the candle closer to my face. "You're so pale. You look like you've seen a—"

We locked eyes. Her face blanched. The word she didn't speak seemed to hover in the air between us: *ghost.*

"I . . ." I searched my brain for a new subject, unwilling to let the conversation veer anywhere near Julius's conception of spirits when I was grappling to understand my own. "Is it morning now? Are you heading to work?"

She drew the candle away from my face. "Yes, and I want you to stay inside all day. You've been out of this house too many times since you've been here. Don't open the windows."

"Are you sure you don't have any books left in the house besides the dictionary? I really need to read."

"That's all I have besides cookbooks. I had to get rid of all the Swiss and German texts I used in my translation work. Even Wilfred's family Bible was in German."

"*How* did you get rid of them?"

"I gave them away."

I scowled. "Did you burn them?"

"It doesn't matter how I got rid of them. Neighbors had seen them on my shelves. They would have questioned my loyalty to the country if I had left them there."

"What type of world are we living in if we're destroying books? Isn't it the Kaiser's job to annihilate German intellectualism?"

"Shh! Don't talk like that." She waved at me to be quiet and glanced at the window, as if the neighbors had climbed the walls and were eavesdropping from behind the lowered panes. "You sound like your father. You've got to keep opinions like that to yourself."

I flopped back down to my pillow with a huff and pulled my blanket over my shoulders.

"I'm sorry you're stuck like this, Mary Shelley. I know you have no one to keep you company."

Ah, but I do. If that wasn't just a dream.

"You'll find a deck of cards in the living room. Why don't you play some solitaire?" Her footsteps retreated across the floorboards, out of my bedroom. She closed the door, leaving me behind in the near darkness.

Her feet pitter-pattered down the stairs. The front door shut. I sat up, relit my bedside lamp, and drew a deep breath.

The compass's arrow pointed at me.

I looked toward the butterfly and lightning photographs on my wall and remembered the burning air from the night before, the distressed movements of the compass, the restlessness, the fear.

"Stephen? Are you here? Are you safe?"

A mourning dove cooed its five-note song outside my window, but nothing else stirred.

"Stephen?"

The compass remained fixed on me. I slouched back down on my bed and felt as alone as Aunt Eva had thought I was.

THE BELLS ON MY AUNT'S WOODEN TELEPHONE RANG ON the kitchen wall as I scrounged around for breakfast in the icebox. I slid the horn-shaped receiver off the side latch and held the cold metal to my ear.

"Hello. Ottinger residence," I said into the gaping black mouthpiece that always reminded me of the lips of a person shouting "Oh!"

Crackling static met my ears. My heart leapt.

Stephen is somehow on the other end of the line.

"Is this Mary Shelley?" asked a male voice that could have been his.

"Yes."

"This is Julius."

"Julius? Oh." I settled back down on my heels, not even realizing I had risen to my toes.

"I'm in between sittings right now," he said, "and I have a line of customers spilling out to the street again, but I wanted to talk to you a moment."

"About what?"

"How are you?"

"I'm all right."

Static buzzed through the silence again before he asked, "Did you really hear him whisper?"

I swallowed. "Yes."

"Do you believe in spirits now?"

I leaned my forehead against the telephone's glossy oak and debated my answer.

"Mary Shelley?"

Another swallow, one that scraped against my throat. "I don't know about other spirits, but I think . . . I might believe . . . I can communicate with Stephen."

"Do you want to come to a séance with me?"

"Why would I want to do that?"

"I know a spirit medium. She holds séances in an apartment over her grandparents' hardware store downtown. Her circles are legitimate—there's no hanky-panky, no flimflamming, no reason to be afraid. She's an upstanding girl who attends the local Spiritualist church."

"I don't want to contact Stephen through a medium."

"You don't have to contact him. Just come as a learning experience and witness the way other people summon spirit phenomena. You're a smart girl, right? Come see what Spiritualism is all about. You'll fit in with everyone else there. You're like them, Mary Shelley."

I bit my lip, troubled by how much I wanted to go, to find people like my strange new self.

"Are you home alone right now?" he asked.

"Why?"

"That's an awful way to live, sequestered like that, hiding from the flu until you die." His voice sounded louder, as if he had moved his lips closer to the mouthpiece to speak more directly into my ear. "Come with me tonight. These people are all well educated and inquisitive. Everyone's young and eager to learn more about the connection between the living world and the afterlife."

"Aunt Eva would have to come, too."

He paused. "Yes, of course."

"What time?"

"The circle doesn't start until nine o'clock. I'll pick you up at eight thirty."

"I'll try it once, but if I find the experience upsetting, I don't want you to ever talk to me about spirits again."

"You have a deal, Mary Shelley. I'll see you this evening. Dress nicely. No goggles."

He hung up.

AFTER BREAKFAST, I STARED AT STEPHEN'S PHOTOGRAPHS in my bedroom and dared myself to contact him as if I were a Spiritualist medium. Maybe a trance was what I needed to understand these teasing glimpses of his life after death. A spiritual state of mind. Full belief in the other side.

I knelt in front of his photos with my eyes closed and my mind open. I even laid my hands against the picture frames and called his name.

"Stephen. Stephen. Are you there? Stephen Elias Embers."

No. Not quite right. I felt like one of those questionable people who advertised public séances in the newspaper.

TODAY ONLY!
MISS MARY SHELLEY BLACK
A REMARKABLE DEMONSTRATION OF SPIRIT COMMUNICATION
HEAR SHAKESPEARE HIMSELF RECITE *MACBETH*!

I opened my eyes. "You're not like that." I got off the floor and plopped onto my bed. "You've got to approach this more like . . . an experiment. Like . . . Phantom."

That's right: Phantom.

When I was ten, Dad and I had a devil of a time finding a mouse that was chewing through the cardboard cookie boxes in Dad's grocery store. I nicknamed the little pest Phantom, for he came and went in the night like a supernatural entity. None of the traps in the usual places worked. We couldn't find his means of entrance and escape anywhere. All we saw were the mysterious visitor's nibble marks and half-eaten cookies.

After a week of fruitless searching, Dad and I became detectives. We lined the perimeter of the store and the backroom with talcum powder and tracked the tiny footsteps we discovered the next morning. Phantom seemed to be creeping out from somewhere behind the barrel of soap chips. We then used steel bars, springs, and peanut butter bait to build the finest mousetrap a father and daughter had ever invented—much safer than the store-bought ones Dad wouldn't allow me to set. Once we had put our equipment in place, we captured that mouse the very next night.

Stephen was certainly no mouse, and I didn't intend to trap him. But he was something to be coaxed out of hiding.

A mystery to explore.

A scientific mind like yours should want to explore the communication between spirits and mortals, Aunt Eva had said the day I arrived at her house. *It's no different than the mystery behind telephone wires and electrical currents.*

She was right. If I could figure out why I was still able to see Stephen, it would be no different than Thomas Edison discovering how to create electric light out of carbon filaments and dreams. Or the Wright brothers proving humans could fly.

The impossible often turned possible.

Scientific detectives and Spiritualists could be one and the same.

COME TALK TO THE SPIRITS

AUNT EVA CAME HOME TO FIND ME DISEMBOWELING HER telephone.

"What on earth are you doing inside my telephone box?" She plunked a crate of onions on the wobbly worktable at the center of the kitchen and put her hands on her hips.

I blew a stray strand of hair out of my eye. "I'm dissecting it."

"What?"

"My brain desperately needs exercise. I decided to see how the wires work."

"Don't play with any wires—not after shocking yourself to kingdom come." She slammed the telephone box closed, just missing the tips of my fingers. "Bolt that up and stay out of there."

I held up the silver bells. "I need to put it back together first."

"Mary Shelley—"

"It'll just take a minute. The phonograph took longer."

"Leave the phonograph alone. It's having trouble as it is."

"Not anymore."

She sighed, pulled down her grease-streaked flu mask, and grabbed two onions from the crate. "While you're cleaning up your mess, I'm going to make supper."

I screwed the bells back into place. "We've been invited to go somewhere tonight."

"We have?"

"Julius wants to take us to a séance."

She let an onion drop to the floor and turned toward me. "A séance?"

"He called about it this morning." I watched her eyes water with disbelief and excitement behind the round frames of her glasses. "I guess you're interested?"

Her cheeks flushed scarlet. "I am not interested in Julius Embers."

"I meant the séance. I already know you're interested in Julius."

"He's four years younger than I am. I'm a recent widow. Don't be ridiculous." She pulled a knife out of a drawer and went to work dicing the onions. The back of her neck glowed a radioactive shade of red. "He knows so many worldly people in downtown San Diego. And it's the night before Halloween.

I bet the séance will be quite the social event. What would I even wear?"

"I have no idea."

"Wait a minute . . ." She turned my way with the knife in her hand. "Why do *you* want to go to a séance with Julius Embers?"

Instead of answering, I shut the telephone box and screwed the front cover into place.

"Oh, Mary Shelley." Her shoulders sagged. "We can't have another episode like the one at the funeral."

"You said it felt like I brought part of the afterlife back with me. What if I have? What if I'm not all the way back from the dead?"

"You look alive enough to me."

"But Stephen—what if he hasn't made it to the other side? What if there's a reason he's not resting in peace?"

"I don't want you causing another scene. It's not healthy to refuse to let someone go."

"Then why have séances? Why have spirit photography? If you think what I'm doing is wrong, why do you support Julius Embers?"

Aunt Eva pursed her lips until she looked far older than her twenty-six years. She resembled photographs of her own late mother, who always puckered her face at cameras like she was sucking on lemons. "It's just . . . different. Julius is a professional." She went back to the onions—*chop, chop, chop, chop, chop.*

I grumbled and put the screwdriver back inside Uncle Wilfred's toolbox, which sat near my feet.

"What time are we supposed to be there?" asked Aunt Eva.

"He's picking us up at eight thirty."

She lifted her head. "In his car?"

"I guess so."

"It's a Cadillac. I've seen it in the garage behind the house." *Chop, chop, chop, chop, chop.* "A Cadillac ride and a downtown séance." She whistled and shook her head. "And here I thought onion soup was going to be the highlight of my night." She rubbed her damp forehead with the back of her hand. "You need to go pick out something nice to wear. I don't know about Spiritualism in Oregon, but séances are formal events here in San Diego. Or so I hear."

"Why don't you let me make the soup, and you go get ready. You're the one who's worked in the shipyard all day." It was my roundabout way of telling her she stank too much to attend a formal social event, but she agreed without offense and hurried off to bathe.

AFTER SUPPER, WHEN THE SUN HAD LONG SINCE SET AND our gas lamps illuminated the house, I sifted through my wardrobe, pushing aside the nicest dress I owned—the black silk taffeta one I'd worn to Stephen's funeral. My second best, a navy-and-white plaid wool dress with a lace-trimmed collar, ended up being the garment I wiggled over my shoulders and buttoned into place. A belt made of the same fabric cinched my waist, and the hem fell mid-calf. I'd have to wear my black Mary Janes instead of my dingy Boy Scout boots. A pair of kid gloves would hide the scaly lightning-burn remnants on my fingertips. I dug around in my doctor's bag for a little beaded coin purse that had belonged to my mother and stocked it with a portion of the money my father had made me pack before I fled Portland.

In the kitchen, where we could heat the curling rod on the stove, my aunt fluffed, knotted, and swirled my long locks into an elaborate style she called a turban coiffure. To be specific, she made me look like I was wearing a fuzzy turban made out of my own chestnut-brown hair. My reflection in her hand mirror didn't even look like me.

"I really regret chopping off all my curls." She nitpicked over the last few pins at the back of my head, jabbing my scalp until I winced. "I feel so ugly these days with my short hair and my red, calloused hands."

"You're not ugly. Your hair is modern and chic, and your job in the shipyard is admirable, both for the country and the women's movement."

Someone rapped on the front door with the metal knocker.

"It's him!" She grabbed her mask and flew down the hall, contradicting everything I'd just said about her being an admirable symbol of the women's movement.

Julius stood on our front porch in a chalk-stripe suit and a charcoal-gray fedora—and again no flu mask, which I found to be arrogant. His face looked pale, and the skin beneath his eyes bulged with bruise-colored bags, as if he hadn't slept the night before. Taking advantage of one of my new peculiarities, I inhaled a deep breath through my mask and tried to detect the emotions rolling off him.

My tongue went numb.

"Good evening, ladies." He took off his hat and revealed slicked-down black hair, stiff and shiny with pomade that smelled like a barbershop. "Are you ready?"

"Yes, we are indeed." Aunt Eva grabbed her handbag and led us out the door. "Thank you so much for inviting us, Julius. How is your mother?"

"Not well. Let's not talk about that."

He placed his hat on his head, and we followed him down the front path to a blue two-door Cadillac roadster convertible with a hood that stretched for miles and a wooden steering wheel as large as a ship's helm. He had parked the car underneath the electric streetlamp in front of the house, and the light shining down through the bulbous globes made the vehicle's paint glisten as bright as sapphires.

"What type of engine does it have?" I asked.

He opened the passenger-side door for us. "Why don't you just try looking pretty for a change?"

I was just about to give him a tart reply when a screaming black police department ambulance sailed around the corner and came to an abrupt stop in front of a house across the street.

Aunt Eva froze. "Oh, dear God. The flu has reached our

block." Her feet skidded on the sidewalk like she was trying to run away on ice, and then she took running leaps back to the porch. "The flu has reached our block!"

"Eva, stop!" called Julius in a voice deep and authoritative enough to keep her from escaping inside the house. "The flu is everywhere. It's not some big, bad monster coming down the street, knocking at each door. It's random, and you and your niece smell enough of onions and camphor mothballs to fight off any germ that gets within ten feet of the two of you."

I watched policemen in high-buttoned green uniforms hustle to the neighbors' front door while maneuvering a beige stretcher. Their clothing reminded me of army tunics. Soldiers engaging in battle against an enemy they couldn't even see.

"Come back down here, Eva." Julius opened the passenger door wider, revealing a plush black seat more luxurious than any sofa my family had ever owned. "We don't want to keep our hostess waiting."

"They're dying right across the street, Julius."

"Eva—come talk to the spirits. They'll tell you there's nothing to fear."

His words acted as an elixir upon my aunt's nerves.

Her shoulders lowered. Her chest rose and fell with a soothing breath. "Oh. I hadn't thought of the séance that way. I suppose you're right." She ventured back to the Cadillac and climbed into the middle section of the seat.

I stepped in next to her with my coin purse dangling off my wrist. Julius helped me push the hem of my skirt into the car so it wouldn't catch in the door when he closed it, and then he strode over to the driver's side.

The officers across the street hauled out a body concealed by a sheet. Long red hair swung off the end of the stretcher.

Aunt Eva turned her face away with pain in her eyes. "That was Mrs. Tennell, the woman who found you dead during the lightning storm, Mary Shelley. The poor thing. She has five children."

I dug my nails into the beads of my handbag. "I should have thanked her for helping me. I should have visited her. I'm too late."

"There's nothing you can do." Julius climbed into the driver's seat and slammed the door shut. "Stop thinking about it." He brought the engine to life with a roar and steered the roadster southward, to the heart of downtown San Diego.

We traveled past houses and storefronts and more black ambulances. On the sidewalk in front of a home as pristine white as a wedding cake lay three bodies a huckleberry shade of blue, dressed in nightclothes. The corpses rested beneath a streetlamp, as if the living had kicked out the dead like garbage. I bent forward and held my forehead in my hands to stave off nausea.

"I heard the Germans snuck the flu into the United States through aspirin," said Julius.

I swallowed down bile. "That's just more anti-German propaganda."

Aunt Eva kicked my ankle. "Don't talk like that."

"I'm not trying to sound un-American," I said, "but the aspirin rumor is stupid. Influenza is an airborne illness. The only way the Germans could have used the flu as a weapon was if they shipped boatloads of sick German people over here and let everyone cough on us. But the flu kills so quickly and randomly that everyone on the boat might have been dead by the time it arrived in an American harbor, like Dracula's victims on the *Demeter*."

"Does she always argue like that?" asked Julius.

Aunt Eva nodded. "Yes, I'm afraid so."

"She sounds like my brother."

A small smile managed to spread across my lips beneath my mask.

Another siren screamed by. That old bully Death breathed down my neck and nipped at my skin, warning, *Don't waste one spare second of time. If there are things you want to accomplish while you're still alive, you'd better do them soon. I'm coming.*

13
UGLY THINGS

JULIUS PARKED THE CADILLAC IN FRONT OF A FIFTH Avenue hardware store. The shop was wedged between a toy store and a restaurant that smelled of juicy grilled hamburgers. The sign in front of the eatery claimed the place specialized in "Liberty Steaks," but that was simply paranoid speak for *We don't want to call anything a name that sounds remotely German, like "hamburger." We're pro-American. We swear!*

A glass door led us to a dark interior staircase that clattered with the echoes of our dress shoes as we climbed the steps. Another door, plain and chipped and brown, waited at the top. Julius knocked.

Someone opened the door a crack and stuck out her head: an unmasked girl, a year or two older than me at most, with long golden ringlets crowned by a sparkling jeweled band. Her eyes were lined in black kohl, her lips rouged a deep red.

"Hello, Julius." She opened the door farther, enough for us to see her wine-colored dress and gargantuan breasts that seemed at odds with the innocent Goldilocks look of her hair. "I didn't know you were bringing two guests."

Julius took off his hat. "Does that throw off your numbers?"

"Sadly, no. Not at all. Francie died over the weekend. We're not sure if Archie and Helen are still alive. Roy saw an ambulance at their house on Monday."

Julius wrinkled his brow. "That's disturbing."

We entered a dim, bare hallway, and the girl shut the door behind us.

"Welcome." She offered her hand to Aunt Eva. "I'm Lena Abberley."

"I'm Eva Ottinger. And this is my niece, Mary Shelley Black."

"Ahh." Lena shook my hand and grinned at Julius. "You've brought your muse, Julius. 'Beauty resides within the sacred studio of Mr. Julius Embers, Spiritualist Photographer.'"

I reddened and let go of her hand, tasting a flavor that stung sharp and hot. "I didn't know he was going to put me on that handbill."

She winked at me. "Don't be modest about the great Julius Embers's interest in a pretty young thing like you. He and I refer clients to one another. You'll find a stack of those hand-bills next to my donation jar in the parlor. Come along." Lena beckoned with her index finger. "Roy is already here." She swished through a doorway to the right of the entry hall with her curls bouncing and her hips swinging beneath her dress.

We followed her into a small living room decorated in fringed electric lamps and paintings of mustard-yellow flowers that weren't particularly pretty. A blond young man with cloudy eyes puffed on a cigarette at a round wooden table in the center of the space. Julius closed the room's door.

"This is my fiancé, Roy." Lena nodded toward the young man at the table. "Roy, this is Julius's muse and her aunt."

"I'm not his muse," I told Roy, who looked straight through me like he didn't care one way or another.

"I have a homemade anti-influenza remedy for you to snack on." Lena picked up a bowl of sugar cubes from the table. "You're going to need to take off your masks for the séance. The gauze scares away the spirits who died before the flu attacked. They worry surgeons are sitting around the table, waiting to operate on them."

Julius snickered. "You just don't want to wear your own mask, Lena. You hate how it looks on you, so you blame the helpless spirits."

"I don't see you spoiling your handsome face with the gauze, either, Mr. Embers."

"If Death is coming for me," said Julius, lifting his chin, "I want him to see my entire face. He's not going to find me cowering behind anything."

Aunt Eva massaged her masked cheek. "Are you sure we

need to take off our gauze? The flu just arrived on my block tonight."

"The flu is *everywhere*," said Roy, sucking on his cigarette.

"That's what I told her." Julius scooted chairs out for each of us. "Sit down, ladies. Take off your masks and eat Miss Abberley's snack so we can begin."

Aunt Eva took the seat next to Julius, so I positioned myself in the chair between her and Roy and dropped my coin purse next to my aunt's bag. I pulled down my mask until it dangled around my throat like a necklace and watched Aunt Eva do the same. Lena presented us with the bowl of sugar cubes, which smelled like my father's hands after he'd fill cans of kerosene in the back storeroom of Black's Groceries.

I sniffed at the cubes again. "Sugar cubes soaked in kerosene? Is that your flu remedy?"

"Precisely." Lena scooted an extra chair between Roy and Julius for herself. "That's how you get rid of germs. You burn them away."

"I'll burn my throat away."

"That's the point." She sat down. "Eat it or leave."

I picked up a glistening cube and studied it.

Aunt Eva placed a piece of sugar on her tongue, grimaced, and swallowed it whole. Her face turned red. Her eyes watered, and I half expected her to breathe fire. "May I have a drink of water, please?"

"Roy, be a gentleman." Lena knocked Roy's arm with her elbow. "Get Mrs. Ottinger a glass of water."

I raised my cube to my mouth but transferred it inside my fist at the last second and pretended to swallow. When Roy hustled back in with the sloshing glass for Aunt Eva, I flicked the cube to the floor beneath the table.

"So, tell me, ladies." Lena leaned forward on her elbows. "Who do you want me to bring to you tonight?"

My jaw dropped. "We can't tell you that information. How will we know whether or not you're a cheat?"

Lena raised an eyebrow. "A cheat?"

"Mary Shelley!" rasped my aunt. "Be polite. We're guests here."

"If I tell you whom I want to see," I said, folding my hands on the table, "and drop clues about what I want him or her to say, we'll have no proof whether or not you genuinely contact the dead."

"Are you insinuating I can't contact the dead?"

"I'm saying, if you can, you don't need to ask whom we want to see."

"Good Lord." Julius rubbed his swollen eyes. "Listen to all those proper *whoms*. No wonder Stephen couldn't keep his hands off her."

Lena's eyes pounced on me. "Stephen? Is that who you want to find?"

I glared at Julius. "I didn't want you saying anything to her about your brother and me. I don't want her summoning him."

"Then why did you agree to come here?" asked Aunt Eva,

her voice struggling back to life after the kerosene. "I thought you wanted to find Stephen."

"I'm here because I'm curious. If you're going to summon a spirit for me, Miss Abberley, I want you to pick someone obscure—someone no one here would have ever mentioned to you. If I see you're genuinely gifted, I'll pay you to show me how you channel your gifts. But I'm not parting with one precious cent if you're going to sit there and ask me to feed you information."

Lena tugged on one of her coiled curls. "Are you setting rules for me?"

"Yes. If I'm to pay you for tutelage, I'd be an employer of sorts."

Roy chuckled and actually spoke more than four words. "You're being challenged, Lena. It's about time, after all that spoiling you get from your doting followers."

"Shut up, Roy. Put out your cigarette." Lena rose from her chair and pressed her hands against the table. "I've got rules for you, too, Miss Black."

"What are they?"

"No getting out of your chair after I turn off the lights. No talking. No breaking the sacred circle. No touching the ectoplasm."

"What's ectoplasm?" I asked.

"Aha! So, you *don't* know everything." She beamed with a show of shiny white teeth. "Ectoplasm is spiritual energy, fully materialized. Imagine an umbilical cord connecting the other side to the mortal world. My body produces ectoplasm that reaches out and moves tables and objects with the strength of human hands. Keep your fingers off it, and while you're at it, keep your fingers off Roy, aside from holding his hand while we create the chain of energy. Are you quite clear on my rules, Miss Black?"

"Yes."

"Good. Then let's begin." Lena plunked the bowl of sugar cubes on a side table that also held a donation jar and Julius's handbills. She *clip-clopped* in her thick heels to a switch by the door and pressed the button that turned off the lights, submerging the room in blackness. Agonizing chills spread down my back and arms. The temperature seemed to drop twenty degrees. I smelled Roy's extinguished cigarette. And mold.

Lena traveled back to her chair in the dark with the same *clip-clop* rhythm as before, which reassured me she hadn't traded places with anyone else. A chair scraped against the floorboards, sounding like she had taken her seat.

"Join hands," she said.

We did as she asked. Roy took my gloved hand tenderly, and Aunt Eva clamped down on my healing fingers until I fidgeted enough for her to loosen her hold.

Lena drew air through her nose and released it through her lips with a slight whistle. "I'm going to fall into my trance now." She breathed in and out again. "Open your mind. Leave your doubts at the door. Turn your thoughts to loved ones who've left this world for the Summerland." She continued her long, audible breaths, each exhalation punctuated by a soft moan that caused Roy's fingers to twitch against mine. I tried to see the outlines of my companions' heads, but the darkness penetrated the room completely. Lena must have sealed off the windows to keep even the slightest hint of moonlight from peeking through the shades.

I didn't turn my thoughts to any loved ones.

The perfume and cigarettes and mold in the air gave the séance a dirty feel. We were not attending a formal social event, as Aunt Eva had said we would. I'd been tricked into another theatrical show, courtesy of Mr. Julius Embers, whose impenetrable emotions reminded me again of Stephen's warnings about opium. Hazy Roy, who sounded like he was starting to snore next to me in the dark, was probably an addict, too.

"Spirits, are you with us?" Lena's new, deep trance voice rumbled up from her belly. "Knock once for yes, twice for no."

Aunt Eva's hand flinched in anticipation.

"Are you with us?" asked Lena again.

SLAM.

A solid knock walloped the table and made me jump.

"How many spirits have joined us tonight?"

SLAM SLAM SLAM SLAM SLAM.

"Five spirits. Marvelous. Do you see your loved ones sitting at this table, spirits? Once for yes, twice for no."

SLAM.

"Do you want to show your beloveds you're here?"

SLAM.

"Then play for us, spirits. Play."

The table vibrated under our hands, as if an electrical current buzzed beneath the wood.

"Join us, spirits. Play. Show us you're here."

The vibrations strengthened, rattling up my arms, jolting my neck, and trembling down my spinal column. The table creaked and shook and tilted back and forth, gaining momentum. Wood crashed against my rib cage, tipped away, and banged against me again. I couldn't breathe. Pain and fear crippled me.

No, no, no, screamed the rational voice inside my head. *This is not what Stephen's spirit feels like.*

The table hit me so hard it knocked the wind out of me. I regained my breath, kicked off my right shoe, stretched out my stocking-covered toe, and felt around in the dark for signs of fraud. After another blow to my ribs, my toes met with something soft and curvy and covered in smooth fabric: a pair of female legs, wrapped around the center post, shaking the table with all their might.

One of the feet gave me a swift kick in the fleshy part of my calf.

"Ow!" I cried.

"Shh," hissed Aunt Eva.

The shaking stopped and Lena called out, "Don't touch the ectoplasm. Keep all hands and legs to yourselves. Behave like proper ladies and gentlemen or you'll do irrevocable harm to the one you want to see." She exhaled five more of her drawn-out breaths, probably to calm herself after my investigative toes. "Close your eyes. Turn all thoughts to the dear souls you miss so much. Don't allow anything else inside your head. No doubts. No fears. *Nothing*."

I closed my eyes and played along, even though my expectations had soured as much as when Stephen had told me about Julius's photography tricks. I turned my thoughts to Mae Tate, the first student at my high school to die of the Spanish flu. No one in the séance room would have known about her. Mae had worn her dark brown hair in loose braids that hung a full foot below her backside, and she always sat at the front of the classroom because her father couldn't afford to buy her eyeglasses. She collapsed on the floor during the first week of English literature, while we were studying William Collins's "The Passions" in our McGuffey Readers. Mrs. Martin rushed us out of the room, as if the girl had caught fire, and we all stared with open mouths at the way Mae convulsed on the hard wooden floor like the victim of a witch's curse.

That's all I could remember about Mae Tate at that moment. My mind clouded over. Other memories—stronger, richer ones; memories that wanted me to see and feel and taste them—invaded my brain.

A room wallpapered in peacock green.

Stephen's mouth on mine.

Mr. Muse.

Lightning striking a sepia sea.

Four words penned in an artistic hand: I DO LOSE INK.

Blue smoke.

A flag-draped coffin.

A whisper: *Blackbirds . . .*

"I see—the letter *W*," said Lena across the table.

W? I shook my head and reoriented myself. *Oh, Christ. She's going to tell Aunt Eva Uncle Wilfred came through.*

I opened my mouth to stop any fake uncles from emerging in the dark, but my voice got stuck in my throat. The air burned with the same stifling firework smoke I had smelled before Stephen showed up next to my bed. My eyes watered from the uncomfortable change in the atmosphere. The weight of suffering pressed down on my body.

"They're killing me," said a voice behind me.

I turned my head but saw only darkness.

"They're killing me," it said again.

"Stephen?" I struggled to break free of the circle, but Roy and my aunt tugged me toward them. "Stephen, I'm here." I sprang loose from their grip with a force that tipped my chair backward. The wood and my elbow banged against the floor.

Aunt Eva shrieked, and Julius cried out, "What was that?"

"It's all right." I untangled myself from the chair and crouched in the dark. "Stephen, where are you?"

"Help me." Stephen's voice came from a few feet away. "I swear to God they're murdering me."

"You're already dead. I went to your funeral. You died in the war."

"They're coming. Oh, God, they're coming!"

"Stephen?" I reached out but grabbed only air. "What happened to you? Who do you see killing you?"

"Ugly things."

"What types of things?"

"Monstrous birds." He gasped, which made my shoulders jerk. "Don't you hear them?"

"Birds are killing you?"

"Blackbirds. They've tied me down. They're torturing me."

My God, I thought. *Is he halfway in hell?*

"Do you know who I am?" I sat up. "Can you see me?"

A pause followed, long enough to swell with questions from the other sitters. *What is she doing? What's happening? What the hell is going on?*

"Shell." Stephen's voice brushed against my ear and shivered through me in the sweetest way. Static sparked across my hair. "My Mary Shelley."

I lowered my eyelids and smiled. "Yes, it's me. You showed up in my bedroom last night, scaring me half to death."

"You've been pulling me toward you like a magnet. Keep me with you. Don't push me back to France and home again. They've got me trapped there."

"You died in battle. No one's going to hurt you anymore."

"No. You've got it all wrong. They haven't finished with me yet. They're never going to finish with me."

A chair scooted away from the table.

"Keep me with you," he said against my neck.

"Keep coming back to me," I whispered. "I'll help you figure out what's wrong, I promise."

Heavy footsteps clomped across the room.

I opened my eyes. "Someone's going to turn on the lights. Be careful, Stephen—"

The electric lamps buzzed back to life and blazed against my corneas. The smell of fire in the air softened to the lingering wisps of Roy's snuffed-out cigarette. My mouth cooled to a normal temperature.

Stephen was gone.

Lena plodded my way, brow pinched, ringlets jostling. She raised her hand, and before I could duck, she slapped my cheek. "How dare you take over my séance? How *dare* you? Who do you think you are, coming in here, questioning me, insulting me, making a scene in the middle of my sacred trance?"

Julius got to his feet. "All right, all right. Calm down, Lena."

She turned on him and smacked him, too. "Why did you bring her here? Are you trying to make fun of my spiritual skills?"

"No—"

"Get her out of here." Lena ran to the door and swung it open with a crash of wood against wall. "Get her out right now. I don't want to see any one of you on my doorstep ever again, and that includes you, Julius. I hope you never find your brother."

I shot to my feet and tried to lunge at Lena, but Aunt Eva

and Julius took hold of me and escorted me out to the entry hall, where Lena pelted the backs of our heads with balled-up handfuls of Julius's flyers.

AUNT EVA CLIMBED INSIDE THE CADILLAC WITH BOTH OF our beaded handbags quaking in her arms. I put my left foot on the running board to step in beside her, but Julius clasped my elbow and steered me down the sidewalk with enough speed to make me trip.

"Where are you taking me?" I asked in a panic.

He stopped below an electric streetlamp near the hamburger restaurant and yanked me close. "You're not just pretending to see him, are you?"

"No. I hate frauds."

He pushed his fingers into my flesh. His pupils looked as small as pinpricks. "Swear upon his grave you're not lying."

"I swear upon his grave. I still believe your photos are fakes, but I've seen him and heard him, and I just felt him whisper against my skin. He thinks something's still killing him."

Julius's face paled. "What did he say?"

"He told me monstrous blackbirds are tying him down and torturing him. The air burns whenever he comes, and he's terrified, like he's reliving his death over and over."

Julius swayed. He dropped my arm and leaned against the lamppost to steady himself, his skin chalky white.

"I'm sorry, Julius. Did they tell you anything about the way he was killed over there?"

"No."

"Did they mention birds? Or capture by the Germans?"

"No."

"If he comes to me again, I'll ask him more. He begged me to keep him with me, but I don't know how to hold on to him. I was hoping your friend would help, but—"

"Just make him leave. Make him go wherever it is he's supposed to go."

"I will if I can. I feel so sorry for him. He's suffering."

Julius pushed himself off the streetlamp and lurched back to his car, where Aunt Eva waited, clinging to the passenger-side door with blanched fingers. I followed, and we all sat in the Cadillac without a word.

Halfway back to the house, Aunt Eva turned to Julius. "Do you think she's going out of her mind with grief?"

He sniffed and wiped at his nose. "She's sitting right there. She can hear you."

"The lightning seemed to change her. She even feels different when I touch her. Is she really seeing him?"

Julius didn't answer. He held the wooden steering wheel with his right hand and rubbed the bottom half of his face with his left, and I could tell from his rigid jaw and troubled eyes that the fraudulent spirit photographer believed in his brother's ghost.

14

STAY SAFE

I COULDN'T SLEEP.

I thumbed through Stephen's envelopes and reread several of his letters to hear his living voice inside my head. Most of his messages were written on stationery as blue as the sea—his favorite color—with his initials, *SEE*, monogrammed at the top.

One letter, from April 1917, stood out because of his discussion of the war and our friendship.

Dear Mary Shelley,

Happy birthday! How old are you now? Fifteen? Are you still as short as you used to be? Were you really short, or am I just remembering you that way because you're two years younger?

You probably already know this, but people teased me for being friends with a brainy girl. If I ever acted cold toward you when the taunting got bad, I apologize for my idiocy. None of those people ever write to me these days, so it seems stupid to have worried what they thought. They disappeared into my past without a trace, but the friend I considered abandoning because of them still makes me laugh with her brutally witty letters and bold honesty. I have never met a single soul like you, Shell.

So this is war. The declaration changed Coronado and San Diego overnight. The men are all enlisting and everyone is hurrying to make sure we all look like real Americans. One of our neighbors held a bonfire in his backyard and invited everyone over to burn their foreign books. I stood at the back of the crowd and watched people destroy the fairy tales of Ludwig Tieck and the brothers Grimm and the poetry of Goethe, Eichendorff, Rilke, and Hesse. They burned sheet music carrying the melodies of Bach, Strauss, Beethoven, and Wagner. Even Brahms's "Lullaby."

I kept wondering what you would have done if you had caught people dropping books into a hissing fire. I imagined you running over, reaching into the flames, and asking, "Have you all gone insane? Do you realize you're killing art and imagination, not the Kaiser's army?" But I stood there like a coward and kept quiet. I was afraid.

I know this letter has turned much darker than what a birthday letter ought to be, but I find it hard to talk to people around here. Everyone wants to categorize the world as good or bad, right or wrong. There is nothing "in between" in their eyes.

Be careful, Shell. It's a dangerous time to have unusual ideas. Make sure you truly know people before you offer them your trust. There are monsters lurking everywhere, it seems, and they sometimes disguise themselves as friends, neighbors, and patriots. God, I hope no one ever finds this letter and accuses me of being a traitor. That's not how I feel at all. I love our country. I just feel we've all gotten a little lost.

Stay safe. Happy birthday.

Your friend,
Stephen

I had forgotten that particular letter. Perhaps I had pushed it aside in my mind because the contents made me uneasy, but I now realized every sentence—from his shame over his thoughts of abandoning me to his curiosity about my reaction to book burning—was a testimony to how much I meant to him.

I tucked the blue stationery back into the envelope and closed my eyes with my fingers folded around the crisp edges.

THE THREE O'CLOCK CALL OF THE CUCKOO DOWNSTAIRS drew me out of sleep again.

My room appeared to be empty and still. The air didn't burn. I rolled onto my back and settled my head deep into the pillow, half drifting back to sleep.

A minute or so later, something sank down beside my

right hip on the bed. The mattress let out one of its accordion moans. A pair of legs settled beside mine.

I opened my eyes.

My breath caught in my throat.

Stephen sat next to me trembling, sweating.

I could see him.

He slouched against the wall in a sleeveless undershirt and trousers a burlap shade of brown. His hair hung in his face, disheveled and grown since I saw him in April, and he held his head in his fists. "Oh, God, Shell. Please make them stop."

My voice escaped me. I wanted to lift my hand to see if I could touch him, but I worried I'd scare him away. I managed to say one word: "Stephen?"

He wouldn't move at first—he just held his head and shuddered. Then something gave him a start. His shoulders flinched like he had heard a gunshot, and he dove down next to me, pressed his cheek against mine, and squirmed closer.

I stroked his hair above his left ear. "Why can I feel you?" A smooth lock slid between my fingers with the crackle of static. His face was covered in clammy sweat that dampened my skin. "I can feel you. Are we both half-dead?"

"They're killing me."

"It's all right. Nobody's here." I wrapped my arms around him and clutched the soft folds of his cotton shirt. His breath warmed my neck, and his heart drummed against me as if he were still alive. My own heart galloped like a quarter horse. "Nobody's here, Ste—"

He gasped and peered over his shoulder.

"What's wrong?"

"Oh, God." He pushed himself to his elbows. "They're coming."

"Who?" My eyes flew to the wall, and I imagined for a moment I caught the shadow of a large bird soaring across the golden paper.

"Oh, Christ." Stephen crawled all the way on top of me, knocking his knees against mine. "Keep me with you."

"How?"

"Let me be a part of you."

"How?"

"Let me inside."

My shoulders tensed. "What do you mean?"

"Close your eyes."

Another shadow flitted across the wall behind him. My eyelids refused to budge.

"Close your eyes." He cupped my cheek with his trembling hand and breathed the scent of burning candles against my face. "Please. Close your eyes and open your mind to me. Help me stay with you."

"Will it hurt?"

"I don't know."

"I'm scared."

"You're safe. I'm not. Help me."

At those words, I shut my eyes. He pressed his mouth against mine and kissed me in that urgent way of his, guiding my lips apart with his own, tasting of smoke and fire. My head went dizzy and buzzed with a violent hum that grew more deafening with every second. I couldn't move beneath him. I couldn't breathe. The oil lamp's flame blew out beside me, which made the dizziness worse, like someone was spinning me around and around on a swing in a pitch-black room. Stephen no longer felt like Stephen but a massive weight I couldn't lift. Lights flashed in front of my face—blinding, fiery explosions that singed the air and clogged my throat. Hungry eyes watched me from the corners of the room, ready to come closer. My wrists and ankles burned with the bite of heavy rope. I was going to die. Oh, my God, I was going to die.

"Get me out of here!" I freed my mouth and tried to get up. "I don't want to be here. Get me out of here." I kicked and fought and struggled, but the bindings dug farther into my skin. Everything burned—my wrists, my lungs, my nose, my stomach. All I could do was shriek and writhe in the black, black world.

A pair of hands reached around my shoulders.

"No! Don't shoot me. Get me out of here. Don't kill me."

Someone scooped me upward, as if pulling me out of water.

I broke through the surface and gasped for air, a light shining bright against my eyes. My room came back into view. My oil lamp glowed beside me again.

Aunt Eva's face hovered in front of mine, as pale as moonstone. She gripped my shoulders and stared at me as though she didn't recognize me. "Mary Shelley? What were you screaming about? Are you all right?"

I fought to catch my breath and looked around the room—the last thing I wanted to see was any creature with wings and a snapping beak—but there was nothing with us. My skin dripped with sweat, and my bones turned as heavy as when I had returned to my flesh after the lightning strike. My eyelids weighed a hundred pounds.

"Mary Shelley?" Aunt Eva pressed her icy hand against my forehead. "Do you have a fever? Is it the flu?"

"No." I fell out of her hands and collapsed against my bed. "No. It was something else. It's as bad as what he said. It's worse. What were those eyes?"

A thermometer jabbed me in the mouth. I tried to fight it at first, but my aunt held me down and wedged the glass beneath my tongue.

"You're talking like you're feverish." She stared at me. "Either that or that séance went to your head. We should have never left the house tonight. We should have never gone inside that trashy room with that cheap-looking girl."

My aunt's spectacles blurred until the two lenses expanded into four wavering bottle caps. My eyelids closed. I fell asleep before she could even take the thermometer out of my mouth. My brain simply slipped away, and I was gone—completely gone without a single dream—for the rest of the night.

THE WEIGHT OF SOULS

A MASKED FACE STARTLED ME IN THE DARK.

"Don't hurt me!"

"Stop saying things like that." Aunt Eva brought her candle closer to her face and walked to the side of my bed. "It's just me. I'm getting ready to leave for work. Are you feeling all right? Can I leave you alone?"

My bleary eyes wandered around the rest of the room and caught sight of the outlines of Stephen's photographs on the wall, my flu mask dangling off a dresser knob, my sturdy Boy Scout boots sitting upright on the floor.

"I said, are you all right?" She leaned over me.

"Yes." I breathed a sigh that rustled her hair. "I'm fine."

"Have you been having nightmares?"

"No. Not since you woke me up last night."

She stroked my cheek with her chilly hand. "Take my phonograph apart again today or do whatever you want inside this house, but don't dwell on that séance."

"I won't," I said. It was a lie.

Her eyes studied my face one more time before she disappeared from my room and down the stairs. Oberon spoke his name to her in his gravelly bird voice, and then I heard the front door shut.

A half hour later, I got dressed and emptied my black doctor's bag of everything but sheets of blank writing paper and some cash. Down in the kitchen I ate an apple and pulled Mr. Darning's business card out of a little silver box my aunt kept next to her cookbooks. I then plunked myself on the living room sofa to yank my boots over my stockinged feet.

"Who's there?" asked Oberon from his cage.

I glared at the bird.

"Who's there?" he asked again.

"I told you to stop saying that. It's not amusing anymore." I laced up my boots, grabbed my mask and bag, and clomped out the door.

A crow cawed from the roof next door and gave me a sideways stare I didn't care for in the slightest. I tied my mask strings around my head, hurried my pace, and glanced over my shoulder, making sure the black bird didn't follow me. The crow flapped away with a whoosh of large wings and disappeared among the browning leaves of an oak tree.

Three blocks to the south I passed the undertaker's wretched-smelling house across the street. Four men in coveralls hustled to assemble more makeshift caskets on the front lawn, and I felt the vibrations of their saws inside my bones.

"Have those boys stopped playing on the caskets?" I called to the workers.

A graying man with a thin, masked face looked up from his sawing. "What's that you said?"

"I saw a group of boys playing on the caskets the last time I walked past here."

"You mean those little scamps we've been chasing away this past week?"

"Yes."

The man nodded toward a pile of smaller coffins beside him. "They're in there now."

His words socked me in the stomach. I turned my eyes toward the ground and pretended I hadn't heard the response.

The reinforced soles of my Boy Scout boots clopped down the sidewalk.

Death snapped at my heels—*I'm coming. Are you watching out for me?*

Five blocks farther south, I dug Mr. Darning's business card out of the black bag, for the addresses were getting close. I scanned the shop windows for the photography studio, passing a hat shop, the Dream Theatre, a grocery store, and hotels. Eventually I found it—Darning Studio—a modest storefront on the northeast corner of Fifth.

Two display windows showcased Mr. Darning's work: a collection of twenty photographs, ten per window, not a single one of them tainted by spirits, flu masks, or even the war. I saw babies in long white christening gowns and plump-cheeked children in sailor outfits. Brides in airy veils posed in front of clean-shaven men in three-piece suits. The members of a high school football team, clad in black jerseys and knee pants, folded their arms and gazed at the camera with stern expressions. A pretty young woman with dark curls piled on her head peered at me with eyes like pools of ink. On a white card below her frame someone had written, *San Diego's beautiful chanteuse Vivienne Boudreaux.*

The photos brought a smile to my face beneath my mask. They were all lovely.

I opened Mr. Darning's glass door, next to a black sign engraved with golden letters:

MR. ALOYSIUS P. DARNING
PHOTOGRAPHER AND RENOWNED DEBUNKER
OF SPIRITUALIST FRAUDS

A jingling brass bell announced my entrance, and I stepped into a small waiting area with three oak chairs.

"I'm with a customer," called Mr. Darning from around a partition. "I'll be with you in a moment."

"Sit still, Billy," said a woman's voice. "Daddy wants to see how big his boy is getting."

More picture frames hung in the lobby, lined in a neat row along gold- and burgundy-striped wallpaper. I perused the contents of the frames while I waited, reading letters thanking Mr. Darning for catching fraudulent photographers. I looked at newspaper photos of well-dressed gentlemen clapped in handcuffs, their arms clutched by unsmiling policemen. A handwritten letter from the mayor of Los Angeles offered Mr. Darning grateful phrases such as "Your display of integrity amid a turbulent era is to be commended, sir." And "It is never easy to stand up for what is right when so many people want to prove you wrong. I thank you from the bottom of my heart for saving countless Los Angeles families from becoming victims of fraud during this current craze for Spiritualism."

The mayor's words gave me chills. They echoed those of my father in his letter: *Sometimes our strength of spirit forces us to choose truth and integrity over comfort and security.*

A burst of light exploded around the corner, and a child screamed.

I peeked around the partition.

Deep in the middle of a dense haze of smoke, a woman and a boy of about two or three posed on a wicker chair in front of a canvas backdrop painted to look like a lush springtime garden. Both mother and child wore flu masks, and the boy choked on tears and flashlamp smoke as he fought to pull off his gauze.

"I think that should do it, Mrs. Irvine," said Mr. Darning, waving the thick white cloud away with a piece of heavy paper. "You're all done, Billy. You were such a good boy, I'm going to give you a stick of candy."

I seated myself in one of the lobby chairs and kicked my black bag under my skirt so no one would ask why I was lugging a doctor's bag around town in the middle of a flu pandemic. For the first time it struck me as being a strange thing to do, and I didn't want Mr. Darning thinking me strange.

The little boy waddled out of the studio first, wiping his red, runny eyes and shoving a purple candy stick under his flu mask. He smelled like a sticky grape mess. The copper-haired photographer, dressed in a black coat and tie and, of course, a gauze mask, escorted the mother out on his arm. Her blue cotton dress hung off her thin body like an empty sack of flour.

"Thank you, Mr. Darning," she said, taking her little boy's hand. "I hope my William appreciates the photograph. His letters have turned so somber since he fought at Belleau Wood."

"I'm sure he'll adore the photograph. And I'm sure he's fine over there. I wish I could be there myself, but I'm prone to asthma."

"I know I look a fright after the flu, so I'm not sure I'll be much comfort to him."

"Nonsense—you're enchanting. Your husband will love seeing the two of you alive and well." Mr. Darning opened the door for the pair. "I'll have the photograph ready in two days, and then you can put a wonderful little package in the mail to raise his spirits."

"Thank you."

They said their good-byes, and Mr. Darning closed the door and swiveled toward me. "Miss Black. How are you?"

I pushed myself out of the chair. "I'm all right."

His blue eyes warmed with compassion. "Are you sure?"

"Yes, I—" I remembered that the last time Mr. Darning had seen me, Julius and Grant were dragging me away from Stephen's casket while I kicked and screamed about Stephen's whispers. "Um . . . you offered me a free photograph when you visited my aunt's house, and I would like to take you up on that opportunity."

"Certainly. But didn't your aunt want to come along, too?"

"She's at work, so I'm here on my own. If you don't mind, I also have some questions I'd like to ask you about spirit photography."

"Ah, I see. Well, I'd be happy to answer them." He waved for me to join him in the studio. "Come on back and you can ask me whatever you'd like while we set up your portrait."

I followed him around the corner, and the familiar atmosphere in that main room knocked me off balance. I had to hold on to the back of a nearby armchair to recover from a painful wave of nostalgia for Stephen's father's old studio up in Portland. The assortment of props piled next to the staging area—fake boulders, parasols, teddy bears, Parisian fans with long white feathers—summoned memories of rainy Oregon weekends spent inside Mr. Embers's workplace. Stephen and I would wear grown-up-size costume hats and read books or play games while lounging on the studio's velvet-upholstered chairs and settees. I remembered the scents of darkroom chemicals and smoke and the lingering sweetness of customers' perfumes, as well as the sacred silence of Stephen's father developing his photographs.

"Are you sure you're all right, Miss Black?" asked Mr. Darning.

I nodded. "I'm fine."

He slid a rectangular wooden holder containing the used photographic plate out of the back of his boxy camera. "Let me go put this glass plate in my darkroom. I'll be right with you." He strolled through a doorway to the left, but he was back in less than a minute, rubbing his hands, ready to jump into work. "Now," he began as he scooted the wicker chair he had been using for the previous portrait to an empty spot at the side of the studio, "what did you want to know about spirit photography?"

"Well . . ." I picked at a navy string dangling off my right cuff and tried to figure out where to start. "My aunt said you've been exposing fake spirit photographers across the country."

"That's right." He rolled up the backdrop with the painted garden. "I traveled during the summer mostly, before the flu started shutting down cities. Far too many photographers have added spirit images to their repertoire, I'm afraid. The wave of grief sweeping across the land has resulted in desperation and gullibility."

"'Like rummies chasing bottles.'"

He peeked over his shoulder. "What was that?"

"That's how Stephen Embers described the desperation when he talked about his brother's customers. He said he'd hear them crying downstairs and it broke his heart. It's sickening to think of people preying upon grief."

"It is sickening, but the crooked photographers all use the same tricks, so they're easy to catch. They believe they're skilled enough to fool me." He pulled down a plain gray canvas. "The only one who's proven to be a challenge is our own Julius Embers."

"I'm guessing you'll catch him one day, though."

"Perhaps."

I stopped picking at my sleeve. "You don't think he's telling the truth, do you?"

"Part of me wants to believe."

"Really?"

Mr. Darning didn't respond at first. Instead, he dragged a large silver urn holding a silk cherry tree into the center of his staging area. I noticed his eyes glistened with tears. The bitter bite of grief scoured my tongue—it had a flavor similar to vinegar and was equally painful.

I cocked my head at him. "Are you OK, Mr. Darning?"

He stopped tugging on the urn and put his hands on his hips, exhaling a muffled sigh into his mask. "A close female friend of mine was one of the first San Diegans to die from the flu. A beautiful young singer, only twenty-four years old."

"Oh. I'm so sorry." I stepped forward two feet. "Is she the

dark-haired woman in the photograph in the window?"

He nodded and drew a handkerchief out of his breast pocket. "I started off so skeptical about spirits when I first hunted down frauds." He wiped his left eye. "But now I'm compelled to find tangible proof that we all go somewhere when we die. It hurts more than anything to think of a sweet soul like Viv's"—he pressed his handkerchief over his right eye and squeezed the other one closed; a stifled sob escaped his lips as a pained moan—"as being gone forever. I'm so sorry. I don't mean to break down like this. It's highly unprofessional."

My throat stung from the grief and embarrassment saturating that room, and it took me several seconds before I could respond without a hoarse voice.

"It's—it's all right." I rubbed my swollen throat. "I understand completely."

"I'm sure you do." He sniffed back his emotions and struggled to tuck his handkerchief back inside his pocket.

"Have you found any other possible true spirits?"

"I've read about scientists investigating the spirit world." He cleared his throat and fussed with the arrangement of silk flowers. "A physician named MacDougall conducted experiments involving the measurement of weight loss at the moment of death. He theorized he was demonstrating the loss of the soul, which, according to his studies, weighs about three-fourths of an ounce."

My eyes widened. "How in the world did he get volunteers to die on a scale?"

"At a home for incurable tuberculosis patients. He would push a cot holding a dying man onto an industrial-sized silk-weighing scale, and he kept his eyes on the numbers while his assistants watched for the final breath."

"Holy smoke." I shook my head in disbelief. "My uncle died in a home like that, but he certainly didn't have people hovering over him, waiting with bated breath for him to go."

"He received their written consent beforehand. It's not as cold and unfeeling as it sounds. Other men have conducted similar research on mice. Some are using X-rays and cylindrical tubes to study the physical manifestation of the soul."

"Maybe I should show them my compass."

"I beg your pardon?"

"Nothing." I looked down at the toes of my brown boots. "Just a thought I had about turning myself over to a laboratory."

"Are you referring to anything related to your experience with Stephen Embers?"

I played with the exposed pink skin of my lightning-burned fingers.

"I'm not scrutinizing you as if you were a trickster photographer, Miss Black. I'd honestly like to know what happened at his funeral. I was there, remember? I heard you insist he was talking to you."

"I know." I covered my eyes with my hands. "You probably think I'm either crazy or a liar."

"No. You seem an honest girl." He walked closer to me

with footsteps that scarcely made a sound. "Do you believe you're communicating with Stephen?"

I dropped my arms to my sides and decided to be truthful. "Yes. I'm positive I am."

Hope burned in his eyes. "Really?"

"That's partly why I want you to photograph me today. I don't want to go to Julius, because I'm afraid he'll tamper with the image. But I'm so curious to see if a camera can capture any sign that Stephen is here with me."

Mr. Darning glanced around the room. "Do you think he's here with you right now?"

"No. I don't know." I shrugged and shook my head. "Oh, this all sounds so crazy when I talk about it out loud. I know how hard it is to listen to someone who sounds like she's full of bunk, but everything changed after I died—after I was struck by lightning. I experience the world in an entirely different manner."

"What other types of things do you experience?"

"I taste emotions. Your grief just now when you were discussing your loss felt as though I were swallowing a bottle of vinegar."

"Really?"

"And I affect a compass. The needle follows me around the room, like I'm a ghost. Unless Stephen is there. Then it follows him."

He stared at me without saying a word.

I pulled at the edges of my gauze mask, which rubbed

against my chin. "It sounds insane, I know. I never believed in spirits before this happened, and I'd love to find a scientific explanation. I'm planning to go to the library today."

"Would you show me the compass phenomenon?"

"Yes." I sighed in relief. "Yes, definitely—that would be really nice, actually. I'd love to get a professional's opinion."

"May I come over this weekend?"

"Hmm . . ." I rubbed my forehead and tried to remember what day of the week it was. "Oh, today's Halloween, isn't it? A strange day to be discussing spirits. That means tomorrow's Friday. Aunt Eva will be home by five thirty. I suppose you could come over any time after six. You could stay for supper, if you'd like—although Aunt Eva mainly prepares onion dishes that incinerate taste buds and stomach linings."

He laughed. "No, no, I don't want to impose. I'd just take a look at you and the compass and be on my way."

"That would be fine."

"Well, this is indeed intriguing." He rested his hand on the top of his camera. "Shall we take your photograph, then? See what happens?"

I nodded. "I'm ready."

He showed me the entire process as we went along, demonstrating the prepackaged glass plates he purchased directly from Kodak, which he tucked into a protective wooden holder in the darkroom before sliding the holder into the slot behind the bellows. "This is the stage where the phonies typically cheat," he said. "A trickster's plate will contain a previously photographed image, and that image will look like a transparent ghost when the picture is developed."

"A double exposure."

He nodded. "That's correct. Now, I don't guarantee anything will come of this photograph. I make no claims to possess mediumistic skills."

"I know. But let's just try it and see what happens. For the sake of science."

The skin around his eyes crinkled in a way that told me he was smiling behind his mask. "For the sake of science."

He positioned me in front of the gray backdrop with my arms folded behind my back. I gave a weak smile while he prepared the shot with his head ducked beneath a black cloth, and he took my photograph with nothing but the kindest display of professionalism.

Yet, in the aftermath of the violent flash, an empty feeling pestered me.

Stephen doesn't want to use his energy to show up for a casual picture, you idiot, I realized as stinging tendrils of smoke crept over my hair and skin. *Why would he pose for a photograph when he's suffering? You're wasting your time trying to satisfy your own curiosity.*

Stop playing.

Go help him figure out what's wrong.

OF RATS AND CROWS

ON THE CORNER OF EIGHTH AND E STOOD A GORGEOUS white mansion with Grecian pillars flanking the entrance. A trim green lawn lined with rustling, feathery palms led to castle-sized wooden doors that promised knowledge, adventure, and hope. This was San Diego's library.

Inside, the same surreal sulfur smoke as at Stephen's funeral emerged from burning buckets of coal and blurred the view of the central desk and the pale green walls. Sunshine tried to stream through long windows, but the blue clouds blocked the light and cast drifting shadows across the solid oak furniture. I choked on a sulfuric stench that reminded me of rotten eggs, even with the gauze covering my face.

A masked brunette with a soft splay of wrinkles at the

edges of her eyes walked toward me through the burning haze. "May I help you?" she asked in that eager way of speaking all librarians possess.

"I need to look up quite a few subjects."

She noticed my black bag. "You're not a physician, are you?"

"No, I just brought this to hold my notes. It used to be my mother's bag."

"Ah, I thought you looked a little too young to be saving lives. You made me feel better for a moment, thinking you'd be able to help if anyone falls ill. Quite frankly"—she peered over her shoulder and lowered her voice to a conspiratorial tone—"I'm surprised the city hasn't shut us down entirely. Only the reading rooms are closed."

"Oh . . . they're closed?" My posture wilted. "I was really hoping to do some studying here this morning. I need to read through too many books to carry home."

"What subjects did you need to find?"

I ran through my mental list of categories. "Well, I'd like to find books on modern war poetry, trench warfare, German military practices, prisoners of war, blackbirds, birds in mythology . . ." I stopped for a moment to take stock of everything else. "Lightning injuries, electricity, magnetic fields, spirit photography, Spiritualism, and true experiences of life after death."

Her eyes stopped blinking. She looked like a mouse that had been cornered by a cat. "Are you familiar with card catalogs and the Dewey decimal system?"

I nodded. "Yes."

"We allow our patrons to find their own books from the stacks. You seem an ambitious girl. Why don't you try looking up these subjects on your own? I'll even sneak you into the women's reading room to make up for your troubles."

"You will?"

"Yes."

I exhaled an appreciative breath. "Thank you so much. Where is the card catalog?"

She pointed to the wooden files beyond the wall of smoke behind me. "Right over there."

"I don't have a library card yet. I'm new to the city."

"I'll leave an application for you in the reading room."

I thanked her again and headed over to the drawers of cards that indexed books by subject matter.

By the time I reached the empty women's reading room, I carried a stack of ten books in my arms, my muscles quivering from the weight of all those cloth- and leather-bound volumes. The handles of my black bag dangled from my right hand beneath the pile and cut off circulation to my fingertips. I parked myself at an oak table, all alone save for those blue sulfur-dioxide phantoms.

The librarian had left me both the library card application and a copy of the day's newspaper. A story below the latest flu death tolls caught my eye: the opening of a Red Cross House for healing war veterans, whom the paper described as "Uncle Sam's convalescent nephews." In the accompanying photograph, two local women in tailored black dresses served tea to a young man who looked like he'd just been dragged off the battlefield. His hair was as wild as mine after the lightning blasted through me, and his eyes seemed to be saying, *What I don't need after a war is two crazy society bats pushing cups of tea my way.*

An urge to visit those healing soldiers and sailors welled up inside me. I wanted to learn how the war that snatched away Stephen had affected other boys—and to find some sort of clue that would explain why he claimed to be tortured by birds. Plus that soldier's distressed face saddened me. I felt compelled to help people like him, to lend a sympathetic ear and offer comfort that extended beyond cups of tea.

At the top of my first sheet of writing paper, I scribbled, *Visit the Red Cross House and talk to returning men.*

Next, I opened *A Treasury of War Poetry*, published just the year before, and read firsthand accounts of the trauma of the trenches, told through bold and brutal poems such as "The Death of Peace," "I Have a Rendezvous with Death," and "The Hell-Gate of Soissons."

"Into Battle," by Julian Grenfell, mentioned a blackbird:

The blackbird sings to him, "Brother, brother,
If this be the last song you shall sing,
Sing well, for you may not sing another;
Brother, sing."

A chilling reference to crows appeared in Frederic Manning's "The Trenches":

Dead are the lips where love laughed or sang,
The hands of youth eager to lay hold of life,
Eyes that have laughed to eyes,
And these were begotten,
O Love, and lived lightly, and burnt
With the lust of a man's first strength: ere they were rent,
Almost at unawares, savagely; and strewn
In bloody fragments, to be the carrion
Of rats and crows.

With shaking fingers I transcribed *to be the carrion of rats and crows*, and gagged on both the mental image of birds feasting on dismembered dead soldiers and the rotten-egg fumes stealing through my mask. I put the poems aside and continued through the rest of the books, reading about lightning strikes, magnets, prisoners of war, and modern battle strategies. I studied trench combat, gas warfare, and a condition called shell shock that affected soldiers' minds. I investigated Spiritualism and found stories of desperate, educated men like the novelist Sir Arthur Conan Doyle and the physician Duncan MacDougall, he of the soul-weighing experiment, who were risking their reputations to find proof of the afterlife.

Desperate, I wrote on my paper. *They're always desperate.*

I read about ectoplasm that was proved to be cheesecloth, unexplained spirit voices, spirit lovers, spirit writings, spirit photographs, spirit manifestations, and even two girls in Cottingley, England, who claimed to be photographing fairies. My brain raced, and my sheets of paper filled with notes and diagrams and formulas and poetry.

But I still had no idea why Stephen thought monstrous birds were tying him down and killing him.

"DO YOU KNOW HOW I CAN GET TO THE NEW RED CROSS House in Balboa Park?" I asked the same brunette librarian who had helped me before.

She slid my stack of five checked-out books across the polished countertop. "Take the Fifth Avenue streetcar up to Laurel. You'll find a bridge crossing the canyon to Balboa Park."

"Is the park small? Will it be hard to find?"

She raised her eyebrows. "You've never been there?"

I shook my head.

She laughed. "Well, I guarantee you won't miss it when you get to the bridge. It's the former site of the Panama-California Exposition. The military owns the area now, but somebody could probably direct you to the Red Cross House. Do you know someone recuperating there?"

"No, but I'd like to volunteer."

She leaned her gauze-swathed chin against her fist and studied me. "How old are you?"

"Sixteen."

"Does anyone know you're wandering around in the quarantined city by yourself?"

"I said I'm sixteen, not six."

"That doesn't answer my question."

Instead of responding, I opened the wide mouth of my mother's black bag and crammed it full of books.

The librarian ducked below the counter. "Here." She stood up straight again and slid a red pack of garlic-flavored gum across to me. "Take a stick or two. I can't stand the thought of sending a kid across town without some flu protection."

"You sound like my aunt. If she had her way, I'd be bathing in onion soup every night."

"Just take it, please. Take the whole pack. I can buy another." She folded her slender hands on the counter. "It would be a shame to waste all that curiosity to the flu."

I took the pack, and to make her feel better, I even slipped my mask down for a moment and popped one of the foul sticks of gum in my mouth. Instant tears careened down my cheeks. "Ugh." I spit the gum out in my hand. "This is awful."

"Just chew it, OK? Stay safe out there." She nodded toward the exit. "Now go on. I'm getting tired of crying over kids who don't have anyone to watch over them anymore." She turned away from me and stooped down to a collection of books on a low shelf behind her.

I hesitated, soothed by the taste of concern trailing off her, almost tempted to stay. She looked back to see if I had gone, her eyes shining with tears, so I thanked her and slipped away.

Hold up your end!

WAR FUND WEEK
One Hundred Million Dollars

KEEP YOUR NIGHTMARES TO YOURSELF

I GAGGED ON THE TASTE OF THE GARLIC GUM WHILE A bright yellow streetcar carried me along the rails to the hills above San Diego. Three businessmen in smart felt hats rode with me, probably on their lunch break. They buried their gauze-covered noses in the *San Diego Union*, and one of them read the October influenza death tolls out loud.

"Philadelphia: over eleven thousand dead and counting—just this month. Holy Moses! Boston: four thousand dead."

The use of cold statistics to describe the loss of precious lives made me ill. I crossed my fingers and hoped that Portland wasn't a big enough city to mention. Hearing the death toll up there—worrying about my father in that crowded jail—would have probably killed me.

"New York City: eight hundred and fifty-one in just one day—*eight hundred and fifty-one*! Can you believe that?"

"Laurel Street," called the conductor from his post by the center doors.

I pressed a fancy little nickel-plate button inlaid in mother-of-pearl, relieved for the chance to escape. The car came to a gentle stop on a flat part of the street.

"Where's the bridge to Balboa Park?" I asked the conductor before heading down the steps.

"Straight to the east." He pointed with a long arm, and like the librarian, he added, "You can't miss it."

He was right. A nearsighted person without glasses could have spotted it from more than a block away: an elaborate arched concrete bridge spanned a pond and a canyon, and on the other side of the hundred-foot drop rose a city of Spanish colonial palaces, straight from the pages of a fairy tale.

I walked briskly across the bridge, eager to reach the Red Cross House and urged on by a feeling in my gut that someone there would be able to help me with Stephen. I ran below curved balconies, wrought-iron railings, and plaster pillars sculpted with intricate flowers, grapes, and rambling vines. It would have been amazing to simply stand there and gape at the architecture, but not when I had a mission.

The building I sought stood out like a beacon, for a large red cross marked its roof. I slowed my pace as I approached the daunting entrance, my heart thumping as if I were about to come face-to-face with Stephen himself.

Inside, the main room must have stretched two hundred feet across, and bandaged, wounded men were everywhere. They read and slept on sofas and padded leather chairs, or hobbled about on crutches. Others were confined to wicker wheelchairs. A few groups who didn't look as battered as the rest huddled around tables and played cards. Canaries sang from wire cages. Two open fireplaces warmed the air. No one, save those warbling canaries, made much noise.

Along with the garlic fumes heating my tongue, the rancid taste of suffering drenched my mouth, as if someone were pouring week-old soup prepared with spoiled meat and stagnant water down my throat. I yanked off my gauze and threw the wad of gum into a wastebasket.

A woman with eyes as amber and narrow as a cat's came my way in a white Red Cross hat and clip-clopping heels. She straightened her flu mask over a nose that appeared rather large, smoothed out the crisp apron covering her pressed gray uniform, and took a long look at my doctor's bag.

"I'm not a doctor," I said. "I'm just carrying some library books in the bag." I tugged my gauze back over my mouth and nose. "It belonged to my mother."

"Oh." She blinked like she didn't know how to respond to such an introduction.

"My name is Mary Black," I tried again, omitting the "Shelley" to avoid associations with *Frankenstein* and Germany in an American Red Cross building. "I'd like to volunteer to help the men."

She surveyed my appearance, from the childish white ribbon tying back my hair at my neck to the worn-out Boy Scout boots that were coming unlaced. "How old are you?"

"Sixteen. And a half."

"That's a little young to be witnessing the state of some of these men. Most of our volunteers are married women who've seen a bit of life already. They've experienced childbirth. They've lost husbands."

"I just buried a boy who meant the world to me, ma'am. I've seen corpses as blue as ripe huckleberries lying in front yards out there. There's no need to protect me from anything." I shifted my sagging bag to my other hand. "I'm tired of sitting around doing nothing."

She swallowed. "Very well. Are you up to serving the men refreshments and making sure they're comfortable? Helping them write letters and whatnot?"

"Yes."

She stepped closer and softened her voice. "Several of the men are amputees, and some of their faces are quite damaged beneath their bandages. You may see signs of deformed cheeks and chins and missing facial bones. Are you sure you can do this?"

"I'm positive."

"All right, then. Please avert your eyes if you need to, but try not to express disgust. Our goal is to help them recover in the most soothing environment we can offer."

"I understand." I peeked at the quiet gathering of broken

boys beyond us. "Why are so many of their faces disfigured, if you don't mind me asking? Is it the explosive shells they're using over there?"

"I'm told it's the machine guns. Curious soldiers will often lift their heads out of the trenches, thinking they can dodge bullets in time, but there's no way they can possibly avoid the hail of machine-gun fire." She glanced over her shoulder. "We tend to also see several missing left arms because of the way they position themselves for shooting in the trenches. Their bones shatter into tiny fragments and their wristwatches become embedded in their wounds. There's no way to save the limbs."

I didn't cringe, for I felt she was testing me, and I was determined to prove I could handle the horrors. "What can I do first?"

Her heels clicked over to a woven tan basket sitting on one of the front tables. "Well, I was just about to pass around these oatmeal cookies. Why don't you give that a try?" She carried the basket my way. "Heaven knows, these boys would probably love to be offered baked goods by a pretty young girl. Just be careful none of them gets too fresh with you."

I looped the basket handle over my arm and soaked up the scents of baked oatmeal and roasted nuts—a divine combination that curbed the rancidness inside my mouth.

"Is there a particular part of the room where I should start?" I asked.

"It doesn't matter. They're all in need of cheering. If

the men are too much for you to take, come into the back kitchen. We can always have you help bake something or roll bandages."

"I'll be fine. Thank you." I dropped my black bag by the front door, and then I journeyed into the main room, trying to convey confidence in my stride.

Where to start, where to start? I wondered, unsure if I would be more helpful in one direction versus another. At random, I picked the right.

The first two young men I approached were sitting in fat leather armchairs reading outdated copies of the *Saturday Evening Post*. I remembered the picture of the clown on the rightmost cover from way back in May or June. The black-haired boy reading that particular issue was missing both his legs, his trousers sewn to hide the two stumps. The other young man, a handsome devil with golden-brown hair and smoky-gray eyes, wore bandages over his left wrist where his hand ought to have been. An unlit cigarette dangled from the scarred fingers of his surviving hand.

"Would you like a cookie?" I asked the black-haired one.

He looked to be of Mexican descent, with olive skin and dark irises that brightened when he found me standing over him. "Yes, please," he said.

I handed him one of the lumpy oatmeal cookies and kept my attention from straying to his two stumps. "Here you are."

"Thank you." He untied the top strings of his flu mask and revealed a boyish round face with a healing pink gash across his chin. "You're much younger than the ladies who usually help around here," he said. "*Qué bonita.* Very pretty."

"Thank you."

"No, thank you, *querida.*"

"Please excuse Carlos," said the other boy with a cockeyed smirk I could see through a round opening cut in the center of his mask. "They dope him up with morphine so he doesn't feel the . . ." He pointed with his cigarette to Carlos's missing legs. "He's under the delusion he's still a Latin lover."

"I'm twice the man you are, Jones."

"Said the man with no legs," chuckled the blondish boy.

"Not funny, friend. You're just jealous the ladies fuss over you less." Carlos leaned back in his chair and beamed up at me. "Do us lovesick fellows a favor, *querida.* Take down your flu mask. Let us see your entire beautiful face."

"You don't need to see my whole face."

"But I do," said Carlos.

"You'll be sorely disappointed." I lifted another cookie out of the basket. "I have huge warts and buckteeth hiding under my mask."

"Don't tease us." Carlos gave me a pleading look with his big brown eyes. "We're starving for female attention, *querida.* Just one quick peek."

"I'm afraid not." I offered the cookie I was holding to his friend Jones. "Would you like one of these?"

"No." The blondish boy slid his cigarette between his lips through his mask hole. "But I'd love a light." He raised his narrow hips and yanked a matchbook out of his back pocket with a grimace. His other arm, the one with the missing hand, lay across his left leg as if it were something dead.

"They're bad for your breathing, you know," I said, nodding to his cigarette. "And if these masks do help fight the flu, that gaping hole in the front of yours isn't going to do you a lick of good, either."

"Who are you, my aunt Gertie?" He jerked his chin at me and bit down on the cigarette. "I bet you're also part of the noble crusade to outlaw booze."

"I just know some of the easier ways to avoid an early grave." I set his rejected cookie back into the basket. "You should take care of yourself so you can heal. You're still young. What are you, about nineteen? Twenty? Twenty-one at most?"

He stared me down. "Just light my match, sweetheart." The cigarette fluttered in his lips as he spoke. "This little cigarette is the only thing keeping me from putting a bullet in my head."

The chill in his gray eyes made me want to recoil, but I kept my face stoic. I lowered the basket to the ground and lit his cigarette for him with trembling fingers, as if he were an explosive I was afraid of detonating.

He exhaled a stream of smoke out of the side of his mask instead of directly into my face, and his eyes softened. "Thanks. You're a doll."

"You're welcome." I looked at his good hand. "Are those scars from the war?"

He exhaled another white cloud. "Barbed wire. We rolled entanglements between us and the enemy's trenches, and it was sharp as hell. I came back from war a real cutup."

I reached down for the basket, ignoring his dark pun, and felt his gaze burn against the top of my head.

"I'd give you a hand, doll," he said, "but the Krauts already got it."

"Stop it, Jones." Carlos lowered his half-eaten cookie. "Don't pay any attention to him, *querida*. He's got a strange sense of humor."

I picked up the basket. Jones was staring straight at me while he took a long drag on his glowing cigarette. I turned away and left the two of them behind. My back slouched more than before. Confidence left my stride. The harsh scent of bitterness surrounding that boy hurt worse than the smell of kerosene.

The other masked soldiers turned my way, their expressions expectant, as if I could truly do them good with a simple basketful of cookies. They welcomed me with misshapen, bandaged faces, empty sleeves where arms should have been, healing burns, gashes with red, crusted skin, crutches, absent legs, joints throbbing with rheumatism, and the taste of an indescribable weariness that made my own muscles ache.

Unlike Jones, most of the men were polite and sweet, offering quiet words of thanks.

I came upon a boy who was missing his left arm and leg. Between the bandages and his flu mask, his head was a jigsaw puzzle of intermingled gauze that swallowed up more than seventy-five percent of his face. He slept in one of the leather chairs, head tilted to the right, his chest rising and falling with easeful slumber.

"That one's in the arms of Madame Morphine," said the man sitting in the chair across from him—a graying fellow with an eye patch. "I'll take his cookie for him."

"I'll save it for when he wakes up," I said.

"He might not wake up for a couple hours."

"If you were sleeping as peacefully as he is"—I handed the man his own fair share—"wouldn't you be upset if someone else took your cookie?"

The man wrestled down his mask to show a wistful grin. "I would give far more than a cookie to be able to sleep as peacefully as that, little miss."

"You don't sleep well?"

"Not anymore I don't. Not after they dropped me down in the trenches with the rats."

I fetched another cookie out of the basket and nudged it into his hand.

He patted my elbow. "Thank you, miss. I won't tell a soul."

"Get some good sleep," I said. "You're not in the trenches anymore."

My next stop was a table of three young men playing poker, their wounds less visible than the others', although a pair of crutches leaned against the back of the shortest one's chair. They sat with more ease than the rest of the convalescing fellows, and they enjoyed touching my fingers when I handed them their treats.

"Thank you, blue eyes."

"Much obliged, girlie."

"Aren't you a sweet thing?"

The tallest of the group, a scarecrow of a man with a bulging Adam's apple, sang "Pretty Baby" to me, and I blushed and thanked him and wished he would stop. In an armchair next to them, a curly-haired redhead with a leg wrapped in bandages leaned his forehead against the palm of his hand and wept silent tears.

"Would you like a cookie?" I asked him while Mr. Scarecrow kept on singing behind me.

The man didn't answer. He didn't even look my way. Another long tear rolled down his masked cheek and soaked into the gauze.

Mr. Scarecrow cut off his serenade mid-chorus. "That's Mulroney. He cries all the time, which is pretty dang embarrassing to watch. You may as well keep walking so you don't have to look at him."

I bent down closer to the weeping soldier and put my hand on his arm. "I know how you feel. The world's been getting the best of me, too."

The soldier's eyes met mine.

"Would you like to escape from your troubles for a while?" I asked. "I'd be happy to go find a book I can read to you. Maybe we can both take a short vacation from the real world."

He nodded.

"Something funny, maybe?"

He nodded again, with more vigor.

"I'll be right back."

I left a cookie on his lap and sought out the Red Cross woman who had greeted me.

Society ladies were entering the building to start their afternoon shift of administering aid—a glistening, perfumed whirlwind of starched white blouses, feathered hats, waved hair, and jewels.

"Do you know if there are any books to read to the men?" I asked them.

A tall, spindly woman around Aunt Eva's age beckoned with a manicured fingernail. "Over here, dear. How nice to see a young girl giving her time." She led me to a battered crate shoved beneath a table and scooted the box out for me to see. "These were donated just yesterday."

I knelt and thumbed through a dusty pile of clothbound books. Chaucer. Milton. Tolstoy. Melville. Hawthorne. Bunyan. None of them were right for men in need of cheering.

Down at the bottom, a lighter choice caught my eye: *The Adventures of Tom Sawyer*.

"Aha! That's more like it." I maneuvered Twain's novel out from under the stack. It had a red cover and looked to be in fairly new condition.

"A children's tale?" asked the society woman in a tone that told me she was wrinkling her nose beneath her mask.

"I don't feel like reading anything somber." I stood back up. "And I doubt any of them want to hear grim stories of tortured men and tragic women. Let's give them Tom and Huck."

I tucked *Tom Sawyer* under my arm, borrowed a spare chair from the poker players' table, and returned to the side of the weeping curly-haired soldier.

"'Chapter One,'" I read after I gave a comfortable sigh, "'Tom Plays, Fights, and Hides' . . ."

A collective silence hushed the poker table beside me. Knees turned my way. Heads lifted. Every single man nearby perked up his ears and listened to the "children's tale."

While the ladies glided around the room and poured tea into fine bone china without a single spilled drop, the soldiers and sailors leaned on the arms of their chairs and laughed at Tom Sawyer's shenanigans. Their chuckles rumbled around me, growing richer with each chapter, and I thought, *Maybe I am doing some good. Maybe Stephen would be pleased to know I'm helping people like him. Maybe Dad would be proud.*

"'Chapter Four: Showing Off in Sunday School' . . . 'Chapter Six: Tom Meets Becky' . . ."

I read and read until my throat turned dry, and then I took a drink of water and read some more. The canaries and society women and that foul taste of suffering fell away, replaced by Tom's aunt Polly's house with the whitewashed fence, and the island where Tom and Huck pretended to be pirates.

"'Chapter Ten: Dire Prophesy of the Howling Dog' . . ."

Despite the good I seemed to be doing, however, the section of the room where the boy called Jones smoked in his armchair still weighed me down. He was like a dark stain on a delicate fabric, and I couldn't stop my eyes from occasionally drifting his way.

It wasn't until I had read nearly one hundred pages that I finally figured out why he bothered me so.

Jones seemed bright. The way he cracked an instant joke—as dark as the jokes may have been—demonstrated a quick wit. It indicated he could've been someone I'd enjoy as a friend if that brutal bite of bitterness wasn't getting the best of him. Perhaps he had once even been gentle enough to have loved a girl. Maybe he held that girl close the day before he left for training and promised in a voice not fully sure of itself, *I'll be fine.*

He bothered me because if Stephen were sitting in that chair instead of Jones, Stephen might have also stabbed my soul with the chilling stare of a person who now knew things he should have never learned.

AT FOUR THIRTY, I SAID GOOD-BYE TO MY AUDIENCE AND went to the door to fetch my bag.

My pace slowed as I drew nearer the exit. The same feeling of dissatisfaction that had pestered me at Mr. Darning's studio turned my legs sluggish. I hadn't accomplished one single thing for Stephen. I had worried too much about upsetting the men to ask them the questions baffling my brain.

My feet came to a halt.

I turned toward the person in the room who had spoken to me with the most honesty and marched in his direction.

"Ah, Aunt Gertie returns." Jones twirled an unlit cigarette around with his fingers like a baton.

"You seem unafraid of honesty." I stopped in front of him. "I need to ask you a question about the war."

I could see his mouth harden through the hole in his mask. Clenching my fists, I fought off my fear. "What would you think if a soldier told you he was being tortured by birds over in France?" I shifted my weight from one foot to the other. "What would that mean to someone who's been over there?"

Again he studied me with those watchful, penetrating eyes that didn't seem to blink. "I'd say, 'Keep your nightmares to yourself, pal. Those aren't the things we're supposed to be discussing with other people.'"

"You'd think they're just nightmares?"

"If I mentioned out loud half the things that torture me in my dreams, I'd be put in a straitjacket faster than you can say *crackpot*. And I guarantee you every man sitting in this building feels the same way."

I looked out at all the other men and experienced a depth of concern so overwhelming it made me tremble. I took a breath to steady myself and turned back to Jones. "There was nothing over there resembling murderous birds, then? Nothing that could have pinned a soldier down?"

"I don't know." He crossed his right leg over his left knee

and bit the cigarette between his teeth. "Reality and night-mares have a funny way of blurring together when a man's fighting down in the bowels of mother earth." He twitched his foot and kept his gaze on my face. "Why do you want to know this stuff? Who's telling you he's getting pinned down by birds?"

I bit my lower lip and debated whether I should answer.

He gave a short laugh that was more of a shrug. "You're as bad as the doctors, aren't you? Wanting to know what's going on inside our heads but scared sick of the answers. Maybe you shouldn't go asking about things your naive female brain can't handle. Go back to your quilting bees and tea parties or whatever the hell you all concern yourselves with."

This time I was the one who responded with an unflinch-ing glare. "A dead boy is the one telling me," I said. "A dead soldier."

His eyes lost a hint of their chill. "What are you talking about?"

"Even us naive women find ourselves haunted by the war, you see. And some of us have even tried killing ourselves, like you claim you're tempted to do. I can tell you firsthand it's not worth the heartache and pain. So don't do it."

I turned and left the building.

THE PIRATE KING

A ROW OF ELECTRIC LIGHTBULBS BURNED ACROSS THE ceiling of the southbound streetcar, illuminating a green-tinged poster that hung on one of the closed windows.

REMEMBER BELGIUM! BUY BONDS
FOURTH LIBERTY LOAN

Below the boldfaced words, a silhouetted soldier in a spiked German helmet dragged a little girl away from her Belgian village.

I shifted in my seat and stared at the poster while the streetcar rocked back and forth. Conflicting thoughts about the war stabbed behind my eyes like a headache.

In saving U.S. boys from heading overseas, I realized, Dad may have been allowing Germans to kill Belgians.

The U.S. government saved Belgians . . . by allowing Germans to kill and maim our boys.

Lives were being traded for other lives. The line between right and wrong blurred into a haze. Dad and Stephen could be called heroes, murderers, or victims, depending on how you looked at the situation, and the Germans, too, for that matter. Nothing about the war made sense. None of it seemed right. The kaisers, kings, and presidents should have just had a good arm wrestle over their differences instead of bringing regular people into their mess.

The stabbing behind my eyes worsened.

"God, don't let it be the flu," I murmured loud enough for a woman in a maid's uniform to turn my way with fear in her eyes.

I BLEW THROUGH AUNT EVA'S FRONT DOOR JUST AS DARKness was settling over the house, and I was immediately assaulted with another "Who's there?" from Oberon. His feathers rustled in his cage, and I could have sworn a pair of wings brushed against my hair. I swiped at the back of my neck, grabbed a candlestick, and ran upstairs to drop off my black bag and sweat-soaked flu mask. My goggles—my steadfast companions during my last moments with Stephen and my lightning death—lay on my bed amid the other treasures I had taken out to make room for books and notes. I fitted the lenses over my eyes and adjusted the leather straps around my head for old time's sake.

After making the rounds to light the downstairs lamps, I soothed my parched throat with a cup of cool water in the kitchen. My headache began to ease its firm grip on my skull. I filled the glass again and browsed Aunt Eva's collection of phonograph records out in the living room, hunting for the musical equivalent of *The Adventures of Tom Sawyer*. She owned several songs from the opera *The Pirates of Penzance*, which would do nicely.

I wound the phonograph's hand crank and put the needle in place. The record crackled to life. An actor with a dramatic stage voice announced he would live and die a pirate king, and a bouncy harpsichord introduction began. I leaned back in the rickety white rocking chair and listened to the pirate and his harmonious crew fence and sing about how glorious it was to be a pirate king.

Oberon's big bronze cage was starting to smell like it needed to be cleaned. The magpie swallowed seeds from a metal bowl, but I tried to ignore the movements of his crow-like head by gazing out at the empty street through my snug goggles. The world was still for the moment, unless the sirens of ambulances had become so ingrained in my ears that I no longer heard them. A glowing jack-o'-lantern smiled at me from the porch rail of a bungalow across the way, and I remembered it was Halloween. No one else seemed to be celebrating a holiday a little too closely associated with death. And nightmares.

I sighed and held the glass to my chest. "Those poor men and their war dreams," I said to the empty room before taking another sip.

During the song's second verse, I spied a roadster with shining round headlights cruising into view in front of the house. The Pirate King continued to belt out his piratical joy, while the car's driver steered his vehicle in a one-hundred-eighty-degree turn and bumped the front tire into the curb. He backed up two feet, shifted again, and pulled alongside the pavement. The roadster was a Cadillac. Its sapphire-blue paint glimmered beneath the streetlight.

Julius's Cadillac.

I sat up straight and stiff.

Aunt Eva was in the passenger seat—I could see the silhouettes of her work cap and flu mask. I tore off my goggles and ran to the front door.

The two of them climbed out of the vehicle and shut the doors. Julius wore the same gray fedora as the night before, and he lugged a crate of oranges under his arm. Aunt Eva laughed and chatted with so much giddy enthusiasm that she didn't even notice me standing guard in the doorway until they reached the porch steps.

"Mary Shelley!" She grabbed her chest. "You scared me, just standing there. What are you doing without your mask?"

Julius thumped up the porch steps behind her. "Would you look at that? It does have a mouth and a nose." He gave my chin a flick, but I jerked away.

"What are you doing here?" I asked.

"Julius surprised me at the factory and offered to drive me home." Aunt Eva gestured for us to hurry inside. "Come in, both of you. Shut the door, Mary Shelley. Julius, please have a seat in the living room."

Julius sauntered in with his crate.

"Who's there?" asked Oberon.

I grabbed my aunt by her wrist before she could take two steps up the stairs. "Why is he here?"

"He's lonely and grieving, so he picked me up from the shipyard. I invited him to supper. Go in and sit with him."

"Where are you going to be?" I asked.

"Upstairs."

"Why?"

She yanked me toward her and spoke through gritted teeth: "Because I wasn't expecting him, and I need to change out of these awful, smelly work clothes. I'm embarrassed beyond words right now. Please be a kind hostess while I make myself presentable." She pushed me toward the living room and announced in a cheerier voice, "If you'll both excuse me for a moment . . ."

She hurried up the rest of the stairs. A smell of grease and perspiration so thick I could almost see it lingered in her wake.

I headed into the living room and plopped myself in the

rocking chair across from Julius. "Why are you here?"

"Why do you sound upset?"

"I just want to know what you want."

He tossed his hat on a cushion beside him and sank back into Aunt Eva's flowery ivory sofa—a tiny piece of Victorian doll's furniture compared to his long body. As usual, he wore no mask, and a pale and worn appearance soured his entire face. His eyes were bloodshot and his pupils pinprick small, as they were the night before.

"You should be nice to me," he said. "I brought you something."

I turned my attention to the fruit crate sitting at his feet. "Oranges?"

"No." He hoisted the crate with a grunt, carted it over to me, and dropped down on one knee by my side. A chalky flavor numbed my tongue—a feeling emanating from Julius that I couldn't identify.

"I brought you Stephen's books," he said.

I opened my mouth to react, but no words found their way to my lips—only a shaky flutter of air.

He placed a leather-bound volume on my lap: Jules Verne's *Around the World in Eighty Days*. The cover's rich mahogany scent filled my nose, bringing me back to rain-soaked Oregon afternoons spent with Stephen.

A second book followed: *The Mysterious Island*, the novel Stephen had been reading the day we last saw each other. I touched the embossed title and remembered how the book had rested on his knee when he sat at the bottom of the staircase. I smelled briny sea air and heard the low thunder of waves crashing against the beach across from his house, as well as the ticking of the grandfather clock with the pockmarked moon face and the swinging brass pendulum.

A tear burned down my cheek. Julius pulled a handkerchief out of his coat pocket and offered it to me.

"Thank you." I wiped my eyes.

He rose from the floor and sat on the little round end table next to me. "I know how close the two of you were since you were children." His chilly hand settled around my shoulder. "And I've been thinking quite a bit about what you said after last night's séance. I don't think you're crazy."

I kept my eyes on Stephen's books.

"Mary Shelley," said Julius as he moved his fingers to the back of my hand, "will you please help me remove his spirit from my house?"

Those words got me to look straight at him. "Do you see him, too?"

"No, but I hear him. In his room. Sometimes, even in the middle of the day, the floorboards groan, and I know it's him."

"Is that what those noises were when I last posed for you—when you and Gracie kept looking up at the ceiling in horror and your mother got hurt?"

"I—yes, I think it was." His hand trembled against mine. "I can't even sleep in that house anymore. I want to move, but I need money."

"Are you planning to sell the house?"

"I can't. My stepfather left the property to Stephen and my mother."

"What about all the money from the spirit photographs?"

He snorted. "I'm not a fellow who saves up his nickels and dimes. I have an expensive image to maintain. Customers to impress. Hobbies . . ."

"Then don't complain about being stuck there. Maybe if you hadn't tossed out Stephen's photographs or hurt him—"

"I told you before, brothers fight. That's just how it is."

"You've destroyed his work. He called you violent and a fraud."

"I called him meddlesome and spoiled. It's all a matter of perspective."

"I'm going to see if Aunt Eva needs anything—"

He clasped my elbow before I could step past his big feet. "Don't go. I'm sorry. I just want you to help him. Please, Mary Shelley. Put him to rest."

"Why do you even care?" I asked. "You were never nice to him."

"That doesn't mean I want him to suffer. He was just a kid, for Christ's sake. He . . ." Julius's voice cracked, and grief's sharp sting overpowered the ice-cold numbness on my tongue. "He did a stupid thing by running off to war when he could barely even put up a fight here at home." He closed his eyes and clenched his jaw, and I could feel his battle against tears in his squeeze of my arm. "Jesus, look at me." He shook his head and let out a pained laugh. "Who knew that little pip-squeak of a brother would ever make me cry?"

I removed his hand from my elbow with a delicate motion. "I am trying to help him. If you have even the smallest inkling why he thinks birds were killing him overseas . . ."

"Germans shot him. There were no birds."

"But something terrified and hurt him before he died. And I bet he won't ever leave this earth until he understands what happened to him."

"He died in combat. What more does he need to know?" Julius pulled his handkerchief out of my hand and wiped his eyes.

"Maybe he's like Hamlet's father's ghost, needing justice for his murder." I rubbed my arms to fight off an outbreak of gooseflesh. "I still think he may have been a prisoner of war. He seems mistreated—tortured."

The taste of Julius's grief dissolved in my mouth, replaced by numbness again, as if he were retreating from pain.

"What else could possibly help him feel at peace, Julius?" I asked. "You lived with him all his life. What do *you* think I could do to convince him to move on?"

Julius lifted his lashes and regarded me with his deep brown eyes. A strange look of serenity washed over his face, and his breathing softened. "I just heard him."

"What?" I cocked my head and listened for whispers, but I heard only Aunt Eva's footsteps bustling around upstairs. "Are you sure you didn't just—"

"Mary Shelley . . ." Julius took me by the elbow and guided me down to the rocking chair. His voice dropped to a conspiratorial whisper. "He said . . . he knows you threw that photograph into the bay."

I froze.

Julius leaned close, his forehead a few short inches from mine. "He said he wants another picture of the two of you together. Before he goes. That's what he needs."

"How . . . ?" I swallowed. "How do you know I threw that photo in the bay? Did Aunt Eva—"

"He just told me. You shouldn't have done that. It upset him. He thinks you don't want to remember him."

"No . . . he doesn't think that. It's those birds—"

"He wants a photograph."

I searched Julius's face for signs of trickery, but he kept his eyes on mine. His stoic expression showed me nothing.

He gathered both my hands in his freezing palms. "I'll capture you together one last time. I'll give you a copy of it to keep somewhere special. And then you can tell him good-bye."

"But . . ."

"Mary Shelley." He smiled in a pitying sort of way. "What did Stephen want more than anything else in the world? What made his heart beat fastest?"

My face flushed. I turned my eyes toward the floorboards. "To be as skilled a photographer as his father."

"No. You know that's not the right answer." Julius nudged his knee against mine. "He wanted you."

I shut my eyes to stave off more tears.

Julius bent close again, his breath brushing against my cheek. "He doesn't want you to ever forget him."

"I wouldn't."

"Help him. With a photograph. Invite his spirit into another picture with you. Prove you'll always remember him."

"But . . . he hated spirit photography."

"Please, Mary Shelley." Julius strengthened his hold on my hands. "I just need one . . . last . . . picture."

I looked him in the eye again, and this time I saw something wild and unstable staring back. "Wait . . ." I squirmed. "What's all this about, Julius? Why are you really here?"

"It's about you helping Stephen and me get out of that godforsaken place."

"How could one photograph get *you* out of that house?"

"I'm going to send it to a contest. A scientific publication is looking for proof of the existence of spirits." His eyes gleamed like a child's on Christmas morning. "And they're offering a prize of two thousand dollars for solid evidence."

"No." I pulled my hands out of his. "I'm not helping you get any money."

"I'd give you a fair percentage of the prize money if you brought him to me." He clasped my shoulder. "I bet we could produce solid evidence—a photograph of Stephen that would make the judges' scientific eyes pop with fear and awe and respect."

"No!" I shot to my feet. "Absolutely not. Cripes, Julius, I

thought you were here because you truly cared about your brother."

"I do care. If you turn down this opportunity, you're the one abandoning him, not me. Why would you do that to him? Why would you let him suffer?"

I drew in my breath to give myself confidence. "I'm sure one of the reasons he's unsettled inside your house is because he hates what you did to his father's studio."

Julius shrank back, so I summoned the courage to go further. "Stephen said your drug abuse and fraudulence probably led to his father's heart failure. Maybe he wants you to stop lying and to stop doctoring those photographs."

He absorbed my words for another silent moment. His eyes watered and reddened, and he seemed on the verge of either bawling or erupting with rage. He stood up and towered above me at his full, intimidating height. "I am not a fraud. I do not doctor photographs. I did not drive my stepfather to an early grave."

"But you're a drug addict."

"You don't know what you're talking about."

"I can tell just by being next to you." I breathed in again, the chalky scent coating my throat like novocaine. "You're numb. Maybe if you sobered up, you wouldn't feel the need to prey upon innocent people."

He grabbed both of my arms and lifted me to my toes. "You try living with your brother's ghost and sending your mother away half out of her mind. You try growing up with a stepfather who loved your brother more than you and tell me you wouldn't touch one speck of a substance that takes away the pain."

"You're hurting me."

"Don't ever accuse me of being an addict and a fraud again."

"Let go of me."

"I came to you for help." He shook me. "I came to you as the brother of a boy who loved you."

"Let go of her!" Aunt Eva ran up behind Julius and pulled on his shoulders.

"Leave me alone, Eva."

"What are you doing to her?"

"Leave me alone you stupid, clingy woman!" He let go of me and shoved my aunt to the floor.

The room fell silent, aside from my rapid breathing and the clicking of Oberon's talons as he paced his perch.

Aunt Eva slowly propped herself up on her elbows. She was wearing a brown silk dress, and she smelled powdered and perfumed. Little tortoiseshell combs dangled from stray blond strands. Her glasses hung cockeyed on her nose. She wasn't wearing her flu mask.

"Get out of my house." She pushed herself up to a standing position and straightened her spectacles. "I don't ever want you near my niece again."

"No—I can't. I need her to help me!"

"I said get out." She charged at her wall of photographs,

yanked down the picture with the white-draped figure and me, and pitched the frame at Julius's head. He deflected it with his arm, and the frame crashed to the wooden floor in a shower of glass.

He backed away. "You're crazy."

She grabbed the framed article with his soldier spirit photos and threw that at him as well. He jumped away and let the glass shatter at his feet.

"I'm calling the police if you don't get out of here this minute!" She pulled down another photo—the one with Uncle Wilfred's spirit. "I'm sure Mary Shelley has marks on her arms from your fingers."

The third frame whacked him in the temple. She then pelted him with his hat.

He grabbed the fedora, yelled obscenities I'd never even heard before, and bounded down the hall. He must have swung the front door closed with all his might, for the house shook and the rest of the photos on Aunt Eva's living room wall were knocked crooked.

Aunt Eva exhaled in a way that sounded like a sob. She put her hands on her hips and hung her head, taking deep breaths that wheezed from the depths of her lungs.

I hesitated between comforting her and cleaning up the glass.

"Are you hurt, Mary Shelley?" Her voice turned choppy. "Do you need a doctor?"

"No. You got to him before he could hurt me too badly."

"I can't believe—I don't understand." She tromped out of the room and into the kitchen.

I followed after her.

With her back to me, she opened the surface of her tan cookstove, lit a match, and stirred up the smoldering coals like she was jabbing the poker into Julius's heart.

"I can cook, if you'd like," I said.

She kept digging at the coals.

I rubbed my arms, still feeling Julius's finger marks throbbing beneath my sleeves. "I'm sorry about what he did to you."

"I wasted nearly a year of my life wanting that man. I spent Wilfred's last months hoping Julius would be my chance to have someone who wouldn't waste away and die on me. I had no idea he thought so little of me that he could come over and bully us like we were nothing. Why was he hurting you?"

"We were arguing about Stephen."

She shook her head and slammed the stovetop closed. "It's my fault for always pushing you at him. It's my fault for allowing you to see your childhood friend again. I could have saved us both so much heartbreak if I hadn't been swept away by—" She wiped her wet cheeks with a dishcloth. "And here I am, twenty-six years old, with no husband or children of my own."

"I'm surprised you'd still want children after dealing with me."

She sputtered a small laugh. "But I do. And I—I lost my husband just as I was starting to age. I'm not pretty like you and your mother. I'll never find someone to love me again."

"You are pretty, Aunt Eva, even though you never seem to think so. And you're not old. My mother didn't give birth to me until she was thirty."

"But she died when she gave birth to you."

"Because of severe bleeding that had nothing to do with her age. There's still time for children. Isn't it amazing that right now you have the opportunity to head downtown in trousers and short hair to build ships—to join in some of the same adventures as men?"

She blew her nose into the dishcloth. "A job doesn't hold you when you're lonely. It doesn't comfort you when a killer flu comes barreling into town."

I walked over and placed my hand on her smooth, silk-covered shoulder. "I'm here for you, though. We'll take care of each other."

At the hospital my touch had soothed her, and again she relaxed under my palm. She faced me with eyes swollen with tears. "Are you really communicating with Stephen? Did you honestly hear him and feel him in that séance room?"

I pursed my lips and nodded. "Yes."

"Are you sure you're not just imagining him? I know you're desperately lonely, too. You have no friends here. You have no father and no school, which I'm sure can cause—"

"It's truly him, I swear. He seems to need my help in under-standing his death. Otherwise, I doubt he'll ever rest."

Her mouth quivered. "Do you believe he's been with you anywhere else besides that séance room and his funeral?"

I lowered my eyes.

"Mary Shelley, where do you think you've encountered him?" She gulped. "In this house?"

I nodded and met her gaze. "He comes to me at night. I've seen him. I've felt him. I think someone did something terrible to him."

A deep groove of concern formed above the bridge of her nose.

"Don't be afraid of him," I said. "He doesn't seem to want to do any harm. He's just scared. I think between the war and the flu, no one's going to escape getting haunted. We live in a world so horrifying, it frightens even the dead."

She left my side and grabbed an onion and her knife from the worktable. "Go clean up the broken glass while I fix supper. Let's put the subjects of death and the Embers brothers to rest for the evening. I've had enough for one day."

I did as she asked, for the kitchen was drenched with the taste of heartbreak, and I could barely breathe.

A BLOODSTAINED SKY

I BROUGHT *THE MYSTERIOUS ISLAND* TO BED WITH ME THAT
night. My room sweltered with a heat unthinkable for an Oregon girl in fall, so I wore my sleeveless summer nightgown
made of batiste and embroidered lace and stretched out on
my bed beneath the oil lamp's light.

Part One, I read silently to myself, *Dropped from the Clouds*.
Jules Verne and his brilliant writing transported me into a
hot-air balloon that careened toward a South Pacific island
on the winds of a catastrophic storm. The lingering pain of
finger marks on my bare arms faded the further I dove into
the story, and the ache of missing Stephen and my father
softened to a point I could almost tolerate. Warmth spread
like candle wax through my blood. I fell asleep ten chapters

in, with Stephen's book squished between my cheek and the pillow.

An awful dream visited me. A crow as large as a bald eagle sat on my chest. I pushed at its lung-crushing body to get it off me, but it cawed and flapped its black wings and sliced my skin with its snapping beak.

"Don't!" I yelled with enough force to pull myself out of sleep.

My eyes opened.

I gasped.

Stephen was on me—not a bird.

I regained my wits, pushed him off, and crawled backward to the corner of my bed. "Stay back. Don't come any closer."

He lunged toward me, so I stood upright on the mattress and shoved my spine against the wall. "Get back, Stephen!"

"Don't push me away." He clutched my hips and tugged me down.

"Let go of me! You can't get close to me the way you did last night."

"I need you, Shell." He pulled me to my knees. "Come closer."

"No." I shoved him with enough fear-fueled strength to send him falling backward on his elbows. "You're pulling me into your darkness when you get too close." I stood again. "You have to stay back if you want me to help you."

He remained on his back and watched me with eyes black and fearful. He wore that white undershirt again, and I could see an unhealthy thinness in his arms and stomach.

His cheekbones had become more prominent since April.

"I see red marks on your arms," he said. "They're killing you, too."

"I'm all right, Stephen. Just scoot back a few feet so I can think clearly."

He kept staring at Julius's marks on my skin.

"Scoot back if you want to stay with me," I repeated. "You need to listen to what I say so we can keep each other safe. Do you understand?"

He edged backward a foot.

"Do you promise not to come any closer? Look me in the eye."

He did as I asked, and a small spark of the old Stephen inhabited his brown irises again. I could still see the handsome boy I loved inside that changed, haunted person.

"Will you stay right there?" I asked.

He nodded.

"You promise?"

He nodded again.

"Talk to me, Stephen, so we can make sense of the ugly things and send them away." I swallowed. "Tell me about France."

He dropped his gaze, and his photographs behind him shook with an unnerving *tap, tap, tap, tap, tap* against the wall.

"Last night at the séance you asked me to stop you from going either there or to your house," I said. "What parts of the war do you experience?"

"I'm not talking about France."

I lowered myself to a kneeling position. "I need you to tell me what happened so I can help you get some rest. What do you see?"

The picture frames trembled harder.

"Tell me, Stephen."

"Trenches flooded with rainwater. Mud. Filth. Gas masks." He sat upright and pulled his knees to his chest. "Blood-soaked bodies hanging on barbed wire. Artillery shells whistling and screaming overhead. Rats the size of cats crawling over me. Flashes of light that bring out the huge, dark birds."

My flesh went cold. "Tell me more about the birds."

"I don't know where they come from." He buried his face against his knees. "But they're like no creature I've ever seen. I can't tell how many there are. They show up, and I expect them to peck out my eyes, but they just keep watching me and killing me, and they never go away."

"How are they killing you?"

His body shook as if something cold had surrounded him. "It's dark and shadowy. I'm struggling too much to see them through the smoke and flashing lights. My wrists are tied to something. They stick the tube of a copper funnel down my throat and gag me."

"Were you tortured over there? Did the Germans capture you?"

"I don't know."

I inhaled a gust of fiery air. "The air burns whenever you're with me. What do you smell when you're with these birds?"

"Fire, yes. And those goddamned flashes of light explode over and over and over and over."

His lightning photograph whacked against the floor, saved from shattering by the braided rug.

I heard a movement in Aunt Eva's bedroom down the hall—a squeak of her mattress. I held my breath, counted to twenty, and turned my attention back to Stephen. My voice dropped to scarcely above a whisper. "What do you see when you're in your bedroom?"

He lifted his face, his eyes dim and weary. "A bloodstained sky."

"In your bedroom?"

"Yes. And the closed door and windows that won't let me out."

"You feel trapped in your bedroom, then?"

"Yes."

"Is your brother ever there?"

"No, just the birdmen, when it's dark."

"Birdmen? They're part man?"

"I don't know. It's dark. They've got hands and beaks."

"You see them in your room? Not just on the battlefield?"

"I don't know if it's my room or not. It's hot from all that light . . ." He brought his hand to his left temple.

"Are you all right, Stephen?"

He winced. "It hurts my head."

"What does?"

Mr. Muse's frame banged hard enough to make a dent in the wall.

"Oh, God." He opened his eyes. "I want to shoot them."

"Please stop that knocking sound. Aunt Eva will hear you."

"You've got to keep them from getting at your eyes."

"There aren't any birds here, Stephen. Listen—your brother gave me some of your books, and I can feel the warmth you experienced when you read them. I wonder if going inside your house and touching anything left over from your time in France—"

"No! Stay away from that house."

"I can't go to France, but I can get into your bedroom."

"No. Don't go anywhere near there. If they're there, they'll take your beautiful eyes."

"How am I supposed to help you, then?" I raised my voice. "Tell me. What am I supposed to do?"

I heard Aunt Eva running across the floor of her room. I turned toward my door and heard the second frame clatter to the ground. By the time I leapt over to the pictures to hang them back on the wall, Stephen was gone.

Aunt Eva walked in just as I placed the lightning bolt image back on its nail. I saw the expression on her face when she caught my fingers wrapped around his photograph—the slump of her shoulders, the sudden downturn of her mouth. The previous glow of awe in her eyes when I'd mentioned communicating with the spirit world had now dimmed to deep concern.

She didn't say a word about Stephen. She told me to go back to bed and left my room.

The compass's needle followed me again. The smoke and frustration in the air lifted. I tucked myself beneath my blankets, but I couldn't sleep until the early hours of the morning, when the crickets stopped chirping and the first strains of light glowed through the lace of my curtains. I could only lie there and think of a white, bloodstained sky and Stephen's insistence that he was being watched and murdered by those hideous dark birds.

PAUL SPITZ

WITH MY MASK TIED TIGHT AND MY BOOTS LACED FIRMLY in double knots, I returned to the Red Cross House in the morning, an hour after Aunt Eva left for work.

I grabbed *The Adventures of Tom Sawyer* from the donated book pile and headed back into the throng of bandaged men and twittering canaries, the latter of which set my nerves on edge with their erratic, fussy, twitchy bird movements.

"Are you all right?" asked a woman's voice.

I pulled my eyes away from a cage of yellow birds and found the Red Cross nurse with the amber cat eyes standing next to me. "Yes. Why?"

"You've been staring at that cage for at least two minutes. One of the men who's been eagerly awaiting the end of *Tom*

Sawyer called me over and asked what you were doing."

"Oh." I blinked away a foggy haze muddling my head. "I'm sorry. I didn't sleep well last night. I'm sure I'll be fine once I sit down and start reading again."

"If this is too much for you—"

"I'll be fine. I'm happy to be here again. I want to help."

Her eyes seemed to ask, *Are you sure about that?* I gave her a confident nod and watched her walk away.

Then my attention wandered to the part of the room where Jones and Carlos had rested the day before, and I half expected to hear myself called Aunt Gertie again.

Carlos sat in his same leather chair, reading another old issue of the *Saturday Evening Post*.

The seat beside him was empty.

Fear twisted inside my gut. Had Jones killed himself?

I strode over to Carlos, whose dark eyes shimmered above his mask when he saw me. "Good morning, *querida*. You've come back to us."

"Of course I came back." I nodded to the empty chair. "Where's Jones?"

"Jones?" He knitted his eyebrows like he didn't understand. "Oh, the joker there. That wasn't his real name. I just called him that because so many of you gringos are named Jones."

"Oh." I glanced around the room. "Well, where is he? Is he sitting somewhere else today?"

"He's in the influenza ward. They found him burning up with a fever in the middle of the night."

"What?"

"A nurse told me this morning."

I hugged *Tom Sawyer* to my chest and clawed the cloth cover. Tears pricked at my eyes.

"Don't cry for him, *querida*. He was kind of a bastard."

"I'm not crying for him specifically." I wiped my eyes with my fingers. "I don't know. Maybe I am."

"He might not die. Not everyone does."

"I know."

An awful silence passed between us, which made Jones's chair seem all the emptier.

"I heard you say something about a dead soldier yesterday." Carlos reached his hand toward me across the armrest. "Did you lose a sweetheart?"

I nodded. "His funeral was only three days ago." I sniffed and wrapped my fingers around Carlos's. "Oh, this is silly. I'm supposed to be the one comforting all of you. That Red Cross nurse is going to give me the boot at any second."

"Shh. It's all right." He gave my hand a squeeze. "I lost my sweetheart, too. She did not die, but she took one look at my missing legs and ran away. I have not seen her since I got back to San Diego in early October."

"I'm sorry." I sniffed again. "Maybe she'll get braver with time."

"Maybe." He shrugged. "I don't really think so, though." He gave my fingers another squeeze—a gentle gesture that reminded me I wasn't standing there all alone in the world.

"Where was your boy from, *querida*? Around here?"

"Coronado. He was supposed to finish his studies at Coronado High School last spring, but he enlisted instead."

"Oh, I wonder if he knew that Coronado fellow who's convalescing here."

"What? Did you—" My lips couldn't function for a moment. "There—there's a person from Coronado here?"

"You may have seen him—the poor *hombre* missing the left side of his body. I remember Jones making another one of his terrible jokes about the boy. 'That Coronado bugger is *all right*,' he'd say whenever anyone wheeled him by."

I remembered the boy—the sleeping one from the day before whose head was a mess of gauze. *That one's in the arms of Madame Morphine,* the man with the eye patch had said before asking for his cookie.

"Do . . . do you think . . ." My tongue struggled to keep up with my thoughts. "Do you think he might have known my friend Stephen?"

"I don't know." Carlos let go of my hand. "Go ask him yourself."

"Are you sure you don't mind me going over there right now?"

"I'm not going to chase after you." He snickered and gestured with his chin toward his missing legs.

"Thank you so much for telling me about him." I pulled down my mask and kissed the top of Carlos's head through his thick black hair. "Thank you, thank you."

"You're welcome, *querida*. Thank you for not having huge warts and buckteeth."

I slid my mask back up and took off across the room, slowing my pace when I realized how jarring it would be for the Coronado boy to wake up to the crashing of boots against tile.

I found him in the same chair as the day before—a mangled young man who could have been Stephen's age. His head seemed to have caved in on one side and now hid beneath all those crisscrossing bandages, including his left eye, which may or may not have still resided in its socket. The left sleeve of his button-down shirt lay empty and deflated, as did the left leg of his tan trousers. All I could see of his actual body was a hand, a pale eyebrow, and an open right eye the color of green tea.

He drew in his breath beneath his flu mask. "Oh, sweet Jesus." He sounded like he could only talk out of the right side of his mouth; each *s* that he spoke whistled through his teeth. "I thought I was a goner."

"I'm sorry I scared you."

"You looked like an angel." He took a few shallow breaths. "I don't mean that in a flirtatious way. You honestly looked like a golden beam of light. I thought you were going to take me away."

I shook my head. "No, I'm just a person." The chair where the man with the eye patch had been the day before was empty, so I pulled it closer to the boy and lowered myself into its cushion with a squeak of leather. "Are you in much pain?"

"They keep me on morphine. I'm too far gone to care about the pain when I'm doped up like this." He chuckled a little. "It's nighttime that's the worse. That's when everything aches and the nightmares come breathing down my neck."

"I'm sorry to hear that. I've heard the others talk about the nightmares, too. I'm sure it's not easy." I found my hands shaking. "Umm . . . look . . . someone told me you were from Coronado."

"Yes." He pushed himself up a little straighter. "That's where I've lived all my life. Except for my time in the army, of course."

"Did you go to the high school there?"

"Yes. Good old Coronado High."

"Did you know Stephen Embers?"

"Stephen?" He nodded. "Yes, definitely. We've been friends since he first moved to the island."

My heart beat faster. "D-d-did you see him in France?"

"Yeah, a group of us from school joined up at the same time." He cocked his head at me and raised his visible eyebrow, as if he suddenly recognized me, even with my mask covering most of my face. "Say . . . what's your name?"

My entire name counted too much to hide any part of it. "Mary Shelley Black."

"Ohhh . . ." The soldier's eye brightened. "No wonder you look so familiar. Stephen pulled out that photograph of you all the time."

"He did?"

"I was there when he first got it in the mail, and boy, you would have thought you had sent him a pile of gold from the way he reacted." He held his chest and took a longer break to catch up with his breathing.

"Are you all right?" I asked.

"Sorry. It's sometimes hard . . . to get the words out." His labored speech sounded like it was tiring him, and every *s* whistled worse than before, but he kept going. "I was just going to add that Stephen wedged your photo inside his helmet when we were down in the trenches. He mooned over it—when he was feeling well. He told the rest of us boys you were the prettiest and smartest girl in the world."

"He said that?"

"I was even"—the exposed section of the boy's forehead turned pink—"a little jealous of him."

I blushed as well, and smiled so much the strings of my mask tautened enough to hurt. My eyes smarted with tears, but I sniffed and held myself together for the sake of Stephen's friend.

"How's he doing?" asked the boy.

My blood drained to my toes. "What do you mean?"

"Have you seen him yet? Or did they put him in a hospital on the East Coast first? They said that might happen."

My eyes narrowed in confusion. "Weren't you there when it happened? Stephen died in battle in the beginning of October."

"October?" He shook his head. "No, that's not possible. He wasn't even overseas in October."

I clutched the armrest. "Pardon?"

"They had to send him home."

"Alive?"

"Yes."

"When? Why?"

He answered in a tone so hushed I had to balance myself on the last two inches of the chair to understand him. "It was pretty bad. I hate to be the one to tell you."

"Please, just tell me."

The boy swallowed. "Stephen sort of . . . well . . . he lost his mind over there in the trenches. Got to the point where he couldn't even move anymore. He'd just huddle in the mud, shaking. They tried to help him in one of the field hospitals once—examined him to see if he was faking. But then they sent him straight back into battle . . . and he got worse than ever."

I folded my hands to conceal how much they jittered. "What did they do to him then?"

"They discharged him and shipped him home. He wasn't the only one like that. Hell—excuse my language—but hell, most of us went a little off our rockers over there. You couldn't help it. Some of the fellows' bodies and brains just stopped working right. Scary as heck." The soldier rubbed the right side of his bandaged forehead and wheezed a little. "Stephen was so bad off I didn't think anything could fix him. It was like something inside him broke." He turned his eye back to me and looked like a lost pup. "You don't know where they took him once he got back to the States, then?"

I shook my head. "I don't know anything. His brother said he died a hero's death over in France. He never said anything about him coming home."

"I wonder if he died during transport. Maybe it was the flu. The family could be misinformed. The army gets antsy about the men whose minds leave them."

"He died somewhere, somehow. I went to his funeral."

Stephen's friend got quiet. I snapped out of my shock enough to realize I'd just informed a drastically injured boy his close friend was dead.

"I'm so sorry I had to tell you that news," I said.

"He was a good fellow." Tears blurred his visible eye. "A really good fellow."

"Yes." I nodded. "He is. Was."

"Some of the other soldiers gave me trouble because my father was born in Germany and my last name's Spitz. They called me slurs like Kraut and Boche. But Stephen . . ." The boy's eye brightened a moment. "He would tell them all to shut their damned mouths. Oh . . . sorry . . ." He lowered his head. "There goes my language again."

"It's all right. I've heard words far worse than *damned*—sometimes from Stephen."

The soldier wiped away a tear and sniffed. "Oh, Christ, what a waste." He shook his head and squeezed his eye closed. "Such a waste. I hope he went quickly and didn't have to keep suffering." He leaned his elbow on the chair's arm and rested his head against his fist. Another tear spilled from his eye and glistened against his mask.

"What's your name?" I placed my hand around his upper arm, feeling the soft satin of his sleeve and the lack of nourished flesh beneath.

His meager muscle relaxed beneath my fingers. "Paul."

"I hope you heal soon, Paul. I hope the nightmares stop bothering you and your pain leaves your wounds."

I moved to take my hand off him, but he tensed again and said, "Can you keep touching me a little longer? Again, I don't mean that in a flirtatious way, especially now that I know you're Stephen's girl. But . . . you remind me of something I experienced after that shell went off next to me."

"I do?"

He nodded. "I thought I'd died for a while and went somewhere peaceful. I'd forgotten what that felt like until you touched me."

I held his arm again and watched his eyelid fall.

"Can I ask you one last question, Paul?"

"Yes."

"Did Stephen ever seem to be afraid of birds when he was over there?"

Paul didn't answer, and for a minute I thought he'd fallen asleep. I gave up waiting for a response and shifted my legs to get more comfortable, when he drew in his breath and replied, "None of us liked the crows. They ate us when we died. They hovered on the edges of the trenches and stared down at us, watching us, waiting for us to get shot or bombed. Sometimes we even had to fight them off the boys who weren't all the way dead."

My stomach tightened. "Oh. God. I'm so sorry."

"Why do you ask?"

"Just a strange dream I've been having. I'm sorry I brought up such an unpleasant subject. Please rest now, and heal."

"Thank you. I'm sorry to be so blunt. I think . . . I've forgotten . . . how to speak in polite—" His tongue sounded like it had grown too heavy to finish his sentence. His chin sank forward on his chest, and he dozed off.

We sat like that for at least a quarter hour, amid the restless chirps of the flitting canaries, the tinkle of teacups on society women's trays, and the soft swish of cards flipping at the poker game several feet away. Paul's body relaxed until his gentle breathing indicated he was in a deep sleep. Quiet snores snuck out from beneath his mask.

I remained next to him, touching him, holding on to a tangible piece of Stephen's life, haunted by his words. And even when I moved along to the other men and finished reading *Tom Sawyer*, all I could think about—it consumed my entire being—was the image of Stephen shivering in the shadows of hungry dark birds while his mind crumbled.

THE COMPASS PHENOMENON

SOMETHING MOVED ON AUNT EVA'S PORCH.

I snuck up the front path with noiseless footfalls and craned my neck to see beyond the post that blocked my view. I could make out the shape of a crouching person.

"Who is that?" I asked.

The person shot up with a cry of surprise, and I spotted a pair of large round spectacles balanced above a sagging flu mask. Brown hair grew from the top of the stranger's head like a thicket of grass.

"Is that Grant?" I shielded my eyes from the setting sunlight. "Stephen's cousin?"

"That's right." Grant slunk down the porch steps.

"What are you doing here?"

"Julius wanted me to bring you something." He nodded backward to the porch.

"Why didn't he bring it himself?"

"He's busy at his studio." Grant stuck his hands in his pockets and slithered away from the house. "Plus I think he's afraid of you."

"Julius isn't afraid of anyone." I grabbed Grant's arm before he could dart away. "Hey, wait. I need to ask you something."

"What?"

"I just heard something about Stephen's last days in France."

Nervous air pulsated off him. "Why don't you chat with Stephen about it instead?" He tried pulling away from me. "You're the one who's supposed to be summoning him."

I tugged him closer. "Does the family know Stephen was sent home alive?"

His breathing quickened.

"Did he make it home, Grant? Tell me. Do you know what happened to him?"

"Look, Shell—"

"Don't call me Shell. Only Stephen could call me that."

"Look, Frankenstein . . ." He spoke so close to my face he would have spit on me if we weren't wearing masks. "My mother choked to death from the flu right in front of my eyes five weeks ago. My father's drifting around somewhere in the middle of enemy waters with the U.S. Navy. And my sister lost her hair from a fever so high I can't believe she's not buried like our ma." He yanked himself free of me. "Gracie and I are just trying to survive on our own right now. We don't need anyone pestering us about us working in Julius's studio."

"I'm not pestering you about Julius's studio. I'm just asking about Stephen—"

"Stephen's a dead war hero, all right? Leave it at that. I don't know who's telling you otherwise, but they've got their story wrong."

He turned and walked away.

"A friend who was with him overseas told me otherwise," I called after him when he reached the front sidewalk. "Stephen didn't die in battle."

Grant stopped with his shoulders hiked as high as his chin.

"How did he die, Grant? If you know, please tell me."

He stayed stone-still with his back curved into a lazy C and his eyes directed at the sidewalk in front of him. "You ever heard of shell shock?"

I flinched at the question. I had read about that condition at the library. It could have described what Paul told me about Stephen.

"That's what they're calling the psychological trauma from the war, isn't it?" I asked.

"It's a cowardly way to behave. I've heard the British execute their soldiers who get it, because of the shame."

I wrapped my arms around myself and strove to keep my

voice from breaking. "Is our army doing that to our men, too? Is that what happened to Stephen?"

Grant shook his head, still speaking to the ground. "I'm thinking his friend is the one who's shell-shocked. The friend who's lying to you. Stephen died in battle." He squinted up at me through the sun-bright lenses of his glasses. "If you really are seeing his ghost, spooky Frankenstein girl, ask him yourself. I bet he'll swear he's still over in France, picking off Germans."

Before I could even think to respond, Grant hustled down the sidewalk to his black Model T and leapt into the driver's seat. The engine popped and rattled as it sputtered to life, and he sped away in an oily cloud of exhaust.

I watched him careen around the bend with a squeal of tires before I climbed up to the porch to see what he had left.

A gold Nabisco Sugar Wafers tin sat by the front door, an envelope bearing my name resting on its lid. I ripped open the paper and tugged out a note written on letterhead from Julius's studio.

Dear Mary Shelley,

I apologize for my behavior last night. Grief for my brother and concern for my mother are bringing out the worst in me. You're right, I bury my pain in ways I shouldn't, but I swear to you I'm an honest businessman who is doing nothing to tarnish the good name of my stepfather's studio.

I am giving you something of Stephen's I found in his room. You seem the best person to have it. Perhaps it will make a complete set.

Please come to Coronado for another photograph as soon as you can. You know in your heart it would help us all. It is the right thing to do.

Yours with sincerest apologies,
Julius

I knelt and removed the box's lid.

In the golden tin lay Stephen's name and address, scrawled in black ink across a pile of pastel envelopes in my own handwriting. All the letters I'd ever written to Stephen since his move to San Diego—the companions to his own letters from the summer of 1914 to early 1918—were tucked inside the cookie tin. I sifted through the envelopes and postcards and heard the sound of our shared lives in the crisp rustle of paper.

"It's just a bribe for a spirit photograph," I whispered to myself. "Just a bribe. Don't you dare go running over there, Shell. Don't do it."

I snapped the lid closed, rose to my feet, and braced myself to be greeted by the black-and-white bird that dwelled within Aunt Eva's walls.

"OBERON. HELLO. WHO'S THERE? OBERON."

The bird would not shut up. I slammed my bedroom door

against the nonstop whistling and squawking and set to work mapping out what I knew.

June 29
Stephen's last letter, written from France.

Sometime between June 29 and October 1
Stephen sent home.
Taken to East Coast hospital?

Sometime between summer and October 19
Stephen loses his life.
(Grant just mentioned executions of soldiers suffering psychological trauma. Did that happen to Stephen?)

Saturday, October 19
Restless sounds heard above Julius's studio during my sitting.
Julius says that may have been Stephen's ghost.

Monday, October 21
We pick up my photograph in Coronado; the picture includes Stephen's "spirit."
Julius tells us Stephen died a hero's death.
My lightning accident.

Tuesday, October 29
Stephen's funeral.

Seeing all the dates and pertinent information laid out on paper helped my brain feel a little more organized. Yet so many questions jumped out from the gaping holes in the diagram. The unexplained pieces remained just as unexplained as before.

A siren howled outside, blaring loud and close enough for me to abandon my notes and look out a front window in Aunt Eva's bedroom. A black ambulance stopped in front of the house next door, and the neighbors' yard exploded into a scramble of stretchers, officers, and hysterical family members who rushed about in the fading daylight.

Out of the chaos charged my running and screaming aunt.

"The flu is next door!" came her muffled yell from behind the closed pane. "Oh, dear Lord, the flu is next door. Mary Shelley!"

I hurried to meet her downstairs.

"The flu is next door!"

"I know."

"What are we going to do?" She pushed the door closed and locked it tight, as if she were able to barricade us against germs with a dead bolt.

"Don't panic, Aunt Eva."

"It's next door!"

"I'll start boiling onions for supper. Why don't you change out of your uniform and get comfortable?"

"We'll wash ourselves in the onion water." Her eyes bulged. "I want to smell the onion fumes in my hair."

"That sounds fine." I patted her shoulder. "Go get changed."

She clambered upstairs and climbed out of her grubby work clothes while I lit the gaslights and cookstove with more matches that smelled like Stephen's funeral.

When my aunt tromped back downstairs, she wore an apron and carried a sponge, and she insisted we scrub the insides of all the windows with hot water. I stuffed salt up my nose at her urging and wiped down the kitchen windowpanes while the scent of boiling onions overpowered the air. My stomach cramped and groaned.

Someone knocked on the front door, and only then did I remember my invitation to Mr. Darning to come over and view the compass phenomenon. I thundered down the main hall to get to him before my aunt, but she was already opening the door.

"Who's there?" asked Oberon. "Hello. Hello."

"Oh. Mr. Darning." Aunt Eva wiped her hands on her apron. "This is a surprise. Please, come in—quickly." She grabbed the photographer's arm and yanked him across the threshold. "The flu just hit next door. I don't want to leave the house open." She slammed the door closed and locked it tight again. "Oh, good heavens, I just washed my mask and won't be able to wear it."

"Is this a bad time?" he asked.

"Hello. Who's there?" said the blasted magpie.

I sidled up next to Aunt Eva. "I'm sorry, Mr. Darning. I forgot to tell her I invited you over."

"You invited him over?" asked my aunt.

Mr. Darning removed his hat. "She was going to show me the compass phenomenon."

Aunt Eva raised her brows. "The compass phenomenon?"

"I haven't yet mentioned my compass experiences to Aunt Eva." I backed up the stairs. "Again, I'm sorry—I've been preoccupied. I'll go get it and bring it to the living room." My feet sounded like an elephant stampede as I scrambled up to fetch Uncle Wilfred's mahogany case with the weighted brass compass mounted inside.

"Did she call you on the telephone to invite you over?" I heard Aunt Eva ask when I returned to the top steps.

"No," said Mr. Darning.

I came to a halt.

"She invited me when she came to my studio for her portrait yesterday."

Oh no.

"What?" squawked my aunt, as loud as Oberon. "She left this house?"

"Was she not supposed to?"

"No. I thought she was at home all day. Mary Shelley Black! Get down here this instant."

"I'm coming, Aunt Eva." I squeezed the compass to my chest.

She and the photographer stood together in the living room, and the glare she shot my way could have frozen the Sahara. "What were you thinking? Why don't you just go to the hospital and let flu patients cough in your mouth, get it over with? Is that what you want?"

"I'll go crazy if I just bury myself in onions at home all day. I have to get out."

"I'm going to write your father."

"Fine—write him. He'd be proud of me. I've been helping convalescing veterans at the Red Cross House."

"What?"

"Should I go?" asked Mr. Darning.

"No, please, not yet." I lugged the case over to the game table in front of the windows. "I want you to see the compass, and I want Aunt Eva to witness it, too."

With hesitation, Mr. Darning rested his brown derby hat on the sofa and approached the compass. Aunt Eva crept our way with her mouth pinched tight and her hands on her hips. Oberon whistled and squeaked.

The photographer leaned over the device and rubbed his gauze-covered chin, and I noticed he smelled like the fine leather seats of an automobile. Out the window, I could see a shiny red touring car with a foldable top parked beneath our streetlamp.

He drew a sharp breath. "Ahhh, yes. I see what you mean."

The needle pointed squarely at me.

"Ahhh, yes! This is absolutely fascinating, Miss Black. Absolutely fascinating."

"The needle even stays on me when I move." I stepped around to the right side of the table, holding out my arms as if I were walking a tightrope. Mr. Darning backed out of the way for me, and I crossed over to the left. The needle followed my movement like a devoted duckling.

Aunt Eva watched and gasped. "I had no idea that was happening. When did you discover this?"

"When I came home from the hospital."

"Hmm, I wonder . . ." Mr. Darning returned to the compass and pressed his hands against the case. "Did the lightning change your magnetic field? Or did your experience of momentarily dying—of becoming a temporary spirit, as it were—do this to you? Is your soul having trouble settling back inside your body?"

I shook my head. "I don't know. I haven't yet found any information about the otherworldly effects of getting struck by lightning."

"You say the needle also follows Stephen when you think he's around?" he asked.

Aunt Eva gasped again. "What?"

"It does." I nodded. "Once, the needle moved everywhere, like he was upset or confused. Another time it pointed to his photographs hanging on my wall."

Mr. Darning shook his head in amazement. "This is remarkable. Like MacDougall's scale experiments on the dying. I'm so impressed with all of this." He rubbed his arms and tittered like a schoolboy. "You've given me gooseflesh."

"You don't think I'm going out of my head with grief, then?" I asked.

"This needle seems to be telling us otherwise, doesn't it?" His eyes beamed at me. "Would you bring the compass to my studio Monday and let me photograph the way you affect it? Better yet, I'll bring my own compass so I know nothing's being rigged."

"But you dislike supernatural photography," said Aunt Eva.

"I dislike fakes. As with everyone else, I'd love to find proof of the survival of the spirit beyond death. Maybe Mary Shelley's body is demonstrating that the soul exists as a magnetic field." He leaned his elbows against the table and bent even closer to the apparatus. "Come to my studio Monday, say around ten o'clock in the morning, and I'll record what you're experiencing. Bring Stephen's photographs as well, and we'll see if we can attract signs of him."

"All right." I peeked at my aunt's bloodless face. "As long as Aunt Eva doesn't mind me leaving the house again."

"Let's see what the flu does to our block first. We might not even be here Monday." She massaged her forehead with her hands balled into fists. "I hate to be rude, Mr. Darning, but I'm overwhelmed by everything that's been happening and really need to feed Mary Shelley her onions."

"Please, don't let me keep you." Mr. Darning tore his eyes off the needle and fetched his hat from the sofa. "I'm sorry to interrupt your evening, but this has been remarkable. Thank you for allowing me to be a witness."

"You're welcome, Mr. Darning." I followed Aunt Eva and him to the door. "Did my other photograph reveal anything?"

"No—oh, I forgot to bring that with me. I'll give that to you on Monday as well."

"Nothing peculiar showed up, then?"

"I'm afraid not. But let's not give up. I think we're on to something here. Perhaps we'll open an unchecked door in the world of psychical research."

I smiled. "Thank you so much for coming. I feel better now that I've shown the compass to someone with your background."

We said our good-byes, and Aunt Eva allowed him to slip out a small crack in the door before she locked us up again.

She grabbed me by the sleeve and pulled me close. "You should have told me he was coming."

"I'm sorry. I've been distracted and forgot."

"That's the second day in a row a man has shown up while I look a mess."

"You look fine."

"I have salt hanging out my nose." She brushed at her nostril.

"I'm sure he understands."

"That doesn't make it any less embarrassing." She pushed me away. "I'm so furious at you for leaving this house, Mary Shelley. What is wrong with you?"

"Stephen didn't die in battle in October."

She gawked at me like I was speaking in tongues. *"What?"*

"I met one of his friends at the Red Cross House today, a boy named Paul from Coronado. He said Stephen lost his mind over in France and the army sent him home before Oc- tober. Julius lied—Stephen didn't die heroically."

She closed her gaping mouth. "Well . . . perhaps the family was embarrassed about the actual cause of death. The push to have a war hero might make people say things that aren't true."

"Why was he tortured, then?"

"You don't know that he was. Maybe he caught the flu on the way home."

"He probably came home before the flu even spread. He might not have lived long enough to know about the pandemic. And that doesn't explain the birds and the burning air."

"What birds?"

"He's haunted by birds. They troubled the men in the trenches because they ate the dead."

My aunt stepped back with terror in her eyes. "You need to let this morbid fascination go, Mary Shelley."

"I told you, he's coming to me—I'm not making it up. He needs my help."

"Even if he does, how on earth is a sixteen-year-old girl supposed to help a dead young man who lost his mind in France? There's nothing you can do for him."

"That's not good enough." I stormed back into the living room to fetch the compass and accidentally knocked an elbow into Oberon's cage, which sent the bird flapping and screeching. "Oh, be quiet, you awful bird."

"Don't take out your anger on Oberon." Aunt Eva placed

protective arms over the magpie's cage. "Maybe you should speak to the minister at church. You're starting to scare me."

I hoisted the compass. "A minister would think I'm either crazy or possessed by the devil. I'm tempted to speak to Julius."

"No." She blocked my path to the stairs. "Don't you dare speak to Julius after what he did to us yesterday."

"I want him to tell me how Stephen died."

"I told you, the family might be embarrassed and too upset to discuss it. Maybe that's why Mrs. Embers lost her nerves. Sometimes the truth is too terrible to discuss. Do you truly believe I tell the girls at work the real reason why you came to live with me?"

The compass slipped in my sweaty hands, but I caught it before it fell.

"I tell my friends your father went to war," she said, "just like Stephen's family is saying he's a hero. The world is an ugly place right now, and some things need to be hidden. Don't go poking around in other people's business."

I sighed in disgust.

She squeezed my arms. "Will you promise me you won't contact Julius?"

I gritted my teeth and nodded.

"Good." She jutted out her chin. "Now let's go eat our onions. Put Wilfred's compass away and then come right back downstairs—but be careful with that. It's been in his family for years."

"I will."

Oberon jabbered and screeched as I took the compass upstairs, and my mind replayed Paul's conversation about the birds.

They ate us when we died. They hovered on the edges of the trenches and stared down at us, watching us, waiting for us to get shot or bombed.

You've got to keep them from getting at your eyes, Stephen had told me when he spoke from the shadows of my bed. *They'll take your beautiful eyes.*

At the top of the stairs, I murmured under my breath, "'And strewn in bloody fragments, to be the carrion of rats and crows.' No wonder they haunt you so much, Stephen. But did they really kill you?"

I set the compass on the end table next to my bed, and the needle jerked away.

"What . . . ?" My blood sped through my veins. "Are you . . . ?" I turned and searched the room for signs of Stephen, but saw only furniture and his crate of books.

"Are you here?" I asked. "Are you with me right now?"

The arrow swayed and shifted in every direction. Pressure mounted in the air like a kettle about to boil. Smoke engulfed my nose.

I clutched the compass's case. "I'm sorry if I scared you with that poem. Please don't be upset. Please come back and talk to me."

Something whacked against the floor.

I jumped and turned again.

At first I didn't see anything out of place. Nothing moved. Nothing rustled in the quieting, rapidly cooling atmosphere.

I poked around the room and discovered the source of the sound—Stephen's lightning bolt photograph lay facedown on the braided rug, stiff and motionless, like the dark blue bodies on the sidewalk when Julius drove us to the séance. I held my unsettled stomach and picked up the frame. The fall had cracked the wood, but the glass remained intact, as did the photograph beneath. I hung the picture back on its nail, and the anagram Stephen had written between the golden waves caught my attention:

I DO LOSE INK

"Link," I whispered, picking out the verbs. "Soil. Lend. Nod. Sink. Don. Die—"

A headache flared between my eyes. I rubbed my forehead above my nose.

"Mary Shelley," called Aunt Eva from downstairs. "Are you all right? Did something fall up there?"

"Everything's fine. I'm coming." I straightened the lightning bolt's frame and whispered, "I'll figure it out, Stephen. I'll figure everything out. I just need to think. I'm sure the answers will come."

LIVING AND BREATHING

DRESSED IN MY WHITE NIGHTGOWN, MY HAIR FREED FROM its ribbon, I gathered the strength to write my father a letter by the oil lamp's light.

November 1, 1918

My Dearest Father,

I received your letter, and I am relieved to hear you are well. Are they giving you enough food? I would feel better knowing that you are eating properly. If I sound like a little mother, perhaps that's because Aunt Eva fusses over me night and day and shows me how to be an expert worrier. She's caring for me well, but you can probably guess which one of us is the braver member of the household.

Is there any chance they'll drop the charges before your trial? Do you have a lawyer? If there's any possibility you won't stay in jail, please tell me as soon as you can. I really miss you. I was just remembering the other day about the time we built that mousetrap together and hunted all over the store for that little pest Phantom. And remember when you taught me how to fix our phonograph? I figured out how to make the same repairs on Aunt Eva's machine just two days ago. You would have been proud.

Now for the hardest part of this letter: my sad news.

Stephen died. Can you believe that, Dad? Stephen Embers died. I am doing better than expected, so please do not worry. His funeral was lovely. Everyone treated him like a proper war hero.

I have been reading quite a bit to keep my brain active—and to help me understand the war better. I have a question for you: when you were in the Spanish-American War, did you see soldiers whose bodies and brains had stopped working right? They're calling it shell shock now, but I'm sure it happened before they invented shells. I'm curious about that subject and would like more information. Perhaps when I am older, I will try to learn how to repair broken minds in addition to exploring the inner workings of machines and electrical devices. These damaged men need help, and figuring out how to heal them seems a worthy challenge.

I am healthy and safe, Dad. Please keep yourself the same way.

Your loving daughter,
Mary Shelley

My hand cramped from the tension coursing through my fingers. I had kept the tone of the letter somewhat optimistic for Dad's sake, but I longed to say so much more. Penning the words *Portland City Jail* on the envelope made the muscles burn even worse.

I set Dad's letter aside and fetched the stack of Stephen's envelopes—the ones he had addressed to me—so I could read words written by the boy whose mind was still intact. What could his voice from the past tell me?

At the bottom of the stack lay the very first letter Stephen had written after he moved to California. I opened the blue envelope and pored over his message.

June 21, 1914

Dear Mary Shelley,

We finally unpacked enough for me to find my writing paper and pen. The house is just as I remembered from when I visited my grandparents: large and drafty, with the wind whipping through the boards at night, making the walls creak.

The house faces southwest, with a view of the wide-open Pacific. L. Frank Baum wrote the last books of his Oz series when he wintered down here, just a few blocks away from where I'm sitting right now. If I ever see him walking down the street, I'll tell him I know a crazy girl up in Oregon who's read all his books at least five times apiece.

Glenn Curtiss, the aviation genius, owns a naval flight school on North Coronado Island, and his airplanes buzz over our house and rattle the china cabinet several times a day. My mother worries that all the plates and cups will shatter from the ruckus. It scares her something awful. I've seen Curtiss's flying boats, which are normal biplanes with pontoons attached to the bottom. They take off from the Spanish Bight, the strip of water that separates the two Coronados, and the pilots circle them over the Pacific outside my bedroom windows (yes, windows, plural—you should see this place, Shell!). Imagine what it would be like to feel that free, flying through the air, gazing down at the earth like a seagull. Maybe one day I'll join the navy and learn how to fly. I bet you would, too, if they allowed women. Better yet, Curtiss would hire you to work for him, and you could lecture him about all the ways he could improve his engines.

Are you lonely up there without me, Shell? I already miss our chats. I genuinely doubt I'll find any girl around here who spends her spare time fiddling with clocks and poring over electrician's manuals. Have you read any good novels I should know about? Is it still raining in Portland, or did summer weather finally arrive? Summer lasts year-round here. While you shiver up there this winter, I'll be swimming in the ocean and basking in the sunshine on the beach. I'll send you a sand crab.

Write soon.

Your friend,
Stephen

I sputtered up a laugh and remarked aloud, "I remember telling you *exactly* what you could do with your sand crab."

I laid the letter next to the lamp and sighed into my hands, my elbows digging into the table. "Are you in the room with me right now, Stephen? Can you hear me?" A quick check with the compass told me I was the only magnetic force gripping the atmosphere at the moment. "Why can't you come when I call you? Why do I have to be half-drunk with sleep for you to completely show up? In fact . . ." I stood. "I'm going to bring a chair upstairs so I can sleep sitting up."

After the long day at the Red Cross House and all the bickering with Aunt Eva, my arms shook with exhaustion as I lugged a dining room chair up to my bedroom. Aunt Eva's door was shut, the space beneath it dark, so she didn't have to witness my preventive measures against waking up with a boy or a bird on my chest.

I sat on the scratchy needlepoint cushion and attempted to get comfortable. "All right." I nestled my head against my arms on the table. "Come if you can, but don't scare me." I closed my eyes.

At first only the soft whisper of the oil lamp's flame met my ears—a soothing nothingness. Minutes later an entire brigade of sirens tore through the streets like an invasion of wailing banshees. Their cries made the hairs on the back of my neck bristle. I must have drifted off counting how many ambulances there were—at least four of them—while the oil lamp turned the backs of my eyelids orange.

A dream ran through my head: I lay on my back somewhere outside and watched the blackness of the nighttime sky dissolve into a milky shade of white. A gunshot hurt my ears. Streaks of red splattered across the heavens.

I awoke with a gasp, fear blazing across my tongue and static snapping in my hair. I heard another gasp, and Stephen thrust his arms around my waist and buried his cheek against my stomach as if I were a life preserver, his face pale and damp in the lamplight. He shivered against me.

I wrapped my arms around his head. "Are you all right, Stephen?"

He didn't answer. He could barely breathe.

"It's OK. I'm here. You're safe. It was just a dream." I lowered my right hand to his shoulder and found the wide cotton strap of the sleeveless undershirt he was always wearing. To soothe him, I ran my fingers down the curve of his bare arm, meeting with cold flesh and scars that reminded me of the barbed-wire wounds on Jones's hand. I puzzled over Stephen's lack of a proper shirt. "Where were you when you put on these clothes?"

I bit my lip in anticipation of his answer. The question seemed like a stroke of genius for the five or six seconds after I asked it.

He didn't respond—he just quaked and panted—so I elaborated. "You're wearing a sleeveless undershirt, a brown pair of pants that look like civilian trousers, and gray socks without any shoes. Do you remember where you were when you put on this clothing? Do you remember why you're not wearing a regular shirt?"

He slowed his breathing enough to answer. "No."

"Are you sure? Please think hard, Stephen. Think back to the moments before the birds arrived. Where were you?"

"I don't know." He closed his eyes and tightened his grip around my waist. "I just remember it being hot. There was too much sunlight. Too many windows. I didn't like wearing sleeves."

"Were you in a hospital?"

"Maybe. I just . . ." His eyes opened wide. "Oh . . ." He exhaled a sigh heavy with remembrance.

My heart raced. "Oh what?"

"I just remembered something."

"What?"

"I think I hurt her."

"Her?" I swallowed down my jealousy. "A girl was there?"

"The Huns flew over us. Their planes were practically right on me. The bombs were about to drop. I don't know why she was there."

"Who was there?"

"My mother."

"Your mother?"

"She was reaching over me, and I kicked her so hard she stumbled several feet backward and landed on the ground. I heard her cry out in pain."

"Your mother was in a hospital with you? Is that what you

mean? Or was there a nurse who looked like her?"

"It was her. She said my name."

"But—that can't be." I shook my head.

"She was there. I was panicking about the plane, but she was there, and I hurt her."

"Wait a second . . . wait . . ." The little clock gears inside my head clicked into place. "Oh, God." My diagram of the events leading up to his death repositioned itself in a brand-new order in my mind. A sentence from Stephen's letter sitting right there next to me on the bedside table leapt off the page: *airplanes buzz over our house and rattle the china cabinet several times a day . . .*

"Oh, my God."

I remembered back to the day I posed for that second spirit photograph in the Emberses' house—the biplane soaring over the roof, footsteps scrambling across the room above our heads, dust shaking loose from the beams, Mrs. Embers tearing into the studio, saying, *I need your help, Julius. I'm hurt.* She had grabbed her stomach as if she had just been kicked, and Julius shouted, *Christ! Get them out of here, Gracie.*

It wasn't a ghost that made everyone stare up at the ceiling with whitened faces. A spirit didn't somehow hurt Mrs. Embers.

It was an eighteen-year-old boy, deep in shock from the war, reacting to a sound that reminded him of battle.

"You were still alive that day." I grabbed the sides of Stephen's face. "When Julius took my photograph and Gracie gave me the package, you were living and breathing in the bedroom directly above my head."

He scowled and shook his head. "I'm still alive, Shell. Stop saying I'm not."

"You came home, Stephen. You're not still in the trenches."

"But the minute you let me go, I'll be back in the mud and the dark and the shit and the blood. I hear them whispering right now." He peered over his shoulder. "Don't you hear them?"

"What are they saying?"

"All sorts of things. One of them wants to know how long it's going to take."

I pulled his head against my stomach and buried my face in his brown hair. "Tell them to go away. Tell them you haven't been on the battlefield for a long while. Tell them you came home."

His fear seeped inside me, pounding in my pulse and drumming against my ears. Our breaths blended into a staccato beat. All I could think about was Julius standing next to his camera while patriotic music blared from the phonograph to cover the bangs and thumps from the room above the studio.

"What happened to you?" I asked. "Did someone do something to you in your own house?"

"They're killing me."

"I know." I kissed the top of his head through his smoke-laced hair. "I know."

He breathed into the folds of my nightgown. "Keep me with you."

"I'll try."

"Keep me close." His lips kissed my stomach through the airy fabric—a flutter of pleasure that penetrated the pain. "I want you so much, Shell."

"I want you, too. More than anything else."

The room trembled with frustration and longing until even the curtains swayed, and my mouth filled with the rich flavor of a feast I could only taste but never, ever consume.

"I wonder what would happen if you pushed the darkness out of your thoughts." I drew in a deep, quivering breath. "If you remembered the parts of your life that had nothing to do with death. I wonder what it would feel like if you moved closer to me without those suffocating memories weighing us down."

He looked up at me, his eyes dark and curious.

"I wonder . . ." I pushed myself off the chair and grabbed his hand to help him to his feet, even though my own legs shook. "Can you stand up with me?"

He rose up above me, and we stood face-to-face for the first time since the morning we held *Mr. Muse* between us in his house. I cupped his cool cheek and guided him toward me by his waist. His hands ran across my back and seemed to grow warmer against my fabric. For a moment, the fear throbbing through him faded to a mere whisper of trepidation, barely there, like a weak heartbeat.

His attention switched to the ceiling. He tensed against me and held his breath.

"No, come back." I grabbed both sides of his face again. "Come back to me. Think of something good. Think about kissing me in your house. Do you remember that?"

His eyes wouldn't leave the dark air above us, and I, too, heard the flapping of restless wings.

"Think about how it felt when we kissed with your photograph tucked between us. Do you remember that?" I lowered his face until his forehead bumped against mine. "Did your heart beat as much as mine did, Stephen? Do you remember your lips on my mouth and neck? Do you remember the way you made me breathe?"

He closed his eyes with a sigh that shuddered straight through me.

"You remember, don't you?" I whispered.

"Of course I remember."

"I'm here now." I brushed his lips with a kiss that tasted far less like smoke than the other night. "Stay with me. Don't think of anything else. Not a single thing. Let's see if I can keep you with me."

He caressed the back of my neck, and we kissed again. The sensation was stirring and sweet. The closer we got, the more the feeling bloomed into a rush of pleasure far more delicious than even the bliss of flesh against flesh. My head clouded over with a dizzying sense of exhilaration. My legs lost their ability to stand.

"I need to sit down." I pulled away from him but grabbed his arm so he wouldn't disappear. "Come with me." I guided him back toward my bed with careful footsteps. "Are you still with me?"

"Yes."

We sat on the edge of the bed, and our mouths returned to each other. His fingers explored the curves of my body from my neck to my chest, and down to my waist. Lovely breezes shivered across my skin. He slid my nightgown up past my knees and kissed the small of my throat.

"Is this all right?" he asked. "Can I pull your skirt up farther?"

I nodded, and he kissed my neck again with a touch that melted straight through me. His hands edged my nightgown up to my hips.

I lay back against the cool quilt and allowed him to climb on top of me.

His lips warmed my chest through the nightgown's fabric. "For some reason, Shell, I can't ever take off these clothes. I don't know why."

"It's all right. Just be close to me."

"I want to be as close as I can."

"We'll make the best of it."

I held on to his back and felt him push against me with a sigh that traveled deep inside my own lungs. I still wore my cotton drawers, and he kept his trousers buttoned, but an electrifying current pulsed between us.

"See," I murmured, "we're even closer than we could have been before."

Energy coursed through my blood and brought a smile to my face, and I could tell by the way Stephen breathed and lowered his eyelids that he was experiencing the same rapture. We toyed with the provocative sensation, his trousers brushing against my legs in a hushed rhythm, until he broke the silence with another whisper.

"This is the way Julius told them he found us."

"No—don't bring up anything upsetting right now." I gripped his arm to keep him from slipping back into the darkness.

"I was just going to say I sometimes wish he had actually found us this way." He eased himself all the way on top of me and breathed into my hair. "Even though it would have been wrong and it could have led to trouble, it would have been nice to have felt that with you, even just once."

I closed my eyes and pulled him closer still, until he surrounded me completely. Until I felt him inside my soul.

THE CAGE

A NOISE INTERRUPTED US.

A squawk.

Somehow we heard it, beyond the walls and the floor, and the noise sent blood streaming back into my brain. I opened my eyes.

"What was that?" Stephen lifted his head and stared at me as if I had just stabbed him in the gut. His pupils swelled as wide as saucers.

I gulped. "I think it was a bird."

His lips twitched. "A bird?"

I nodded. "There's a pet bird downstairs."

He looked over his shoulder, and the flame of the oil lamp rose and danced, streaking topsy-turvy shadows across the wall. The needle of Uncle Wilfred's compass quivered beneath the glass.

Stephen's eyes returned to mine. "We've got to kill it."

Like the lamp and the needle, I trembled with his terror.

The bird squawked again, and we both jumped.

"It hears us," he said. "Kill it before it finds us."

"It's a pet."

"Have you ever seen what their beaks can do to a person, Shell? Do you know what they'll do to your eyes?"

I winced.

"It's either you or him," he said. "Get a gun."

"I don't have a gun."

"Then get a knife. Or even a pair of scissors." His hot breath against my face fanned a fire inside me. All I could think of was a crow as large as a bald eagle bearing down on my chest. The stringy taste of feathers filled my mouth.

"Kill it," he said in a voice that vibrated inside my brain, as if the thought were coming from my own mind instead of his lips. "Hurry."

I rose from the bed.

Part of me knew what I was doing was wrong—so very wrong—but that other part, the part getting louder and more anxious, powered my feet across the bedroom rug. I peeked over my shoulder and no longer saw Stephen on the bed, but his fear continued to burn in my lungs. He was still with me.

I twisted the doorknob and left the room, tense with anticipation of another sound emerging from the thing downstairs.

The pitch-black stairs groaned under my weight, but I kept going, oblivious to anything but that squawking, violent, sharp-beaked creature.

When my feet reached the bottom of the stairs, the house itself seemed to rumble with apprehension. The *click click click* of talons scuttled somewhere unseen.

"Who's there?" asked a voice in the dark.

I froze against the banister behind me.

"Who's there?"

The bird was talking to me. I gagged and clutched my stomach, smelling death and mud and poisonous fumes.

Kill it, Shell.

"There's a pair of scissors in the sewing box in the living room," I whispered. "But I have to go past the cage."

Run past. They're coming. Hurry!

I leapt into the living room but took a bad step, which sent me crashing against the floorboards on my hands and knees. The thing beneath the covered cage beat its wings and screeched, "Who's there? Hello. Hello."

They're coming. Oh, God, they're coming.

I scrambled across the room to the shadow of a wooden sewing box next to the rocking chair and dug out a pair of scissors that glinted in the moonlight.

"Who's there?"

Bile rose in my throat as I tiptoed toward the cage.

"Who's there? Who's there? Hello."

Just do it, Shell! Kill it!

I held my breath and reached out to the beige cloth covering the bronze wires.

"Who's there?"

Do it!

I pulled. The cloth tumbled down.

An ear-shattering screech pierced the night, and I stumbled backward and fell to the ground in horror. A huge black crow-faced bird with a luminous white beak and hands like a man's gripped the bronze bars. It raised its back feathers and bit at the cage with its furious mouth, and the air from its wings beat down on me, sending a wall of stinging smoke burning down to my stomach.

"What's happening?" asked a female voice.

I saw a candle out of the corner of my eye, but all I could do was lean back on my elbows with tremors convulsing my body.

"Mary Shelley?"

"Kill it!" I managed to shout, the scissors feeling sturdier in my hands. "Kill it before it kills me. Shoot it!"

"What's wrong with you?"

"Give me a gun." I sprang to my feet.

"No." A woman with short blond hair pulled the cage away from me and swung open a door to a world screaming with ambulance sirens.

My legs gave way and I fell to the ground again. My mouth tasted dirt and blood from a cracked lip. The sound of machine-gun fire reverberated around my head, as well as shouts and commands and the whistle of a shell about to hit. The earth rocked below me. A woman cried and yelled something about telephoning a minister. Nothing made sense. It was far too much to bear—far too much to keep living through, so I shut myself off to the world and curled into a ball until nothing but stark silence echoed in my ears.

24

DISCOVERIES

SOMEONE WAS KNOCKING ON A DOOR.

I opened my eyes and stared up at the crisscrossing white beams of Aunt Eva's living room ceiling. The batiste fabric of my nightgown clung to my legs and stomach like a film. My sweat smelled of onions. My head, thick with sleep, felt disoriented by the morning sunlight as well as the fact that I was lying on the floor in the middle of a room.

The flu, I thought. *Did I just have a flu fever?*

I sprang up to my elbows and checked for blue-black feet.

The toes wiggling beyond the hem of my nightclothes were still their normal shade of pasty Oregon white. Plus I sweated instead of shivered, and people with the flu always shivered like they were freezing from the inside out.

Not the flu. It wasn't a fever dream that lay with me in my bed the night before and urged me to go downstairs to kill a bird. Not at all.

Another five-beat knock came from the back of the house, sounding like someone was at the kitchen door. I wobbled up to my feet and lurched past the empty space where Oberon's cage used to sit.

Through the kitchen window I could see a masked girl with red braids. She stood beside a wooden pull wagon full of food crates and looked harmless enough, so I opened the door.

She leapt back when she saw me. "Oh no! Do you have the flu?"

"No." I wiped damp hair off my cheek. "What I have isn't contagious."

"Oh." With a worried brow, the girl pulled a crate stuffed with golden onions off her wagon. "Mrs. Ottinger orders her groceries to be delivered every Saturday morning. You need to tell her we could only give her one dozen onions instead of two because there's a shortage."

"All right." I glanced over my shoulder for signs of my missing aunt, but I neither heard nor saw any trace of her.

The girl set the box of onions at my feet, then pulled out a larger crate packed with carrots, potatoes, string beans, apples, and eggs.

"Do you need me to pay you now?" I asked.

"Mrs. Ottinger usually pays on credit. But with everyone getting sick . . ."

"All right. I'll get you some cash." I remembered seeing Aunt Eva fetch taxi money from a Gibson's Cough Lozenge tin kept on top of the icebox, so I paid the girl her two dollars and sixty-three cents and brought the crates inside.

The girl went on her way to the tune of squeaky wagon axles that needed a good oiling. I would have helped her out by liquefying some soap and slicking up the metal if I didn't need to hunt down my aunt. It was Saturday, so Aunt Eva wouldn't have been at work. Normally she was up long before I was—and I doubted she would've left me lying on the living room floor.

"Aunt Eva?"

My voice bounced off the ceiling of the empty house. No one responded.

I sprinted upstairs.

"Aunt Eva?" I crashed open her door, and she screamed from her bed, clutching a two-foot-tall crucifix that looked like some medieval relic. Garlic and onions rolled off her pillow and bounced across the floor.

"Stay away from me!" she cried.

"I'm sorry, Aunt Eva."

"Sorry's not good enough. What type of person crouches in the dark in the middle of the night, scissors in hand, yelling about killing a poor, innocent bird?"

"Where is Oberon?" I entered her room.

"Don't come near me!" She scooted against her headboard with wild eyes.

"It's just me now. Everything's fine."

"Everything is *not* fine."

"Where's Oberon?"

"I set him free before you could hurt him." Two loud coughs shook her chest, then transformed into a fit of hysterical tears. "The poor thing's wings were clipped, so I don't know how far he made it. Hopefully, far enough that he'll never come back here again."

"I'm so sorry—"

"Your voice sounded like yours, but those words coming out of your mouth . . ." She sniffed and sobbed. "I hid all the scissors and knives in the house, and then I tried calling my minister, but his whole family is sick. His wife referred me to another minister, but he was sick, too. The doctors wouldn't come, because they're too busy, and even that Mr. Darning wasn't answering his telephone." She hugged her crucifix against her cheek and wept thick tears across the tarnished gold. "We're all alone. It's just you and me and that lunatic boy."

"Don't say that about him."

"What do you expect me to say? If he truly returned to this earth as a spirit, why are you letting him near you? Why aren't you sending him away?"

"I can't."

"Try."

"Even if I tell him to leave me alone," I said, wringing my hands and venturing closer to her, "I know in my heart he'll keep reliving his death until he understands who or what hurt him. It's terrifying him and infuriating him."

"There's no possible way you can learn that information."

"Yes, there is. He was still alive when Julius took my last picture, Aunt Eva. Those noises coming from upstairs—that force that hurt Mrs. Embers—that was *him*. I bet they were hiding him up in his room."

"You don't know that."

"Wait right here. I want to show you something."

I raced off to my bedroom, where I pulled my diagram of Stephen's last months out of the drawer beneath Uncle Wilfred's compass. With careful strokes to avoid messing up my work with inkblots, I crossed off information that no longer seemed accurate and added new discoveries.

June 29
Stephen's last letter, written from France.

Sometime between June 29 and October 1
Stephen sent home.
Taken to East Coast hospital?

Sometime between summer and October 19
Stephen loses his life.
(Grant just mentioned executions of soldiers suffering psychological trauma. Did that happen to Stephen?)

Saturday, October 19

Restless sounds heard above Julius's studio during my sitting.

~~*Julius says that may have been Stephen's ghost.*~~

MRS. EMBERS COMES DOWNSTAIRS, LOOKING LIKE SOMEONE HAS JUST HURT HER.

STEPHEN IN CORONADO AND STILL ALIVE AS OF MY 10:00 A.M. PHOTOGRAPHY APPOINTMENT!

Monday, October 21

We pick up my photograph in Coronado; the picture includes Stephen's "spirit."

Julius tells us Stephen died a hero's death.

MRS. EMBERS SCREAMS STEPHEN'S NAME UPSTAIRS. (DID SHE JUST FIND HIM DEAD??)

I returned to my aunt with my notes. "See? I think he died somewhere between October nineteenth and twenty-first—somewhere between my Saturday morning sitting and the Monday morning we picked up the photograph."

Her eyes scanned the paper forced into her lap, and her lips whitened. She shook her head. "What are you implying?"

"Remember the state Julius was in when we picked up my photograph early that morning? He seemed dazed and upset, and I asked you if he was on opium. Then their mother screamed Stephen's name upstairs, and she hasn't been seen again."

"Julius . . . he's not a murderer. He can't be. He wouldn't

kill his brother *or* his mother." She shoved the paper off her lap. "He even cried at Stephen's funeral—remember?"

"Were they tears of sorrow or guilt?"

"Why would he risk finding his brother's spirit at a séance if there was a chance Stephen would call him a murderer?"

"But Stephen doesn't know who killed him." I picked up my diagram from the floor. "The war and reality seem to have blurred together into a jumbled mess in his head. All he talks about are bird creatures attacking him."

"Don't talk to me about birds, Mary Shelley," she warned with a stony glare.

"I need to go to his house."

"No!" She grabbed my arm. "Even if I get the flu and drop dead, promise me you won't ever go over to Julius's. Promise you won't let him pour his honey into your ears."

"You're not going to drop dead from the flu, Aunt Eva."

"Promise me."

I squished my lips together. "I don't think I can promise that. Julius is probably one of the only people who knows what really happened to Stephen."

Lines of concern wrinkled her forehead, making her look older. "But while you're helping Stephen, who's going to help you? Why don't you ever think about saving yourself?"

"My mother saved other people. I thought you wanted me to be like her."

"Your mother was a trained physician. You're a sixteen-year-old girl." She pointed to the window. "Listen to the world out there. Do you hear all the sirens? It's not safe to go any-where. You stay inside this house."

"Then Stephen will be staying inside with me. I've got to find out how he died."

"No, you don't." She erupted into another mess of soggy tears. "You don't need to do anything but listen to me for once in your life. Take all his belongings out of your room, throw them into the backyard—"

"No!"

"I feel like the only adult left in this world right now, and I don't know what else to do. Please just stay in this house and rid yourself of anything that has to do with that boy." She began to sob so hard that her face turned a disconcerting shade of purple.

I rubbed my face and steadied my breath. "All right. I'll stay inside for now to make you happy. Please stop crying so much. You're going to make yourself sick." I dropped my arms to my sides and watched her wipe her eyes and leaking nose with a handkerchief pulled from beneath her covers. "If we're not going anywhere, can I please make us a breakfast that doesn't involve onions?"

She hiccupped. "Take a bath first. You look and smell aw-ful. Unless you think that boy will show up in the tub with you—"

"He's not going to show up in the tub, for pity's sake." My skin sizzled with a blush. "You stay here and calm down, and I'll go get washed up. Everything will be fine."

· · · · ·

AUNT EVA'S FEAR OF STEPHEN SHOWING UP IN MY BATH got me thinking.

If I tipped the back of my head against the porcelain-enameled rim of the tub and let my body go limp in the sudsy water, would my mind grow drowsy enough to see him? Would he get too close again and fill the house with his terror? Or could I lure him for just a breath of a moment?

He had come to me in the daylight before—when his whispers burned at my ear at his funeral and when his photograph dropped to my floor just the previous afternoon. If I pushed away the commotion of the sirens outside and let myself sink downward, downward, downward . . .

My arms relaxed over the tub's curved lip.

My chin tilted upward. My head lightened. The center of the earth dragged me toward it, as if I were riding in an unlit elevator on a rushed descent.

Down.

Down.

Down.

The world above me faded to white. Pain seized my head. Something exploded across the clouds, and the sky turned a deep red. I rose toward the bloodstained surface. Voices cried out in panic below.

"Mary Shelley."

I jolted upright with a frantic splash of water. Fresh air rushed into my lungs, and my slippery fingers clutched the sides of the tub to regain my bearings.

"Gracie is here, Mary Shelley," called my aunt through the door. "Can you be out and dressed in a few minutes?"

"Gracie?" I slicked back my wet hair. "Stephen's cousin Gracie?"

"Yes."

"Did she say why she came?"

"I told her she can't have what she came for, but she wanted to talk to you just the same."

"What did she come for?"

My aunt didn't respond.

"I said, what did she come for, Aunt Eva?"

"A séance. To find Stephen."

I leapt out of the tub with a loud cascade of water and grabbed my towel. "Let me just get dressed. I'll be right there."

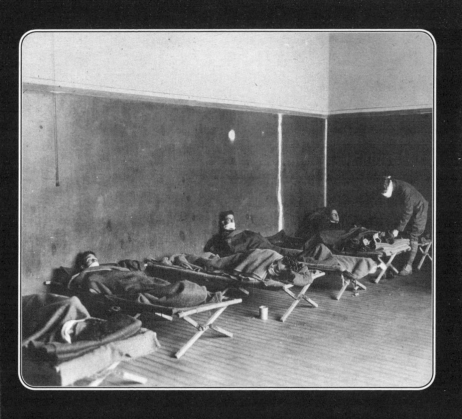

25

COUSIN GRACIE

I PADDED OUT TO THE LIVING ROOM ON BARE FEET AND twisted my hair into a braid to avoid dripping all over my navy-blue dress with the sailor-style collar. I had worn the same garment the first time I met Gracie, I realized, when she had bustled about Julius's studio, changing phonograph records to smother the sounds of Stephen upstairs.

Gracie watched me approach with round, inquisitive eyes—the look of a captured owl. She sat, shoulders stiff, in the middle of Aunt Eva's sofa, her flu mask lowered to her throat, hands clasped in her lap as if they had been locked together with a key.

My aunt looked equally rigid and uncomfortable in the rocking chair across from her.

"Hello, Gracie." I parked myself beside our guest, which made the girl stiffen even further. "It's good to see you again."

"It's good to see you, too." Gracie dropped her gaze. "I've wanted to come over here ever since I heard about what happened at that séance the other night. Grant heard about what happened from Julius, actually, and then Grant told me. I haven't been working in the studio lately."

"Why not?" I asked.

That nasty, curdled taste of spoiled milk I remembered from the funeral spread across my tongue.

"I haven't . . ." Gracie sniffed. "I haven't wanted to go back to that house since Stephen . . ."

I sat up straight with the realization that she may have just confirmed my suspicion that Stephen died in that house. "But Grant still works there?" I asked.

"He says he has to. When our mother died, he quit his job at a restaurant downtown. He said we both needed to work at Julius's studio to be with family and to earn decent money. Our father is off in the navy, you see, so it's just the two of us right now."

Aunt Eva rocked in her chair with soft creaks of wood. "Don't you live on Coronado as well?"

Gracie shook her head and grinned, embarrassed. "We're the poor relations. Our father used to be the swim instructor at the Hotel del Coronado—that's how he met our mother. She used to go swimming in the hotel's pool when the Emberses wintered in that big house over there. Mama didn't get to inherit the house, because she was the female heir. Stephen's dad got it, so we've always lived right here in San Diego."

I squirmed at the idea of Stephen being part of the rich side of the family. "I don't think Stephen ever felt comfortable living on the island," I said. "He told me he was heading to war to avoid becoming corrupted by his surroundings. He probably would have preferred switching houses with you."

"Many people would give their right arm to live in such a beautiful community," said Aunt Eva.

"I've seen men with missing arms," I muttered. "I'm sure they'd choose intact bodies over ocean views any day."

My aunt frowned and changed the subject. "Would you like some breakfast, Gracie? Mary Shelley and I haven't yet had ours."

Gracie shrugged. "I guess breakfast would be nice. But what I really want is a séance."

Aunt Eva stopped rocking.

Gracie looked at me from the corners of her eyes. "Like I said, I've wanted to visit you ever since I learned you spoke with Stephen at that séance." She fidgeted with her interlocked fingers. "That's not true, actually. I've wanted to come ever since Grant and Julius dragged you away from Stephen's casket."

"Oh?" I squirmed again. "Why didn't you come sooner?"

"I've been nervous. I didn't want to bother you."

"You're not bothering me." I pressed my fingers over the back of her clammy hand. "I'm glad you came."

She turned her face away from me. "Last night I dreamed you died of the flu."

"Oh," Aunt Eva and I said in unison.

"I'm sorry if that's a terrible thing to dream, but I realized I should come before it's too late. I know you and Stephen were close—he told me stories about you ever since he used to come down to visit as a child. I . . . need to speak to him."

My heart beat faster. "What did you want to say to him?"

"I want to tell him . . ." Her eyes brimmed with tears. "I just want to say . . . I'm sorry."

"Sorry?"

"I—I want to tell him I miss him."

I looked to Aunt Eva, who scowled and shook her head.

"My aunt is uncomfortable with the idea of me summoning him." I stroked Gracie's wrist. "Maybe you should join us in the kitchen for some breakfast, like she said, and we could chat for a while. I'll tell you the types of things Stephen has been saying to me, and you can help me figure out what's troubling him."

Gracie lifted her head. "He's troubled?"

I scraped my teeth against my bottom lip. "Yes. Very much so."

"Contact him for me, please!" She squeezed my hand. "Please let me speak to him. What if you do get this flu? How am I going to communicate with him then?"

Aunt Eva rose from her chair. "Let's go have some breakfast—"

"No—look at me." Gracie pulled off her wig and revealed a startling bald head with a downy covering of new white hair. "Look what the flu did to me. I'm one of the survivors, and look what it did. Grant thought I was dead one night, and he even laid a sheet over me and called an undertaker. I'm one of the lucky ones, and look what I'm like. When this flu gets you, I might never get a chance to talk to my poor cousin."

"Come into the kitchen." I stood and pulled Gracie to her feet. "We'll contact him out there."

Aunt Eva blanched. "No!"

"Keep all the knives and scissors hidden." I brushed past her. "Open the windows so the neighbors can hear you scream if something goes wrong, but let me help him."

"I don't want him in this house."

"Then let us put him to rest, Aunt Eva, so he can leave. You can talk to him yourself if you'd like, or go hide in your room, but this needs to be done."

Gracie tugged her wig back over her head, and I led our guest back to the pea-soup-green kitchen, where the little circular table would make a fine spot for a séance.

"Do we need candles?" asked Gracie.

"That doesn't seem to matter." I pulled out a chair for Stephen's cousin and lowered myself into a seat that faced away from the windows. I didn't want to see any crows or blackbirds perched on the orange trees out there . . . or even banished Oberon, trying to find his way back in.

To my utter shock, Aunt Eva rushed into the room and

slipped into one of the two remaining chairs. "Do it quickly. I swear, if anyone gets hurt—"

"He doesn't want to hurt any people. Everyone will be safe."

"Should we hold hands?" asked Gracie.

"Not yet." I placed my palms on the table. "I'd actually like to start by asking you some questions, Gracie."

"Me?" Gracie recoiled. "What types of questions?"

"Be kind, Mary Shelley," warned Aunt Eva. "Remember what I said about prying into other people's business."

"I know. But I need answers." I peered straight into Gracie's pale brown eyes. "Tell me the truth—does Julius seem like an honest person to you?"

Gracie flinched, and an avalanche of curdled milk sloshed down my throat. I gagged on the stomach-souring awfulness and braced my hands against the table to keep from retching.

Aunt Eva reached out to me. "What's wrong?"

I gulped down the guilt-soaked flavor with a grimace. "I'm fine. Just a moment . . ."

"Are you going to get sick?" asked Aunt Eva.

"I'm fine." I cleared my throat with a deep, uncomfortable sound. "Um . . . all right . . . let me be more specific, Gracie. When you helped Julius at his studio, did you ever see him cheat?"

Gracie shook her head, and the sour taste softened. "I didn't ever go into Julius's darkroom with him, but I was there when Mr. Darning came to investigate him one time."

"What did Mr. Darning do?" I asked.

"He marked his initials on blank photographic plates to make sure Julius wasn't switching them with used ones. And Julius passed all his tests, which seemed to puzzle Mr. Darning. There were reporters there and everything. Oh, and look." She popped open a silver locket dangling around her neck below her flu mask. "Here's a photo Julius took of me and my mother's spirit."

I leaned in close, but I saw only a fuzzy streak of light behind a somber image of Gracie, who was seated in front of Julius's black background curtain. "I just see a blur."

"That's probably her."

"Oh." I sank back in my chair and furrowed my brow. "So. He seems an honest man to you, then?"

Gracie snapped the locket shut. "I don't know about that." She bowed her head. "He wasn't always nice to Stephen."

"What did you see him do to Stephen?"

"I know . . . ," said Gracie, scratching the back of her neck. "He sometimes stole Stephen's photographs off the wall and burned them."

Aunt Eva's jaw dropped. "He burned his brother's photographs?"

Gracie nodded. "Stephen was worried that all of his work would be gone by the time he returned from the war, so he packed up most of his pictures and negatives and hid them about a week before he left."

I leaned forward. "Do you know where he put them?"

She shook her head. "He wouldn't even tell his mother what he was doing with them. He was probably afraid she'd slip and mention their whereabouts to Julius. She thought he might have purchased a safe-deposit box in a bank or a post office and stored them there."

"Why did Julius destroy Stephen's photographs?" asked Aunt Eva.

Gracie's eyes moistened again. "My cousins always fought like a pack of wild dogs, and their fights turned vicious after Stephen's father passed away. Aunt Eleanor considered asking Julius to move out, but she always favored him a little, even if she never said so out loud. She and Julius escaped her terrible drunk of a first husband together. She always felt sorry for him starting life with a bully for a father."

I traced my fingernail along a scratch in the tabletop and pondered the missing photos. "Stephen gave me two of his pictures before he left for training . . . but the rest must have already been stored away. He never mentioned anything about hiding the others, but we didn't have all that much time together . . . I don't think that's why he's troubled. I don't know . . ." I looked to Gracie. "I met one of his friends from his battalion at the Red Cross House yesterday."

Gracie hunched her back the same way her brother had when I questioned him about Stephen's condition.

"What that friend told me about Stephen's last days in France was upsetting and confusing to hear," I continued. "May I mention what I heard?"

She gave a nod that was more a quiver of her round chin.

"He said Stephen didn't die in battle." I hesitated a moment, for the air was thickening. "He said he lost his mind over there in the trenches. The army tried to help him in a field hospital, but he just got worse. They had to send him home." A searing pain clogged my lungs, but I breathed through it and forced myself to keep talking. "Did you know about his discharge?"

Gracie's lips shook. Her eyes watered until a flood of tears ran down her cheeks. "We were supposed to keep it a secret."

"Why?" I asked.

"All the Emberses' friends boasted about their boys receiving medals, or they could at least say their sons died in combat, fighting for liberty." She sniffed. "None of their young men were sent home in shame. Aunt Eleanor . . . she worried Stephen would be viewed as a coward . . . and a traitor. She even blamed herself for the way she raised him. Stephen was always so quiet and artistic. I can't even imagine a gun"—Gracie squeezed her face into a pained expression as the flow of tears streamed harder—"in that boy's hands."

I held on to her wrist. "He made it back to Coronado, didn't he?"

She sniffled and attempted to steady her voice. "His mother had to fetch him from a hospital on the East Coast. A nurse went with her. They found him sitting in a bed, not speaking, shaking, just staring with eyes that looked like he was watching Death breathe in his face."

I winced.

"They brought him home sedated," she continued, "and hid him up in his room. Aunt Eleanor investigated the nearest asylums, but she said they all used barbaric water treatments. Patients were chained to beds. The doctors wanted to sterilize them all so they couldn't transfer their madness to future generations." She stopped and wiped her eyes with a handkerchief tucked inside the black sash of her dress. "Aunt Eleanor insisted on keeping him at home, waiting until he came out of his shock enough to go to some of the places offering to help recuperating servicemen."

I lifted my face. "How did Julius feel about that decision?"

"Well . . ." Gracie sniffed. "He said he didn't like it, but Stephen didn't make any noise during the first week. None of Julius's customers knew he was up there. Julius told us to keep saying Stephen was still overseas. This was all around the time Mother died from the flu, and I didn't know what to do. Julius said if Stephen got bad enough we should just tell people he'd gotten shot in combat and put him away."

A profound sadness settled in my bones. I wanted to lower my head and cry for everything I'd ever lost in my life, but I pushed my arms against the table, elbows locked, to keep myself upright. "What happened after the first week? Did he start making noise?"

"Yes." Gracie sniffed again. "He started to wake out of his fog a little. He wasn't yet talking, but he started yelling whenever he heard certain noises—the buzz of the doorbell, the telephone ringing, the flashlamp, the Naval Air Station planes. Anything loud and sudden panicked him. He even kicked his mother in the stomach once when one of the planes flew over the house. Julius had to take her to the hospital to make sure she didn't have any internal damage."

"That was the day we were there for my most recent photograph," I said.

"Yes."

"Did you see Stephen when he was up in his room?"

"No, I stayed away from him. I didn't want to see him that way."

I rubbed my eyes, which throbbed and burned with phantom smoke. "Stephen says he often sees creatures watching over him while he's strapped down. No one tied him to his bed, did they? Either in that East Coast hospital or at home?"

"Oh, heavens. I don't know. He may have been chained to that hospital bed. I didn't ask Aunt Eleanor how they were keeping him calm after he kicked her." Gracie tugged my hand away from my eye with a firm grip. "Is he here? Does he know what I'm saying?"

"I think he's trying to come, but I don't want him to get any closer until you answer the most important question—the one that may help him rest in peace." My throat and mouth ached from the smoke and the fight to hold back tears. I realized the cause of his death, spoken aloud, might make him disappear from my life, so selfishly I let a few more seconds tick by before I asked my question: "How did he die, Gracie?"

Gracie's face contorted again. She tried to hold on to my hand, but her tears ran down to the bodice of her black dress at such a rate, she had to let go to wipe them. My aunt just sat there, stunned and mute.

"What happened?" I asked. "Please tell him. He needs to know."

"Stephen . . ." Gracie lowered her eyes. "My poor cousin . . . You shot yourself."

My head slammed against the table. My neck simply refused to hold up my skull any longer, and I found myself lying there with my cheek pressed against the wood. A terrific headache erupted in my left temple.

"Are you all right, Mary Shelley?" Aunt Eva grabbed at my shoulders. "I told you not to do this. Sit up. Sit up, and tell me you're all right."

"How did he get a gun?" I somehow found the strength to ask.

"Julius kept one to protect the house from intruders," said Gracie.

"Where was Julius?"

"He slept at our house that night. He rode over from Coronado on the last ferry and showed up at our door after getting a drink in the city. He said he needed a break from taking care of Stephen."

"What time was that?"

"I don't know—maybe eleven o'clock. He's always coming over to stay the night so he can be in the city."

"And he was there all night?"

"Well . . . he was in San Diego all night, I know that for sure. I went to bed shortly after he arrived, and I found him lying on our living room floor early the next morning. He was . . . he and Grant . . . they sometimes . . ."

My eyes widened. "They sometimes what?"

"They sometimes go to—please don't tell Grant I'm telling you this . . ."

"Where do they go?" asked Aunt Eva for me. "Please just tell her so she'll sit up and act like a normal person again."

"I'll wake up in the morning," said Gracie, "and find them passed out in various parts of the house, and their eyes don't look right. They're like pale sleepwalkers who can barely move. Grant says he's only been smoking pipes in that den with Julius since our mother died—he says it helps him with his grief. Please don't call the police on him. I know it's opium, but he'll stop using it soon. I swear he will."

I tried to piece the timeline together in my head. "So . . . after you found Julius on the floor that morning, Grant must have driven him home to Coronado. Aunt Eva and I saw Grant drop him off when we were waiting to pick up my picture."

"Yes." Gracie nodded. "Then Grant drove straight back to our place. Julius didn't feel like opening the studio that day."

"Why not?"

"More and more people were hearing Stephen upstairs. Customers got frightened. Some of them left before sitting for their photos." Gracie pressed her handkerchief over her eyes and exhaled a long sigh. "Julius telephoned—later that Monday morning. He was in tears. He said their mother had found Stephen, dead, with the gun in his hand, and there was blood everywhere. The police had to come. My aunt hasn't been the same ever since."

I massaged my temple and kept going. "Where is Mrs. Embers now, Gracie?"

"In a local sanitarium . . . one of those health resorts with fresh springwater and relaxation treatments. She probably needs more care, but we couldn't imagine putting her in an asylum. Not after she fought so hard to keep Stephen out of one."

"Is she any better?" asked Aunt Eva, now clinging to my shoulders as if her safety depended on it.

Gracie shook her head. "I've gone to visit her every day. She grabs my hand and mutters something about poison and a gunshot and her strong sleeping pills. Other times she's quiet and looks like a lost little girl. I wish I could help her. I don't know what I can possibly do to make her come back to us."

I knitted my brow. "Why is she talking about poison?"

"I don't know." Gracie mopped her face with her cloth. "Maybe Stephen tried poisoning himself first."

"You're sure no one else was in the house when Stephen died?" I asked.

"I'm positive. Grant and Julius were in San Diego."

"They couldn't have gone to Coronado after you went to bed?"

"No. The ferries were closed for the night, and the drive around the bay is too long and risky in the dark. The peninsula leading to Coronado is just a thin strip of land." She wiped her tears again and knocked her wig off center. "The police confirmed it was a suicide, but Julius paid them to keep quiet so he could keep insisting Stephen had been in France the whole time. The undertakers were so overwhelmed by the number of funerals for flu victims that we delayed his burial by more than a week. That allowed Julius time to tell people we were waiting for Stephen's body to come home. It was all so horrifying." Gracie balled her cloth between her hands. "To lose a loved one at such a young age is unthinkable, but then to have to lie about the circumstances and watch his mother go out of her mind with grief . . . I don't know what to do, Mary Shelley. Is Stephen here yet? Will he speak to me and forgive me for going along with the war hero charade?"

I closed my eyes and drew in a deep breath of the smoke working its way into my lungs and under my skin. An exhausting weight curled around my back and pressed against my spine.

"Stephen," I whispered to him, feeling my aunt's fingers pull away from my shoulders. "I know this all must be disturbing for you, but now you know what really happened. Is there anything else you need us to do to help you rest? Is there anything you want me to tell your cousin before—"

Rage singed my tongue. Without warning, violent tremors seized my torso and legs, and the window behind me rattled in response to my movements. Every object hanging on the walls—from the cuckoo clock to the spice rack—soon clanked and shuddered and sounded like a living creature struggling to break free from its nails, and there was nothing I could do to stop the shaking.

Gracie whimpered. "Stephen?"

"I don't believe it," he growled, so close to me—so very, very close. "And I know exactly why my mother's talking about poison." His anger churned in my veins, and his voice took on a raspy tone that didn't even sound like him. "The blackbirds pour it down my throat."

"Stop it, Mary Shelley," begged Aunt Eva.

"Stephen?" asked Gracie. "Stephen, I'm so sorry we couldn't help you. I'm so sorry."

"Tell her, Shell," said Stephen over the cacophony of rumbling glass and gas pipes groaning at their seams. "Tell her I didn't kill myself. Tell her someone pours poison down my throat. They're killing me. They won't stop killing me."

The window cracked, shocking me out of my convulsions.

The shaking stopped.

The room fell silent.

Aunt Eva thumped against the floor. Gracie's skin turned a seasick green, and she swayed like she'd also faint at any minute. She gripped the table's edge and lowered her forehead to the surface to keep from toppling over.

I didn't blame either of them. I nearly fell unconscious myself.

For Stephen's voice hadn't burned against my ear or emerged from the air a few feet away from my head. His shouts weren't something for me alone to hear in the private confines of my brain.

His voice—his actual deep voice—came directly from my mouth.

26

SOLDIER'S HEART

I WAITED ON THE COLD FLOOR OUTSIDE AUNT EVA'S ROOM with my face pressed into my sweating palms. Gracie had helped revive my aunt and steer her to bed, but after that she simply shut down, as if someone had closed up shop inside of her. She wandered from our house with an empty stare.

Waves of dizziness threatened to knock me over, but I kept my wits about me and tried to fit Gracie's account of suicide into Stephen's blackbirds story. Did he shoot himself because he was convinced birds from the battlefields had followed him home to haunt him? If that was the case, why did both Stephen and Mrs. Embers insist poison played a role?

"What if his mother killed him to put him out of his misery?" I asked myself aloud.

The echo of my theory banged around my brain until a vein in my forehead pulsated. I fidgeted with guilt for even considering the possibility. But, still . . . what if Mrs. Embers didn't want her son to suffer? Perhaps that's why she had to be taken away after his death. Maybe Stephen's mind transformed his mother into a monstrous creature to protect him from the truth.

A HAND NUDGED THE BACK OF MY ARM. "WHO ARE YOU right now?"

I blinked away my drowsiness and found my aunt standing over me with her crucifix in her hands like a baseball bat. The lengthening shadows of late afternoon stretched outside her bedroom door behind her.

"You're not going to hit me with that, are you?" I asked.

"Are you Mary Shelley?"

"Yes, it's me. Please put that down."

Her arms relaxed around the cross, but her face remained tense. "I don't want you out here."

"Do you feel better?"

"Go to your room and lie down. I'm fetching a glass of water for myself. I'll bring one to you in a moment."

"All right. Thank you."

I made my way to my room and flopped facedown on the mattress.

Aunt Eva went downstairs and made a commotion in the kitchen, slamming cupboard doors and yelling about the crack in the window. She thumped back up and plunked herself down on my bed with enough force to rock me back and forth. "Don't ever talk like him again." She set a glass of sloshing water on the table beside me.

I buried my face in my goose-down pillow. "Grant looks strong enough to be of use to someone trying to get rid of an embarrassing family member."

"Stephen took his own life. You heard what Gracie said—his mother found him holding the gun. I'm sure it's hard to fathom the boy you knew doing something like that to himself, but it sounds like he wasn't even remotely the same person by the time he got home."

"I don't believe he committed suicide. I think they killed him."

"People don't commit murder because of embarrassment."

"They didn't know what else to do with him." I turned my head to the side to look at her and her cross. "Do you think a mother could be capable of killing her own son to put him out of his misery?"

"No!" Her eyes got huge. "That's a horrible thought. I'm sure Mrs. Embers held hope in her heart for Stephen's recovery. Please, Mary Shelley, I don't want him to keep coming to you. Tell him to stay away. Tell him if he has any decency left, he'll leave you alone."

"I can't let him go until I find out why he's still partway here."

"It was as if the devil himself possessed you."

"That wasn't the devil."

"He was no angel."

I exhaled a long breath through my nose. "Do you know what my father told me about monsters and devils?"

She shook her head. "I almost hate to think what your father's opinion on that subject would be."

"He said the only real monsters in this world are human beings." I licked my parched lips. "It was a frightening thing to learn, but it makes so much sense. We can be terrible to one another." I dug my cheek deeper into the pillow. "And do you know the oddest thing about murder and war and violence?"

"Oh, Mary Shelley, please stop talking about those types of things."

"The oddest thing is that they all go against the lessons that grown-ups teach children. *Don't hurt anyone. Solve your problems with language instead of fists. Share your things. Don't take something that belongs to someone else without asking. Use your manners. Do unto others as you would have them do unto you.* Why do mothers and fathers bother spending so much time teaching children these lessons when grown-ups don't pay any attention to the words themselves?"

Aunt Eva nuzzled her chin against the crucifix. "Not every grown-up forgets those teachings."

"But enough of them do. If someone killed Stephen, they didn't treat him as they'd want to be treated. And those men who arrested my father punched him in the gut before they hauled him away. The Espionage Act already allowed them to take him away from me, but they also hurt him to teach him a lesson. He sank to his knees and couldn't breathe after they were done with him."

"Wartime isn't like normal times."

"But that's the point. We wouldn't even have wars if adults followed the rules they learned as children. A four-year-old would be able to see how foolish grown men are behaving if you explained the war in a child's terms. A boy named Germany started causing problems all over the playground that included beating up a girl named Belgium on his way to hurt a kid named France. Then England tried to beat up Germany to help France and Belgium, and when that didn't work, they called over a kid named America, and people started pounding on him, too."

My aunt lowered her cross to her lap. "It's not that simple. Africa and Russia are involved, Germany and England were competing to build bigger navies, the Serbs assassinated Archduke Ferdinand—you can't break down the causes in a child's terms. And you better not say those things in public. That's exactly why your father went to jail." She leaned forward. "You have to realize, he was once like Stephen. That's where his anger comes from."

My arms and legs went cold. "What are you talking about? How was he like Stephen?"

"They called the condition names like soldier's heart during the Spanish-American War, this thing they're saying is shell shock nowadays. The unexplained effects of war upon a person's mind. Your father still had it when he met your mother."

I lifted my shoulders and head. "Are you sure? He's never shown any signs . . ."

"I remember him coming over to visit your mother when I was about seven. We'd all be talking about something that didn't even have anything to do with the war, and he'd sort of drift away. He'd look off into the air in front of him and not say a word for at least five minutes. Your mother would take his wrist, check his pulse, and call his name, and eventually he'd shake out of it and ask what we were just talking about." Aunt Eva sat up straight and put the cross aside. "My parents worried about my sister's relationship with him. They thought she was confusing concern for a sick man with love, and they feared she considered him the ultimate test of her skills as a physician."

"But they did love each other, didn't they?"

"I'm sure they loved each other. Your father gradually got better, and they seemed happy enough. His own father worked him hard in that store to make sure he kept up a routine in his life. The marriage lifted his spirits, certainly. But I didn't stop seeing those fading-away episodes until after you were born. Maybe he realized you were too important to lose."

I sighed in disbelief and sank my head back down on the pillow. "Then if Stephen's family had just given him a chance and found him help, he might have eventually recovered, too."

"His family didn't kill him."

"But—"

"No." She pressed her hand against my back. "He's dead because he wanted to be dead. There's nothing you can do for him. I know it sounds cruel, but he chose to leave. And he should stay gone."

I NAPPED FITFULLY AFTER AUNT EVA STOPPED RUBBING my back and left me alone in the room. I kept dreaming about that bloodstained sky. A gunshot would ring through my head, and the world above me would be splattered in the darkest red. I'd awaken with the sensation of a bird pressing down on my lungs, yet nothing was there but the taste of smoke and copper and Stephen's photographs staring at me from the wall beyond the foot of my bed.

Those photographs. *Mr. Muse* and the mysterious *I Do Lose Ink*.

"I Idle Nooks," I murmured, trying to decipher the lightning bolt's anagram to keep my mind from drifting back to blood. "In Kilo Dose. Oilskin Ode . . . No, that doesn't sound like a title at all. None of it makes sense. Nothing makes sense. I've got to work on my diagram again . . ."

I'd fall back to sleep, and the nightmare would haunt me again, like a motion picture running on an endless loop.

When darkness swallowed up daylight and I couldn't stand the thought of any more dreams, I pushed myself upright, lit the oil lamp, and shook the sleep out of my head.

"Think, Shell, think," I told myself in my own clear voice. "Put together a new set of notes. You can do this."

I grabbed a fresh sheet of paper from the drawer and went to work.

Saturday, October 19

1. Stephen panicked about an airplane and kicked his mother during my 10:00 a.m. photography appointment.

2. Julius was so worried about Mrs. Embers's injury that he risked taking her to a hospital during this plague. (I wonder, did he want Stephen to leave the house more than ever after Stephen harmed their mother?)

Sunday, October 20

1. Julius showed up at Grant and Gracie's house, around 11:00 p.m., saying he had first stopped for a drink after taking the last ferry.

2. Between approximately 11:00 p.m. and the following morning, Julius and Grant presumably visited an opium den.

3. Meanwhile, Mrs. Embers was in her bed in Coronado, having taken a sleeping pill.

Monday, October 21

1. Gracie found Julius lying on her living room floor in the morning.

2. Grant drove Julius home.

3. Julius handed me the "spirit photo" and told us Stephen died a hero's death.

4. Mrs. Embers screamed Stephen's name upstairs.

Key Observations/Questions:

1. Did Julius prepare the photo before Stephen's death, knowing Stephen would either be killed or taken to an asylum after their mother's injury? Gracie said Julius wanted to start telling people his brother was dead if Stephen got bad enough.

2. Why were Mrs. Embers's pills so strong that night? Did someone give her an increased dose?

3. What did Mrs. Embers hear or know about a gun and poison? Was she on her pills in her room, or was she there with Stephen?

And at the bottom of the page I wrote the one question I'd been asking all along but still couldn't completely answer, which frustrated me to no end:

HOW DID STEPHEN EMBERS DIE?

THE DARKEST HOURS

AFTER A SILENT SUPPER OF ONION SOUP WITH AUNT EVA, I returned to my bed and read Stephen's Verne novels until my eyes no longer stayed open.

I dreamed of the little boys who played on top of the coffins in front of the undertaker's house. Flies buzzed around their brown caps as they climbed over the foul-smelling caskets and pretended to hunt Germans. This time they sang the nursery rhyme "Sing a Song of Sixpence."

> *The king was in the counting house, counting out his money,*
> *The queen was in the parlor, eating bread and honey,*
> *The maid was in the garden, hanging out the clothes,*
> *When down came a blackbird and pecked off her nose.*

I jerked awake, paranoid once again that a bird was on my chest, watching me while I slept.

I turned to my side, blinked through the dim glow of my oil lamp's light and saw nothing but my bedroom, quiet and still. My lungs breathed without the burden of anything squashing the life out of them. Stephen's photographs hung on the wall across the way, undisturbed.

Yet the air burned with his presence.

I heard a sound—something wet, splashing against my bedsheet behind my back. I clenched my eyelids shut and dreaded flipping over, for I didn't hear any rain outside my window, and so the ceiling couldn't have been leaking.

I counted five more drips before Stephen's beaten-down voice emerged from behind me in the bed. "Please keep me with you. I can't stand it anymore."

I kept my eyes closed. "We'll figure this out soon so you can have some peace. We're so close now."

"I didn't kill myself."

"I know."

"They're killing me."

"I know." I shut my eyes tighter. A warm liquid seeped across the sheets and soaked my nightgown, but I swallowed down my fear and kept talking to him. "Stephen, does one of the blackbirds look like your mother?"

Three more drips. "What?"

"Is your mother ever there when you're suffering from the poison?"

"No."

"Are you sure?"

"She isn't there."

"What about your brother and cousin?"

"They're blackbirds. Enormous, vicious creatures. I see their beaks—huge, luminous scissors that could tear you to shreds."

"You keep saying that, but I don't understand. I need to touch the place where you—"

"No—they'll rip you to pieces. Don't you dare go anywhere near that bed, Shell. You'll see them."

"I want to see them. I want to know who did this to you."

"Please, no." He flinched enough to jerk the mattress. "Don't go to my room. Swear to me you won't."

"Then tell me what I'm supposed to do. I can't keep you with me. It's—scary. It's dangerous. I can't do it, Stephen." My eyes welled with tears. "I've got to let you go." I covered my face with quivering fingers and cried.

Stephen wept as well—I could hear him shaking and sniffing behind me, which made me sputter sobs into my pillow all the more.

"Don't . . ." He choked on tears. "Please don't cry, Shell—"

"I should have stopped you from leaving for the war that day. I should have done something."

"There was nothing else you could have done. I had already signed the papers to go."

"We should have had the chance to be together again. You shouldn't be dead. I've lost my entire life." The pillow beneath my cheek absorbed my tears until the fabric felt drenched—and all the while the dripping liquid oozed its damp and sticky heat across the left side of my body. I coughed and struggled to find my voice. "Are you bleeding, Stephen?"

He sniffed again. "My head really hurts."

I wiped my eyes with a corner of the quilt. "I'm going to get off the bed now. I'll move slowly."

"Don't let me go yet. I'm not ready."

"I'm just standing up so I can see what you look like." My blood turned sluggish in my veins. I had to fight against the weight of his sadness to rise to a standing position. But I made it. I stood upright.

With the softest of steps, I turned around and faced him.

"Oh, Stephen." I slapped my palm over my mouth and burst into tears again.

Blood, thick and dark and blackish red, caked his face and shirt. I couldn't even see his eyes and mouth—only the innards of his head. He huddled against the wall and held his hand against his left temple, but a stream of crimson seeped through his fingers and fell to a puddle on my sheets.

My legs buckled. My knees slammed to the floor. I lowered my head to the rug and fought against black spots buzzing in front of my eyes.

"It's too late," he said while my brain swayed on a swelling sea of dizziness. "They're here."

Unconsciousness stole me away before I could see who "they" were.

DOWNSTAIRS, THE CUCKOO ANNOUNCED HALF PAST FIVE in the morning.

I opened my eyes, and after several more minutes spent on the floor regaining my strength, I pushed myself to a standing position with the wobbling legs of a newborn deer.

Stephen was gone. My empty sheets looked clean and white, without one speck of blood staining them.

But I remembered what he looked like.

I staggered out to the dark hallway with nothing but the feel of the wall under my hand guiding me to my aunt's half-open door. "Aunt Eva? Can I sleep with you until you have to get up?"

She didn't answer, so I entered her unlit room.

"Aunt Eva?"

Strange little breathing noises rasped from her bed, as if she were crying but trying to stifle her sobs.

"Did you hear him?" I asked her. The soles of my feet found their way across her unseen floorboards. "Is that why you're crying? I'm sorry. I'm trying to let him go. I know I need to."

She kept breathing in that odd way. My stomach sank. The sounds didn't resemble sobs anymore.

She was shivering.

"Oh no." I lunged toward her bedside table and lit a match. "Oh, Christ."

She was curled in a ball beneath her covers and trembled as if all the blankets in the world couldn't warm her. Her face had turned tomato red, and her sweaty hair clung to her cheeks and lips. Her eyes stared at nothing.

I covered my mouth and nostrils with my hand to protect myself, even though the germs were just as likely to be waiting on my skin as traveling through the air. The match burned down to my fingers, searing my flesh, so I blew it out, struck another one, and lifted the glass chimney of her oil lamp to ignite the wick.

"The flu got inside the house," she wheezed. "Leave before it finds you."

Every square inch of my skin went cold at the way she described the flu like one of Stephen's blackbirds. "I've got to help you, Aunt Eva."

"Go."

I laid my palm against her forehead. "You're hotter than that match that just burned me."

"Don't touch me." She tried to swipe her hand at my arm. "Pack your things and leave before it gets you, too."

"I don't have anywhere else to go."

"Go. Leave. Get out of the house." She shut her eyes against a violent bout of shivering that gripped her the same way Mae Tate had convulsed on the floor of our high school English classroom.

"I'm going to make you some tea and onion soup—"

"Go!"

I jumped backward at the force of her words. "Who's going to take care of you?"

"It doesn't matter. I can't face your mother and tell her I let you die. She'd never forgive me. She'd want you to live." She grimaced through the pain of her chills. "Go. Go!"

I backed out of the room, unsure what to do. At any second I might drop to the floor with the same convulsions. My life could end in a matter of hours. Stephen would never be free.

But I couldn't leave my aunt. I couldn't—not when I could possibly save her.

The day before my father's arrest, I read an article about a Portland woman who cured her four-year-old daughter of the flu by burying her in raw onions for three days. The mother had fed the child onion syrup and smothered her in pungent bulbs from head to toe. Dad had remarked, "It's like the Gypsies hanging garlic above their doors to ward off evil," and I shook my head in dismay at the woman's desperation.

But that Portland girl survived. She lived. Her mother saved her.

I could save Aunt Eva.

I ran downstairs, switched on the main gas valve outside the back door, and poked matches inside the globes of the kitchen wall lamps to set them glowing. Light burned through the darkness in that cold, still room.

The pile of onions delivered the day before sat in a crate on the kitchen floor. Eleven of the dozen remained. I plunked three of them on the kitchen worktable.

"The knives!" I smacked my forehead. "She hid all the kitchen knives."

I charged back upstairs to Aunt Eva's room. "Where are the kitchen knives?"

"Go away."

"I need to chop onions. Where are they?"

"Wilfred's violin case."

"I don't see a violin case." I pulled at my hair. "Where is it?"

"Under the bed." She groaned through her spasms. "It's so cold in here. Why is it so cold in San Diego? The weather was supposed to cure Wilfred."

"I'll get more blankets. I'll be right back." I dashed away and tugged my blankets and Grandma Ernestine's quilt off my own bed, dragged them down the hall, and laid them over Aunt Eva's twitching body. "Here you go. Nice and warm."

"*Kalt.*"

"What?" I asked.

"*Kalt.*"

"I don't know what you're saying, Aunt Eva."

"*Eiskalt.*"

"Are you speaking German?"

"Don't speak German, Mary Shelley." She whimpered through her chills. "They'll arrest you. *Gefängnis.*"

"I've got to find the knives. Where's his blasted violin case?" I dug through shoes and boxes stuffed beneath the bed. "Here it is. Cripes, you really wanted to hide it, didn't you?" I popped open the latch of a curved leather case.

The knives and scissors were tucked around Uncle Wilfred's cherrywood violin. I snatched a knife with an accidental strum of the E string and returned downstairs, so fueled by fear I didn't yet feel tired from being up so early.

My fingers chopped those golden bulbs as fast as they could without severing a thumb. I stuck an onion wedge in my mouth and sucked on its potent fumes to keep my own body from breaking down. Water blurred my eyes.

"Wait—why am I chopping them?" I spit the onion out of my mouth. "She needs to be buried in them. This is crazy. What do I need to do?" I paced the kitchen floor and yanked my hair again until my scalp hurt. "All right . . . let's make the chopped ones into soup and syrup and cut the other ones in half to stir up the odors. We'll put the halved ones in her bed. Her feet—oh, damn, I forgot to check her feet!"

Another frenzied dash upstairs. I flapped the ends of her blankets off her legs and fell to my knees in thanks at the sight of shivering white feet.

"Oh, thank God. They're not black."

But some of the victims die within a matter of hours, I remembered the newspapers warning. *Some last for days before a deadly pneumonia sets in, and there's nothing you can do to free their lungs from that suffocating blood-tinged fluid.*

Aunt Eva coughed a wicked cough that rattled inside her chest. Her nose bled into her pillowcase.

"Why is there blood?" I mopped her up with a handkerchief, but the flow kept coming. "Hold this against your nostrils with as much strength as you can give. I have to get the onions. We've got to get you covered."

I took off again, and I heard my father's words of advice from his letter in the rhythm of my footsteps pounding through the halls.

Human beings have always managed to find the greatest strength within themselves during the darkest hours.

The phrase spurred me onward to the kitchen.

Human beings have always managed to find . . .

It sliced through the onions with eight swift beats.

. . . The. Great. Est. Strength. With. In. Them. Selves . . .

It rustled in the papery onion skins shuffling in a pouch made of my nightgown's skirt.

. . . during the darkest hours. Human beings have always managed to find the greatest strength within themselves during the darkest hours.

I lifted the blankets off my aunt.

"No," she screamed. "It's too cold. *Kalt! Kalt!*"

"I'm smothering you in onions. You'd do the same for me, and you know it."

I scattered the onion halves over her upper body while she pulled her knees to her stomach and hacked and shivered. More blood gushed out of her nose, this time in a stronger flow. I wiped her up again and changed her pillowcase, but she stained the new case within five seconds. I attempted to give her an aspirin for the fever, but she threw it up.

"I should call a doctor."

Human beings have always managed to find the greatest strength within themselves during the darkest hours.

Back in the kitchen I picked up the telephone's black, horn-shaped earpiece and turned the crank on its boxy oak body. It took a hundred years for the operator to answer.

"Number, please," said a female voice at the other end.

"I need a doctor."

"A specific doctor?"

"Any doctor. My aunt's sick with the flu, and her nose won't stop bleeding."

"Is it a dangerous level of blood loss?"

"I don't . . ." I massaged my eyes. "Yes—it seems dangerous. She's burning up with a fever and throwing up, too. I can't give her an aspirin."

"I'm afraid most doctors are too busy to answer their phones right now. I'll try connecting you to an ambulance dispatcher. One moment, please."

A series of clicks traveled down the line, and all I could think about was how swiftly time was passing. The cuckoo clock would be striking six in the morning in three minutes.

A man from the San Diego Police Department picked up, but he told me I'd have to wait at least twelve hours before an ambulance would be available.

"I hear sirens outside my house," I shouted into the mouthpiece. "Why can't one of those ambulances just stop by and get my aunt?"

"Because they're already being used to transport other patients. We'll put her name and address on a list and get a car there as soon as possible."

"What if she dies before then?"

"Then cover her with a sheet and put her outside. A separate ambulance is making the rounds to pick up bodies."

I hung up on the man and pressed my forehead against the telephone's sharp wooden edge. "This can't be happening. It's too much." I whacked the green wall with my fist. The sensation felt exquisite, so I whacked it again until the cuckoo clock bounced off its nail and splintered on the floor. The second hand still ticked, so I stomped on the clock's face with my bare foot and kicked the contraption across the kitchen, where it cracked against the icebox with a terrific *crash*.

The ticking stopped.

I had killed a clock.

I should have been saving my aunt and my dead first love, but instead I had murdered a beautiful Swiss timepiece, handmade in the nineteenth century by one of my great-grandfathers up in the Alps. My fist throbbed. Little clock handprints bruised the sole of my foot.

Death gave a good chuckle. *I'm beating you, little girl. You see? You can't fight me. Why even try?*

I grabbed clean cloths and returned upstairs to Aunt Eva.

THE REST OF THE DAY UNFOLDED MUCH THE SAME: NON-stop running up and down the stairs with soup and tea and cold compresses. Fruitless telephone calls to find doctors and ambulances. Bloody noses. Rasping coughs that sounded like the last gasps of a drowning person. Skin color checks. Onions. Vomit. Curse words that would have made my father cringe. Clothing changes when I couldn't stand the mess of fluids on my own skirts.

I opened a cookbook and learned how to make onion syrup by filling a jar with alternating layers of onions, brown sugar, and honey, but the concoction would need to sit overnight to be ready to consume. When my stomach growled, I stopped to eat an apple and drink a glass of water, but my breaks couldn't have lasted more than two minutes apiece. There was no time to slow down.

Somehow, night returned before it seemed due. Aunt Eva had made it onto a list for an ambulance, but every time I called for an update, the dispatcher added another twelve hours to the wait.

"I'll pay you money," I told the man near midnight. "I'll pay you to pick her up sooner. I bet you're fetching rich people faster than the poor souls who slave away in the shipyard. That poor woman worked her fingers to the bone to keep the navy safe, and you're just letting her die up there."

"Miss, her name is on our list. We'll get her as soon as we can."

"You're not a true patriot. You're not one hundred percent American."

"Miss—"

"I'm sorry, that was a terrible thing to say. I hate when people say that. I'm sure you're a fine person."

"Miss, you sound tired. Are you ill as well?"

"I'm fit as a fiddle. I've never been better. It's lovely weather we're having, too, isn't it? A grand day for a cup of tea with my beautiful dead boy and my dying aunt."

"Miss, get some sleep. We'll send an ambulance."

"He was just eighteen."

"Get some sleep."

"She's twenty-six."

"Miss . . ."

"All right." I rested the earpiece on its hook and tottered on my feet. "All right."

I STRUGGLED TO STAY AWAKE, TO KEEP HELPING AUNT Eva, but my arms and legs refused to move at a normal rate. A snail of a girl was what I'd become. An old woman shuffling about in the stooped body of a sixteen-year-old.

Candlelight illuminated a little porcelain clock on Aunt Eva's bedside table. The morning ticked its way toward five o'clock. Almost twenty-four hours had passed since I'd first found her with the flu. The oil for her lamp had run out, so I hunkered down on her floor in the shadows with my arms wrapped around my bent legs.

"I wonder how that Jones boy is doing, or whatever his name was," I said to my aunt's wheezing, weakening body. "The one who unsettled me at the convalescent home. Is his flu as bad as yours? And I wonder about Carlos and Mr. Darning, and Stephen's friend Paul. Are they still alive? Is my dad alive? Will today be the end of the world? Because it sure feels like it." I sank my head against my knees and smelled onions and blood on my black skirt. "It wasn't all that frightening to die, come to think of it. Returning was the hard part, landing back inside this broken body and waking up to the war and the flu and people who do cruel things to other people." I bit my lip and tasted dry skin. "Why did I even return? What a nasty joke to send a girl back inside her body, only to show her there's nothing she can do for anyone in the world."

Aunt Eva muttered something in German and gibberish.

"Hmm . . . maybe the onion syrup is ready. I should give that a try." I grabbed the side of her bed with one hand and hoisted myself off her floor. "Let's give that a try, shall we?"

A cry of shock escaped my lips.

My aunt's face was brown. Those mahogany spots—the purplish, brownish signs of a body losing oxygen—were overrunning her cheeks and ears. She gurgled and sputtered, and blood again leaked from her nose.

"No, that's not fair!" I dug my fingers into her mattress. "I'm trying my hardest to save you, so you can't turn purple. Don't you dare let this beat you, Aunt Eva. Don't you dare—"

An ambulance wailed through the neighborhood outside.

What would happen if I jumped in front of the vehicle to make it come to a stop? What would happen?

"Let's find out." I left my aunt's side and galloped down the stairs in the dark, somehow arriving at the bottom without breaking my neck. Outside a salty breeze blew through my hair and skirt, and the moon was a thumbnail sliver in the still-black sky. A cluster of voices murmured down the street, and I turned and smiled for the first time that day.

There would be no need to jump in front of an ambulance, for there an ambulance sat—one block down.

"Thank you!" I took off running to make sure I reached the driver before he could drive away or fade from sight. "Don't be a hallucination. Please don't be a hallucination."

Two uniformed policemen hauled a young woman out of an adobe-style bungalow with a red-tiled roof. Her unshaven husband ran his hand through his tousled brown hair while holding a toddler in his other arm. A grandmotherly woman beside him rocked a crying infant.

"Please take my aunt, too!" I ran at the officers at the speed of hurricane winds. "Take my aunt; she's in my house."

"There's no room," said one of them—an ugly man with squinty eyes and enormous ears.

"She's not very big. You can make room." I was aware of my arms waving around me as if they had a mind of their own, but I couldn't control them. "Please! Stop telling me to wait twelve more hours. This woman here isn't nearly as sick as my aunt. Her face isn't even close to turning purple."

"We don't have another stretcher."

"Then I'll carry her myself, you lazy, useless—"

"I can help." The flu victim's husband put down the toddler and came my way. "I'll help you carry her."

I stepped back, caught off guard by his kindness. "What?"

"Stay right here," he told the officers. "Where is she?"

"This way. Thank you. Thank you." With tears turning the road ahead of me into a blurry, bobbing streak, I led the man to our house, and we tore up the dark stairs together. "Thank you. She's in here. She's turning that brownish-purple color."

The man scooped my shivering aunt into his arms by the light of the candle.

"*Kalt*," she muttered. "So *kalt. Grippe*. Wilfredededed . . . *mein Liebchen*."

"Don't speak German, Aunt Eva. She's not even German, she's Swiss." I followed the man and my aunt out of her room, back into the blackness of the upper hallway. "She was born in America, and I killed her Swiss cuckoo clock. I kicked it clear across the kitchen as though it were causing our problems. Just like Oberon and those scissors that nearly got him."

"Do you have the flu, too?" asked the man on our way down the stairs. "You sound feverish."

"No, I'm fine. I just haven't slept in twenty-four hours, and no one would come get her, and Stephen's waiting for me."

He maneuvered Aunt Eva out the front door. "Where is someone waiting for you?"

"He's probably shivering down in the shadow of blackbirds again . . . um . . . Coronado, I mean. Did I just tell a stranger about the blackbirds?"

Something rustled in the white branches of the eucalyptus when we passed beneath its long, fragrant leaves, and I wondered if Oberon was perched up there, waiting for the door to open again so he could fly inside.

"Where are your parents?" asked the man. We were half-way back to his house.

"Gone. Dad said the flu wouldn't be so bad in San Diego with all the warm, fresh air, but that's not the first time he made a mistake. Why are you helping my aunt when you must be sick with worry about your wife?"

"It's better than thinking I allowed someone to die."

"That's good of you." Goodness—there was still goodness in the world. "I started thinking I was the only one left alive."

The ugly officer waved at us to move faster. "Hurry up—we need to get going."

The man nestled Aunt Eva in the back of the ambulance, squeezing her between his shaking wife and a white-haired woman with a face too young for her hair. They all wore dainty ivory nightgowns. Three sleeping angels. The last thing I saw before the officers shut the door was three pairs of bare feet, lined up in a row. Aunt Eva's looked darker than the others.

"Wait!" I lunged for the door. "Her feet looked black."

The ugly officer grabbed my arms and pushed me away. "We can't wait any longer."

"Her feet looked black."

"It's too dark to tell."

"They looked black. Let me see."

"We've got to go!" He forced me down to a seated position on the street. "Stay right there, and don't you dare get up. You're not helping anyone right now." He took off toward the driver's seat.

"Let them go." The man who had carried my aunt seized my elbow before I could shoot back toward the ambulance. "Your aunt is in good hands."

"Her feet looked black."

"It may have just been the lack of light."

"I didn't even say good-bye."

"She'll be all right . . . It's all right." The man put his arm around my shoulders and led me over to his crying children and the grandmotherly woman, while the sirens blared. "Do you want to come inside with us? None of us are feeling well, but at least we can be sick together. You seem to be alone."

I shook my head. "Stephen told me in that letter about the war to be careful offering my trust to people. He's waiting for me. If I'm going to drop dead from the flu, I need to go to his house while I'm still able. I'm so tired."

"Why don't you get some sleep before you find this person? You really look like you're getting the flu."

"I'm not sick. I'm just tired." I pulled myself out from under the man's comforting arm and backed away. "Thank you. I've got to go. I've got to help someone before I die. My mother didn't lose her life just so she could send a useless girl into the world. There's got to be something more."

STEPHEN'S ROOM

BACK IN MY BEDROOM, I STUFFED MY MOTHER'S LEATHER doctor's bag full of my treasures—Stephen's photographs, his letters, my goggles, *The Mysterious Island*, my mother's coin purse, Dad's note. I crammed everything inside the cloth-lined compartments with the same urgency as when I had packed for San Diego the night my father warned me people might be coming for him. The brass gear necklace with the lightning burn went over my head and shimmered on the bodice of my best dress—the black silk taffeta one I'd worn to Stephen's funeral. The garment still smelled of sulfur and sorrow, but my plans for the morning required my finest clothing.

Downstairs, I put on my coat and tucked an onion in my pocket. And a potato. Our next-door neighbor in Portland,

Miss Deily, insisted a potato in the pocket would scare away the flu, and I was willing to do absolutely anything to buy a few more minutes. I tied my flu mask in place and lifted my leather bag by its handles.

Outside, the sky to the east blushed pink, a color that would have looked brilliant in a chemist's glass flask. I pulled my coat around me and headed south to the center of the city, feeling like the earth's sole survivor. Smoke hung across the sky in a cloud that sprinkled ashes on the silent streets and sidewalks. I didn't know if I was smelling chimneys battling the November chill or crematoriums disposing of the dead, but the city looked and felt like the Germans had just bombed us. The stacks of coffins in the undertaker's front yard spilled out to the sidewalk, and the stench was overwhelming. I held my breath and kept walking.

Death bit at the backs of my ears. *I told you I was coming. Get ready. I'm here.*

"You're not here yet," I said. "I'm still upright and walking, aren't I?"

I clutched my mother's bag and walked five more blocks to Mr. Darning's photography studio, not far from the site of the Liberty Loan drive where Aunt Eva had purchased my goggles in another life. The red automobile that had been parked outside our house during the photographer's visit sat next to the curb.

I hurried to the studio's door and banged on the glass. "Mr. Darning? Are you in there?"

I held my breath. A figure moved inside.

"Mr. Darning?" I banged again. "Please open up. It's Mary Shelley Black. I need your help."

The photographer appeared behind the glass with rumpled hair and blinking eyes. With his mask in his hand, he opened the door, and for the first time I saw his entire face, including a trim mustache that matched his copper-wire hair.

"Miss Black. You caught me off guard. I slept here last night because my neighbors all have the flu."

"It got Aunt Eva, too. I'm scared it's going to take me at any minute."

"Oh, Jesus." He pulled away from me.

"I've been breathing the same air she has. I'm dead—I know it. Please take me to Stephen Embers's house before it knocks me down."

"What?"

"Take me over there, and convince Julius to allow me inside Stephen's bedroom. Julius wants to take a picture of me for a contest. We can tell him the best place for a spirit photograph is up in Stephen's room."

"But—"

"I swear to you I'll show you evidence of a soul who's departed his body. I swear you'll feel better about that girl of yours who died."

He tied his mask around his face. "I don't know if I should allow you in my car—"

"That's her picture right there, isn't it?" I pressed my hand against the window that separated me from the photograph of the beautiful dark-haired woman.

"Yes, that's Viv."

"If you had only a few hours left to live," I said, my fingers running pale streaks down the glass, "and you knew you could spend those last precious moments freeing her soul so she could rest in peace, wouldn't you do anything you could to help her?"

His eyes shone with tears. "Of course I would."

"Then help me free a soul I love." The vinegary sting of grief nipped at my taste buds. "Keep me safe from Julius while I call Stephen to me one last time."

He craned his neck toward me. "You're—you're going to let his spirit go?"

I nodded. "It's time. They all need to move on, Mr. Darning."

He blinked, and a tear escaped his left eye.

I took my hand away from the glass. "But I promise you, what you'll witness in Stephen's room will be better than Mac-Dougall's scale experiments, better than my compass, and far better than Julius Embers's usual photographs. You'll have proof your Viv lives on in some other place."

He turned his gaze from me to the picture of the brunette woman, which told me his answer.

He would be coming.

I would be safe to explore Stephen's last memories in the very room where he died.

．．．．．．．．．．．．．

I SPENT MY FINAL CROSSING OF SAN DIEGO BAY IN THE automobile section of the Coronado ferry, seated on the passenger side of Mr. Darning's ruby-red vehicle, my black bag tucked beneath my legs. Once the *Ramona* docked, Mr. Darning slammed his foot on the gas pedal and we sped across the island that wasn't an island, past the streetcar tracks that had carried Aunt Eva and me to the Emberses' house, and alongside the restless Pacific until we reached the two-story cottage with brown shingles.

He pulled the car next to the curb and shut off the motor.

Three crows were perched on the Emberses' roof. Their sinister caws laughed over the ocean's roar, and I swore they stared me in the eye.

"Oh no." A headache erupted across my skull. "You were right." I slunk down in my seat.

Mr. Darning popped open his door. "I was right about what?"

"I can't get out of the car until those birds go away."

"Why not?"

"I see their beaks."

"Pardon?"

"They're like scissors. They could tear me to shreds. I don't like how they're looking at me."

Mr. Darning didn't move.

"Kill them," I shouted in a husky tone that startled the both of us.

He stepped out of the car and smacked his hands together. "Shoo. Go away, birds. Get out of here."

The calculating birds didn't budge.

"Throw something at them." I slid farther down against the leather. "Hurry, before they smell the gore on my clothing."

"What gore? Why are you talking like that? Your voice sounds different."

"Just kill them."

"I can't go throwing rocks at somebody's roof. Let me fetch my box of photographic plates from the backseat so we can go inside. Ignore the birds."

"I can't ignore them. Look at their eyes. They're watching me."

He backed away from the car. "You're starting to scare me. Please . . . let me fetch my plates from the backseat."

The dark thugs on the roof flapped their wings and took flight. I ducked and gasped and covered my head with my arms while their feathers beat against my neck.

Mr. Darning touched my back and made me jump. "The birds are headed east. They're nowhere in sight. You don't need to be afraid of them. All right?"

I lifted my head and made sure the birds were truly gone. "All right." My voice resembled my own again. "I'm sorry. They bother me these days."

He opened my door for me. "Calm yourself and stop shaking so much. There's nothing to fear." Despite his bold words, his own hands trembled.

A disorienting bout of light-headedness threatened to stop me from making my way up to the front porch, but I gulped deep breaths and persevered, still keeping an eye out for crows. And the flu. My dizziness and confusion could have been the first signs of fever.

Mr. Darning's raps against the front door sounded as loud to my ears as cannon blasts. We waited almost a minute, with no results, and then he knocked again.

I reached out to the wall below the porch light for support. "What if Julius isn't home?"

"Shh. Let's listen for his footsteps and make sure he's not avoiding us."

We tipped our ears toward the door and stood stock-still, but I only heard waves breaking on the shore across the street.

Mr. Darning swallowed and looked my way. "He might be dead."

"Oh no." I jiggled the brass doorknob. *Locked.* "No!" I pushed against the door as if I were truly strong enough to break it down. "This can't be happening. His cousin came to our house just yesterday. Julius was alive as of her visit."

Mr. Darning shook his head. "Being alive yesterday doesn't mean a thing with this flu."

"Don't remind me. My aunt . . ."

"I'm sorry."

I glanced behind me at the empty lawn where the lines of photography customers had waited. I thought of the studio . . . and the porthole-style windows.

"Oh . . . wait . . . Stephen's entrance." I tore down the front steps.

"Where are you going?"

"Stephen used to climb through the studio's windows," I said, my feet squishing across the dew-soaked front lawn, "to save the equipment at night when Julius left them open."

Mr. Darning trailed after me with his brown case of glass plates in hand.

Around the corner, beyond the studio's entrance, I saw three round windows—all open to allow the chill from the night to settle inside the house. Or else left open by a man unavailable to shut them.

Stephen's grandparents had built the openings six feet off the ground, so the portholes were more a useless nautical decoration than a means of view or escape. A larger window faced the ocean at the front of the house, but I had always seen its shutters closed and locked, perhaps so Julius could further provide a dim and ghostly atmosphere inside the studio.

Two options existed: a coral tree with thick branches that reached out to the windows and a sturdy white trellis that was attached to the wall next to the leftmost porthole. I didn't feel like shinnying up a tree trunk in my taffeta dress, so I grabbed hold of the trellis's latticed wood and started to climb.

"You can't go into that house alone," said Mr. Darning. "Not when Julius might be in there."

My head still felt dizzy, so I didn't dare look down at him.

My hands brushed past a flowering vine that tickled the backs of my fingers. "I'll run"—I grunted and kept going upward—"straight to the side door . . . and let you in right away. I just hope Stephen isn't furious at me for coming."

"Why would *Stephen* be furious?"

I wrapped my right hand around the bottom edge of the left window. "He believes there are creatures inside the house that want to hurt me. Nightmare creatures." I peeked inside the studio.

"Do—do you see anything in there?"

I shook my head. "It's empty. The lights are off. I'm going in." I clutched the trellis again and went a few inches higher. "Please turn away, Mr. Darning. This won't be ladylike."

"Be careful."

"I'll try." I reached out to a nearby tree branch, gripped it with both hands, and swung my feet to the bottom edge of the round window. I then slid my legs carefully through the opening so I wouldn't take the six-foot drop in one loud go. With my fingers still locked around the branch, I held my breath and listened for Julius's footsteps. Or Stephen's voice.

"Are you all right?" Mr. Darning called from down below.

"I'm fine. I'm going to push the top half of my body through and see if I can twist around and hang on to the ledge before dropping."

Somehow, I did exactly that. With a swish of black taffeta and the thuds of tumbling feet and elbows, I landed on the studio floor—bruised but intact.

The house inside tasted of smoke and poison and blazing-hot metal. It felt wrong to be there, and I would have bolted out the door if I hadn't felt in my gut that Stephen's room hid the missing piece in the puzzle of his death.

"What are you doing in here?" asked someone behind me.

I leapt to my feet.

Julius came toward me through the open pocket doors, but he staggered rather than walked. His pace was slow and his footsteps unsteady, like the movements of a drunk. His pale face had grown thin compared with his appearance just four days earlier, and his wild black hair needed a good brushing.

I ran over to the side door and opened it for Mr. Darning.

Julius stopped in his tracks when he saw the other photographer entering the studio. "Why are you both here?" he asked.

"We thought you were dead from the flu." I grabbed hold of Mr. Darning's arm for support. "You weren't answering the door. We got worried."

Julius took four more labored steps and spoke as if we were idiots. "Why. Are. You. Here?"

I steadied my breathing. "I'm here to put your brother to rest. I'll sit for that photograph you want."

Julius's eyes—so bloodshot they must have burned—blinked as if I'd just woken him from a long sleep. He stood up straight and made his voice deeper. "Why are *you* with her, Darning?"

"I'm curious about her abilities. I agreed to accompany her to ensure you'll be sending a legitimate photograph of your brother's spirit to that contest." Mr. Darning lifted his brown case. "As usual, I've brought my own plates, marked with my initials, to prevent you from switching to your own doctored versions."

Julius scrutinized Mr. Darning through uneasy eyes. "You sure you're not plotting to get me arrested?"

Mr. Darning lowered his case. "I swear I'm only here for the sake of psychical research. I believe this girl is genuinely capable of luring your brother into a photograph. If we can get him to come, there would be no need for you to be arrested, would there?"

I lifted my chin and tried not to let my fear get the best of me. "Please let me help your brother, Julius. I know he'll come to me. *You* know he'll come to me."

Julius leaned his hand against the wall for support, right next to the picture of the white-draped phantom and me. He sniffed and rubbed his nose. "You look terrible, Mary Shelley. Are you sick or something?"

"No—just tired and anxious to contact your brother. Will you let me?"

He shifted his weight from one foot to the other and hesitated some more. My eyes and throat stung as if a cloud of cyanide hovered overhead, and Julius looked equally sickened by the toxic atmosphere.

To speed things along, I spoke to his way of thinking. "Are

we ready to win this prize, Julius? Should we help both you and Stephen get out of this house for good?"

"How much is the prize?" asked Mr. Darning.

I kept my eyes on Julius. "Two thousand dollars for solid proof of the existence of spirits. Isn't that right, Julius?"

Julius stirred back to life once again. He pushed himself off the wall. "Bring Stephen quickly . . . and then send him far away from here. I don't want him anywhere near me, so don't—"

I hurried out to the house's main entryway.

"Hey! Where are you going, Mary Shelley?"

Julius and Mr. Darning followed me out to the hall, their footsteps amplified in the deep, hollow space, which still reminded me of the belly of a ship with its dangling brass lantern and knotty wood walls.

"Why are you out here?" asked Julius. "The studio's back—"

"Shh." I lifted my finger, for I thought I had heard a whisper down the way.

The grandfather clock continued to preside over the far end of the hall, but the second hand ticked louder than I remembered. A shadow hiding the round white moon face seemed to lengthen across the wall to the clock's left and stretch toward the staircase. I remembered what the stairs looked like—the shine of the dark wood, the green runner trailing up the steps behind Stephen. An electrical hum rose in their direction, drowning out the ticking of the clock.

I kept an eye on that back portion of the house. "We have

to photograph him in his bedroom to catch him with your camera."

Julius shook his head. "No! Absolutely not. You are not going into his room."

"Isn't that where you hear him?" I asked.

"I don't want you in there."

"Then there's no point in trying. That's where he is. I bet if I called to him right now, he'd make a sound up there . . ."

"No." Julius ran over and grabbed my shoulder to stop me from going to the staircase. "Don't call him."

"I'd listen to her, Embers," said Mr. Darning. "She seems to know how to find him. He was already coming to her in my car outside your house."

Julius turned even paler. "He was?"

Mr. Darning nodded. "I heard him. This is going to be a spectacular photograph. I can feel it."

Julius gulped like he might throw up. Then he said, "All right. I'll take the photograph upstairs. But I have conditions, too."

I tensed. "What are they?"

"You have to take off that mask. No more photographs of you in goggles or gauze or other bizarre accessories. This has to be a professional sitting. You're here only to pose for the picture and to send him away. No dramatics. No snooping."

I looked to Mr. Darning, who gave me a comforting nod and said in that gentle tone of his, "You know it's probably already too late for gauze masks. The judges would appreciate seeing your face. You don't want to look like you're hiding anything."

I nodded. "I'll take the mask off, then. May I use your washroom to cool my face before the sitting?"

"I—all right." Julius rubbed his eyes and swayed for a moment. "Go make yourself presentable. I'll fetch my equipment and start setting up." He pointed at Mr. Darning. "You wait right here, Darning. I don't want you sniffing around his room before I'm up there." He stumbled back inside his studio, and I half wondered if he'd collapse and pass out.

Mr. Darning set his brown case of photographic plates on a small marble table in the hall and popped open the lid. "Go get yourself comfortable, Miss Black. You're doing well. I've never seen a braver girl."

"Thank you," I said, although I didn't feel brave in the slightest. The vile tastes of poison and blood flowed across my tongue and warned of imminent pain.

I wandered down to the grandfather clock on unsteady legs and stopped for a moment to watch the brass pendulum swing in its hypnotizing rhythm. The second hand journeyed to the bottom of the white moon face, and the gears—those thin cuts of circular metal moving in perfect synchronicity—spun and clicked deep inside the heart of the contraption.

I glanced back at the staircase and longed to hear Stephen ask me again what I saw through my goggles' lenses. I wanted to tell him a new answer: *I see the future, and I know it can all be changed if you stop yourself from heading off to the army when you're still in school. Don't run away from your home life just yet. The battles will rob you of your mind, and someone will destroy your body. Your photographs will be lost. You'll never get to grow up.*

I clenched my fists and continued through the house, past the humming staircase.

The washroom consisted of a pull-chain toilet, a white shell sink, and more cedar wall panels that smelled of wood and toxic fumes. Only a sliver of natural light came through a small window near the ceiling, so the room felt dark and crowded and uncomfortable. I removed my mask and splashed cool water over my sweating cheeks and nose. The peaked face staring back at me in the mirror above the sink belonged to a petrified kid, not a confident spirit medium. My skin lacked all color, and my hair seemed darker than usual. I already looked like a black-and-white photograph.

I dried my face on a limp yellow towel that reeked of dark-room chemicals. The noxious air inside the house kept me from inhaling deep enough to calm my racing heart. With my throat dry, I twisted the doorknob and walked across the hall-way in my double-reinforced Boy Scout boots that could still help me run at a moment's notice.

I approached the bottom of the staircase, my pulse beating in the side of my neck. I could feel Stephen there, sitting the same way as when I saw him back in April. My left foot slipped on a polished floorboard, but I righted myself, regained my balance, and inched farther. The bottom step of the staircase came into view, along with a foot in a gray sock. The buzzing of electricity grew so loud my eardrums felt they would burst.

I stepped around the corner and saw him.

Black-red blood still covered his entire face and shirt, so close and clear and grotesque in the daylight. I shut my eyes and gagged.

"Don't go up there," he told me. "Get out."

"You don't look right." I braced myself against the wall and tried so hard not to ruin everything by vomiting all over the floor.

"Are you ready?" asked Julius in a voice that buzzed as much as the stairs.

I peeled one eye open and couldn't see Stephen anymore.

Julius thumped down the staircase in his huge brown shoes. "Mr. Darning just observed me placing his own plates in the camera upstairs. The equipment and lighting are ready."

"I'm ready, too," I said in a voice that sounded as if my vocal cords had turned to sandpaper. My head pulsated with pain to the beat of the blood churning through my veins. My body wouldn't last much longer—if the flu didn't overtake me, my nerves would. The need to reach Stephen's bedroom fueled my strength to endure the walk up that staircase.

I'd read about pilots describing a change in air pressure when their planes ascended into the sky. That's how it felt climbing up to the Emberses' second story. My stomach rose into my chest the way it did on a Ferris wheel, and the blood vessels in my temples seemed poised to pop. My throat burned hotter. I gripped the rail for support, as my legs melted beneath me.

At the top of the staircase, Julius turned right, toward a bedroom. The broiling air gusting out the opened doorway blew against my face like heat from an oven. The sound of a thousand lightbulbs, restless with electricity, droned within.

"Do you hear the buzzing?" I asked Julius.

"What buzzing?"

I eyed a wooden bed across from the door, below one of three windows that washed the room in an eerie sunlight I'd seen in photographs of empty barns and graveyards.

Mr. Darning waited for us just inside the door, offering me another nod of encouragement. "It's all right, Miss Black. I'm here."

Julius entered ahead of me, and I noticed the unsteadiness of his legs, the hesitancy with which he approached his camera. The leather bellows stretched toward the mattress, which was covered in nothing more than a dusty brown blanket. A chill spread from the nape of my neck to the small of my back. That ratty old cloth was probably hiding Stephen's blood. There was no longer a pillow.

"Well?" Julius steadied himself by holding on to the black box of his camera's body. "Aren't you coming in?" His voice squeaked an octave higher than usual. He kept his neck stiff and his eyes alert, searching for something over his shoulder.

I stepped across the threshold of Stephen's bedroom, which smelled rancid and stale. My legs might as well have been wading through a pool of molasses. The air pushed me backward as if it were alive, forcing me away from that buzzing and angry bed, breathing hot fumes against my face.

I staggered forward and reached my hand out to the brown blanket, the same way I'd try to grab a log if I were drowning in a river. Static stung my palm. I knew touching that mattress would give me a shock as potent as the lightning bolt's, but I bent forward, pushed through the molasses air, and climbed onto that bed.

A jolt of electricity whacked me in the back. I fell and shut my eyes through spine-rattling pain that shuddered through my teeth and made me bite my tongue. The room went black.

When I opened my eyes, I found the world dark and my wrists bound to a bed by coarse ropes that burned through the layers of my skin. I was on my back, and there was whispering near the door.

"Wait until I put on the mask. I don't want him recognizing me."

"Who cares if he recognizes you?"

"I don't want anything in his eyes slowing me down, all right? I didn't smoke enough dope tonight. I'm losing my nerve."

"I told you, too much dope might slow us down. What a waste it would be to forget to photograph him."

"Are you sure something's going to show up?"

"We've got to try, right?"

I struggled against my ropes. Dark figures shuffled around

me, guided by the dull light of a single candle. They wore black clothing and kept the flame far enough from their faces for me to see anything but pure-white surgical masks and the glint of their watchful eyes. One of them positioned a camera near the bed. I heard the turning of the tripod's handle and smelled the firework scent of magnesium powder poured across a flashlamp's tray. Scuttling noises emanated from everywhere, as if rats were scurrying around the room. Every sound was magnified.

One of the figures turned toward me, and his mask mutated into an enormous white beak. I sucked in my breath and blinked my eyes, but he wouldn't change—the creature looked like an ungodly bird with the body of a man.

A light flashed, and I was deep in the belly of a trench in France, cradling my rifle, waiting for the sound of artillery fire alongside other panting men. The mixed stink of rotting flesh, cigarettes, sweat, rum, urine, and stagnant mud turned my stomach into mush. I huddled on the ground at the far end of the line, and not more than six feet down from me lay the body of a soldier with reddish-brown hair, his flesh soft and pale, the blood on his face still drying.

A group of cawing carrion crows descended over the poor soul and pecked at his glassy brown eyes with their scissor-sharp beaks jabbing, jabbing, jabbing—fattening themselves on the ruins of war, gorging on a dead nineteen-year-old boy. One of the birds raised its head and stared at me with its beak smeared red and hunger brightening its ravenous eyes. I'd woken with one of its kind pressed against my rib cage before, digging at my uniform, smelling the blood in the fibers until I fought it off me to prove I was still alive.

I aimed my rifle at the crows on the boy and shot the largest bird dead, which sent a flurry of black wings flying past my face and a spray of machine-gun fire raining down upon us.

Then I was back on the bed in the unlit room, and one of the birdmen propped up my head on a pillow and forced the narrow tube of a copper funnel between my teeth. I gagged and struggled to free my wrists and ankles from the ropes. There was so little light; all I saw were those luminous beaks. I heard a bottle uncork and smelled the sting of darkroom chemicals in the air. Panic charged through me. I tried pushing the funnel out of my mouth with my tongue, but the figure shoved the tube farther inside, making me gag all the more.

"I'll try to keep his head up," said one of the birdmen in a strained whisper. "Unless . . . do we want to drown him with the acid? Maybe he'll look more like a flu victim in the photograph if he's choking."

"I don't know. I just want to get it over with."

The creature tilted a bottle, and then he poured.

Liquid fire careened down my throat and scorched my insides, burning all the way down to my stomach. I choked and coughed and spit out a substance that seared my face with the pain of a thousand pinpricks.

A light exploded, white and fiery like a bomb. I was back in the trench in France, running through the mud with a rifle in my hands, bullets whizzing overhead, a gas mask covering my head and magnifying my wheezing breaths. The man in front of me went down, collapsing in a spray of blood and muck that splattered across my mask. A green mist settled over me, as poisonous as that liquid the dark birds poured inside me.

I was back on the bed again, and the creatures were arguing over whether a picture had just been taken.

"Was I in that picture?"

"No."

"Are you sure about that?"

They shoved the copper funnel back in my mouth, and the volcanic river again sloshed down my throat. I turned my head and coughed out the poison into my pillow, burning my own flesh a second time. I cried out in horror.

The figure jumped out of the way. Another flash of light and smoke erupted five feet away, momentarily illuminating the dark human halves of the birds, who watched me from by the camera.

They were photographing me.

"Why are you poisoning me?" I tried to yell, but my larynx had been so burned by chemicals it made my voice coarse and weak. "Don't peck out my eyes."

"How long is it going to take?" asked one of the creatures in a deep and whispery voice.

"I have no idea. Have patience. Take some more pictures. He really does look like he's dying from the flu. I think the choking helps."

"What about the ropes? Dying flu patients aren't tied to beds."

"Damn it. I didn't think of that. Get those off him."

The creatures surrounded me again, studying me as I writhed and hacked out the stinging poison.

"He looks like he'll still fight. He's strong when he's delirious."

"I thought you were sticking him with morphine."

"Why the hell did I let you talk me into this?"

"Think of the huge impact on the world of psychical research if we capture his soul as it's leaving!"

"You only think that because you're more of a doper than I am, and he's not your brother."

"He's hardly a human being anymore. He's as good as dead, right?"

"Why did he say we were going to peck out his eyes?"

"Because he's a lunatic."

"I'm getting my gun."

"No! His spirit will leave too quickly. We won't have time to photograph it."

"I can't stand this. He's looking at me. I'm getting my gun and putting him out of his misery."

"No!" I cried in a voice that didn't sound human anymore. "Don't shoot me. Get me out of here. Don't kill me."

A flurry of action surrounded me—the rush of feathers, the scuttling of feet, voices arguing whether or not they should speed up the process. One of the creatures released my wrists from the ropes, but the deep-voiced one wrestled him to the ground and cussed him out. The room spun as if I were on a carnival ride. My throat and belly raged with fire. I turned on my side to curl up in pain and saw the silver metal of a gun shining on the bedside table.

My salvation.

I reached out, desperate to kill the squabbling birds with the bullets before they could finish with me. My clumsy fingers grasped the weapon. A brutal force knocked me in the head. The world slowed to a crawl, and a gunshot echoed in the black and heavy atmosphere. A white, bloodstained sky beckoned from overhead, tugging my soul toward it, while someone shouted from below, "Quick! Take a picture. We're going to miss it! We're going to miss it!"

And the scene started over again. I opened my eyes and found the world dark and my wrists bound to a bed by coarse ropes that burned through the layers of my skin. I was on my back, and there was whispering near the door.

This time someone grabbed my arms and shook me. I heard the name "Mary Shelley" and got confused. *Mary Shelley? Why is she here?*

"Leave us alone," I shouted. "Don't poison me. You're killing me."

A hand smacked me across the face. "Stop saying that. Why are you saying that?"

"Don't kill me. Please don't poison me."

"Stop it. I'm not poisoning you. Why are you talking like

you're him?" My attacker shook me until a bare, sunlit room came into view. Julius's face—not a bird's—stared down at me. I didn't see a single bird anywhere.

Beyond Julius's head, dark stains marred the ceiling's white plaster—the shadows of blood. Stephen's own blood was the red and white sky that haunted him.

"Oh, God. Oh, my God." I regained my bearings and tried to sit up, surprised to find my wrists weren't tied with ropes. "Stephen? Can you hear me? Those weren't monsters poisoning you."

"Don't you dare say I was the one poisoning him." Julius shook my shoulders. "Do you hear me? It wasn't me."

"What do you think you saw, Miss Black?"

I jumped at the sound of the other male voice as if I'd heard another gunshot. Mr. Darning stood by the camera and calmly sprinkled a box of powder across the flashlamp's tray as if preparing for a normal studio portrait. "You looked like you were in a trance," he continued. "I took a photograph of your intriguing state and can't wait to see if we've captured a record of your communication with the other side."

My stomach lurched.

Our conversations about spirits and science ran through my mind: *A physician named MacDougall conducted experiments involving the measurement of weight loss at the moment of death . . . at a home for incurable tuberculosis patients . . . He would push a cot holding a dying man onto an industrial-sized silk-weighing scale, and he kept his eyes on the numbers while his assistants watched for the final breath . . . I'm compelled to find tangible proof that we all go somewhere when we die. It hurts more than anything to think of a sweet soul like Viv's as being gone forever.*

"What did you see?" asked Mr. Darning again, his voice eager, his eyebrows raised. He positioned the loaded flashlamp into a holding stand next to the camera. "His spirit?"

"No." I steadied my breathing, even though the truth was falling into place with sickening clarity. "I witnessed two blackbirds experimenting on a delirious war veteran in the confusion of the dark."

Julius squeezed my arms. "Why are you talking about blackbirds, too? There were never any birds in this house."

"His attackers looked like birdmen with their dark clothing and beak-like flu masks. He wanted to shoot them, but he grabbed the gun wrong and must have pulled the trigger. It wasn't a suicide—he was disoriented and fighting for his life. He died struggling to live. He wasn't as good as dead."

"He wanted to shoot them?" asked Mr. Darning.

"Did you hear what she just said, Darning? 'As good as dead.' That's what you kept calling him that night."

"Perhaps you should stop damaging your brain with illegal substances, Julius." Mr. Darning ducked his head under the black cloth behind the camera. "I certainly wasn't anywhere near your brother when he was in the throes of his neuroses."

"Get me off this bed before it happens again." I squirmed

to escape Julius's grip. "I can taste the poison and the smoke from the flash. Don't make me repeat that."

"Let's take another photograph before she gets up," said Mr. Darning. "I've got this new plate ready to go."

"Would you stop taking photographs?" shouted Julius. "Get out from under that cloth and stop treating my house like a laboratory. I'm sick of your morbid psychical research haunting me each night. I'm sick of listening to my brother's bed shaking up here because of you."

Mr. Darning's face reemerged. "Keep your mouth shut, Julius."

"I sometimes hated Stephen, but he was my brother. I never would have done anything so twisted if I'd been in my right mind. You became obsessed with death after your girl-friend died."

"Stop putting ideas into Miss Black's head."

"She already has the ideas in her head. She knows who was in his room, Darning. Didn't you hear her? She felt you poisoning him."

Mr. Darning left the camera and grabbed my shoulder. "Tell me exactly what you think you saw, Mary Shelley. No one's going to hurt you if you tell me the truth. Who did those blackbirds look like?"

"Stephen!" I cried out. "Stephen Embers, where are you?"

"Don't bring him here right now." Julius covered my mouth with his hand, but I sunk my teeth into his flesh and freed my lips.

"It wasn't otherworldly creatures who tortured you." I twisted and tried to get away. "It was two desperate men trying to win a contest. It's in my notes from the library—*they're always desperate*."

"Quiet!" Mr. Darning shoved me by my shoulders down to the scratchy brown blanket. "Just settle down. No one did anything wrong."

"Why did you have to treat him like he was nothing? He was a person—not an experiment."

"Boys in Stephen's condition are better off dead, Miss Black."

"That's not for you to decide."

Mr. Darning pinched my nostrils shut and forced my jaw closed with his free hand. My eyes bulged. My lungs fought to find oxygen. I scraped my nails into his hands, but he only clamped down harder. I kicked my legs and pounded on his knuckles.

"Are you killing her?" asked Julius in a panic.

"She'll tell someone. Why did you have to blabber about everything? She's a nice girl."

"I don't want another kid dying in here."

"Well, I don't want to go to jail. I don't deserve to waste away behind bars for your goddamned lunatic of a brother who ruined our experiment."

The flashlamp exploded.

An eruption of smoke and light attacked the room with the violence of shells blasting in Stephen's war zone.

Mr. Darning jumped off me and gaped at the Cyclops lens staring us down through the dissipating cloud of white. The flashlamp's fiery aftermath—the same burning air Stephen carried with him to his death—invaded my nostrils and lungs.

Julius stumbled toward the camera. "How did that go off by itself?" He covered the lens, as if he could hide everything they'd done by screwing the round cap into place. "What just happened, Mary Shelley?"

I struggled to find my voice through gasps of air. "You wanted me to bring Stephen for a photograph"—I pushed myself to my elbows—"and he came."

The air boiled with rage, and the panes of all three windows shuddered in their frames with a fury that took away my breath. Mr. Darning froze. Julius peered at the restless glass with eyes large and black. I scanned the bedroom to see if Stephen stood anywhere against the wood panels, but I saw only faded rectangles where his pictures used to hang. His anger heightened all around us. The room felt ready to implode.

Somebody pulled me off the mattress and dragged me under the bed, where I buried my face in my arms just moments before the windows shattered with a crash that rang in my ears. Shards of glass skidded across the floor and nipped my hands, and the men cried out in pain. They dropped to the floor with an impact that jolted my elbows.

Then silence.

I lay there beneath the bed, terror-stricken, shaking, my ears still ringing, but the air around me lightened a hundredfold. The bedroom's toxic taste dissolved with the gentleness of cool milk tempering the bitterness of a cup of tea. I realized someone was holding me under the bed, keeping his arm around me, imparting warmth and a feeling of safety to my trembling body. "Grab the photographic plate that shows him trying to kill you," whispered Stephen near my ear. "Tuck it inside that satchel lying next to you and run."

I lifted my head and found, to my right, the silhouette of Stephen's old leather camera satchel caked in dust. I managed to get the tan strap over my shoulder in the cramped space beneath the bed and crawled out, careful not to cut myself on the battlefield of broken glass.

I grabbed for the camera but lost my footing for a moment when I saw Julius and Mr. Darning lying on the floor, streaked in blood. Glass had sliced their faces and clothing and hands, each tiny wound bleeding a stream of bright scarlet. Julius stared at his bleeding palms like he didn't understand what was happening.

I had witnessed enough photography in my life to know to push down the dark slide sticking out of the top of the camera to protect the glass plate inside. I then pulled out the wooden plate holder that carried the fragile piece of evidence.

"Mary Shelley," groaned Julius. "I'm in agony. Get me my painkillers from my bedroom."

I stuck the plate holder in Stephen's empty satchel. "I'll call an ambulance when I'm a few houses down."

"No! Don't call anyone."

"I'm calling the police." I moved to leave, but someone gave me a shove from behind that sent me toppling toward the glass on the ground. All I remembered after hitting the floor was peering over my shoulder and catching the fleeting image of Mr. Darning's face and the camera coming toward my head. Pain walloped my skull.

My spirit slammed up to the far corner of the ceiling.

My body remained below.

ᗪEᗩTᕼ, ᗩᏀᗩIᑎ

DOWN ON THE GROUND, MY FORMER SHELL LAY IN A twisted heap—an empty body with Stephen's satchel still strapped over my shoulder. A welt on my forehead bled and swelled like rising dough. Mr. Darning collapsed with the camera in his hands, crumpled over my feet, and seemed to lose consciousness. Julius curled into a ball four feet away and sobbed.

"I told you to stay away from my house," said a nearby voice.

I looked beside me. Stephen was also crouching up there in the upper corner of the room with his back against the ceiling and his feet pressed against the wall. He looked less wounded and bloodied, although I could see where the bullet had entered his head. Burn marks marred the skin around his mouth.

I edged closer to him. "He hit me with the camera. What if I stay dead? What if no one finds me or understands what happened?" My frustration rumbled down to the room and rocked Stephen's bed against the wall.

Julius sobbed harder. "Stop haunting me, Stephen. Leave me alone. Go away."

"Is everyone all right in there?" asked a woman outside the window, down below on the front lawn.

"Who's that?" I asked Stephen.

"She sounds like our neighbor."

"I heard the glass break," called the woman. "Are you up there, Julius? Is anyone hurt?"

Julius struggled to lift his head. "Get me help! I'm bleeding to death here."

"I don't know if I'll be able to find an ambulance. I'll fetch my husband and bandages."

"I need my painkillers! I'm in agony."

Mr. Darning groaned as if he were coming to but remained limp across my feet.

I turned my attention to the windows with their demolished panes and strained to hear the neighbor's feet running to her house. I thought I detected the squish of heels hurrying across grass.

Stephen wrapped his arms around his legs. "Those weren't birds, then?"

"No." I slid all the way next to him and leaned against his side. "They were people."

"Did they really try to kill me to win a contest?"

"Yes, they did. I'm so sorry." I laced my fingers through his. "Mr. Darning loved a young woman who died. He was desperate for proof of the afterlife, and your brother was desperate for money. I guess they were both out of their minds on drugs. Maybe they became friends because of their addictions, or maybe—" A thought struck me. I remembered the peculiar puzzle of Mr. Darning catching every other flimflamming photographer except for Julius. "No, wait—did they already know each other before Mr. Darning started saying he was a fraud catcher?"

Stephen cocked his head. "You mean Aloysius Darning?"

"Yes. Did you know him?"

"That was the name of a two-bit photographer whose business was about to shut down before I left for the war. I died because of *him*?"

"One played the mysterious photographer. The other played the expert. And both profited. No wonder Mr. Darning always denied finding proof that Julius was a fake. He probably also posed as the spirit soldiers." I looked down at the man who I once thought shared my father's voice. "He was scamming me the entire time. I was just as desperate as everyone else, wasn't I?"

A door opened somewhere downstairs.

Stephen braced himself against the ceiling. "If they find the glass plate inside the satchel, they'll have documented proof of him attacking you while Julius stood by. People will ask questions. They might discover photographs from the night of my death."

"But what if they don't see the plate? What if nobody searches inside the satchel?"

"Go back down there and show them the plate yourself."

I shrank back against the ceiling's plaster, terrified of dropping into that damaged flesh below. Down there, my body grew grayer and colder by the minute.

"Go on," said Stephen. "I can't ever leave, knowing you died because of me. Push yourself back into your body. Stop the world from mucking up everything so badly."

A gray-haired couple blew into the bedroom with rolls of white bandages tucked in the crooks of their arms. They contemplated the blood and the glass and struggled to make sense of the scene. The man knelt beside my body and searched for my pulse.

"Go back, Shell." Stephen stroked my hair with soothing fingers. "You'll be all right."

"What if the world never gets any better?"

"It'll have a far better chance if you're in it. Go on. The only way I can rest is if you survive."

I met his brown eyes. The same sense of urgency that had gripped us in his family's sitting room overcame me.

"Send me off as a happy young woman," I said.

"What?"

"I want to go off to my battles the same way you went to yours. Send me off as a happy woman."

Gravity gave me a sharp tug that threatened to pull me away from him. We clasped hands before I could slide too far.

He leaned down and kissed me, and his touch no longer summoned images of bloodstained skies, battlefields, and murderous blackbirds. Instead of smoke and fire, his mouth tasted of the divine sweetness of icing on a cake when the sugar isn't overdone. The taste of love before any pain gets in the way.

Our lips stayed together until gravity proved too strong.

He held tight to my hand. "Go live a full and amazing life, Shell. Come back when you're an old woman and tell me what you did with the world."

I nodded and clung to his fingers. "Swear to me you'll rest."

"I swear."

My body down below appeared closer than before. At any second I'd plunge into an excruciating pool of ice. Our arms stretched farther apart, and our hands shook against each other. Every precious second we had spent together during our shared lives—from the day he brought his little Brownie camera to school to the morning I spied him through my goggles at the bottom of his Coronado staircase—warmed my soul and killed the darkness. I was ready.

A silent count to three.

A plea that the end wouldn't hurt—for either of us.

I closed my eyes and let him go.

I DO LOSE INK

IN THE MINUTES FOLLOWING MY DROP INTO THAT FRO-
zen, leaden body, I somehow found the strength to reach
inside Stephen's satchel and hand the wooden plate holder to
the Emberses' neighbor, who was shouting to his wife that I
wasn't dead.

"Here." I forced the smooth wood into the man's hand. "Here's
evidence that the people you found me with are monsters."

Before my eyelids drooped closed again, a flood of yellow
warmth brightened the far corner of the ceiling—and disappeared.

MY MEMORIES OF THE MOMENTS AFTER MY BRIEF DEATH
in Stephen's bedroom were a muddled assortment. Chills

that penetrated down to my bones. Pain boring into my skull. Salty broth forced between my lips. Muscle aches. Wheezing. Flooded lungs. Gasps for air. Delirium. Drowning.

Somewhere toward the end of my suffering, I dreamed about the anagram Stephen had written at the bottom of his lightning bolt photograph.

I DO LOSE INK

In the dream, the words stared at me from behind the glass of his battered and splintered picture frame that had fallen to my floor too many times. I tried with all my might to unscramble his hidden meaning, but the letters slid around in the sepia waves and repositioned themselves into dozens of nonsensical phrases.

Oiled oinks. Kid loonies. Doe oilskin. Die ski loon. Ski on oldie.

My brain hurt. I massaged my exhausted eyes and tried to make the real title come into focus.

Sink. Die. Soil. Ink. Look. Slide. Side.

Before the dream ended, I saw it, sharp and clear:

LOOK INSIDE

I AWOKE IN AN UNLIT CORNER OF THE HOSPITAL WITH sweat-soaked bandages wrapped around my head and something stringy tied to my right foot's big toe. Perspiration drenched the hospital gown sticking to my body. My mouth tasted pickled. I strained to lift my head to get a look at the end of my cot and found a toe tag tied around my flesh, awaiting my death.

"Lord, have mercy! She's still fighting to live." The stocky nurse I remembered from my lightning injury waddled toward me with cobalt-blue eyes shining above her mask. "You've been struck down by lightning, given a concussion that knocked you dead, and spent a week getting clobbered by the flu—but here you are, blinking at me like a confused newborn. I wish all my patients possessed your mighty will to live."

I stared at the woman with my lips hanging open. "I had the flu?"

"Yes, you most certainly did." She set her clipboard beside me on the cot and placed her cold hand against my forehead. "Your temperature was one hundred and five degrees when they hauled you in here with that head injury, and you developed a bad case of pneumonia. Some detectives have been asking to speak with you, but I told them they'd need to find a spirit medium if they intended to chat with you anytime soon."

I wiggled my itchy foot. "Is that a toe tag on me?"

"It is. I half wondered if tying it there would make you mad enough to prove me wrong about dying again." She went to the foot of the bed and untied the string. "I guess it worked."

"How long have I been here?"

"Well, it's Sunday, November tenth . . ." She flipped through her clipboard. "You came in November fourth, just about a week ago. Kaiser Wilhelm abdicated the throne and escaped to Holland since then."

"He did? Is the war over?"

"Not yet, but soon, we hope. Very soon." She pulled a thermometer out of her white pocket and gave it a good shake.

"Did anyone bring a doctor's bag that belonged to me?" I asked. "I left it inside a red automobile in front of a house on Coronado."

"It's sitting right below your cot."

"I need to look at a photograph tucked inside."

"I need to take your temperature first."

"Please let me have my—"

She shoved the little glass tube inside my mouth before I could say another word. The thermometer made the insides of my cheeks itch, and I was tempted to pop it out with my tongue, but I needed her help.

She kept track of the time using a wristwatch, and after a grueling wait that seemed to ramble along for an hour, she fetched the stick from my mouth. "Ninety-eight point six." Her eyes glistened. "Congratulations, my little fighter. You're beating the infamous Spanish influenza."

I tried to sit up. "May I have my bag now?"

"Lie down, lie down—you're not completely healed yet." She lowered me back to the cot by my shoulders. "I'll pull out whatever it is you need, but then we need to get you resting and eating and drinking so we can send you on your way. Why do you own a doctor's bag, anyway?"

"My mother was a doctor."

"A lady physician for a mother?" She whistled. "No wonder you're a bold one, missy."

I heard her click open the black bag's clasp beneath me, and I swallowed with anticipation.

"I see a pretty photograph of a butterfly—"

"It's the other one. The lightning bolt."

"Here it is." She set Stephen's picture on my stomach. "My, my, my. That's a beauty. Must have been taken by quite the photographer."

"Yes. It was." I ran my fingers down the chipped frame to his words written at the bottom. The letters—written below an older, scratched-off title—were just as I remembered:

I DO LOSE INK

LOOK INSIDE. Not a title at all.

A request.

The nurse patted my knee. "All right. I'm going to check on some of the other patients, and then I'll bring you clear broth and get a doctor to examine your lungs and head. Don't go anywhere." She chuckled and shuffled away on the soft soles of her shoes.

I pried open the frame's back cover and saw the shine of a gold key—and a note, written on the photo's cardboard backing in Stephen's gorgeous handwriting.

April 29, 1918

My Dearest Mary Shelley,

My mind keeps replaying the events of yesterday and giving our time together a new ending, one that doesn't involve Julius ruining everything for us. That morning feels like an unfinished work of art, interrupted and spoiled. If I could have had just five more minutes with you, I would have kissed you until our lips ached, and I would have told you I've loved you from the moment you fixed my camera on those church steps when we were little kids.

Even when the world seems like it's spinning out of control, you're always there for me, Shell, whether in person or through your letters. During my darkest moments, you have always reminded me that life is interesting as hell (pardon my French, but there's no other way to put it). If nothing else, I will fight in this war to ensure people like you remain free to dream your dreams and become whatever you desire.

This photograph is for you—a small compensation for putting up with my brother's spirit games and for sending me off to battle with a contented soul. I photographed the lightning storm from my bedroom window last winter. I'm guessing you would have loved seeing the bolts pierce the Pacific. I wish you had been here beside me.

You'll also find a key to a safe-deposit box at the main San Diego post office (I've written the box number, as well as my military address, below). I don't have time to put this parcel in the mail myself, unfortunately. The idea of giving this key to you just struck me as I was getting dressed to leave this morning. Hopefully, my mother will send it before Julius snoops and you'll be as skilled at this anagram as you were with Mr. Muse. A regular letter would likely disappear in Julius's hands.

Please take the contents of the box and do with them what you like. I don't want to risk writing them into a will or leaving them in my house. Julius would get to them somehow. My mother has copies of her favorites, but the negatives are in the box. You may keep the photographs or sell them if you can. Never send any profits to my brother.

If I lose my life in France, perhaps show my work to a few people as proof that I was once in this world. It's hard to imagine disappearing without a shred of evidence that I existed. I would be eternally grateful.

Thank you for coming back into my life before my departure to the unknown. I will never forget you, Mary Shelley Black.

Yours with all my love,
Stephen

P.S. Don't ever worry what the boys who don't appreciate originality think of you. They're fools.

MARY SHELLEY BLACK

A DOCTOR SIGNED MY HOSPITAL RELEASE PAPERS THE same day the war ended: November 11, 1918.

Fireworks whistled and exploded somewhere out in the city, and when I flinched from the commotion, the nurses told me a German delegation had signed the armistice to end the fighting. Faraway battles would stop snatching the minds and lives of our boys and men in the dark bellies of the trenches. The carrion crows would have to fly to other hunting grounds.

During the twenty-four hours before my release, I'd been subjected to oversalted soup, cold fingers and stethoscopes prodding at my skull and chest, eye exams, mental exams, and stiff detectives in dark suits questioning me about Julius and Mr. Darning. The detectives told me Grant and Gracie were being cooperative about their knowledge of Julius's whereabouts during the night of Stephen's death. Yet the men warned there'd be trials and potential ugliness.

"We discovered some grisly photographs in our searches through the two men's studios," said the older detective with the least compassionate voice. "The road ahead may be rather upsetting for a sixteen-year-old girl. I'm afraid your delicate female eyes and ears will experience some ugliness."

"Oh, you silly, naive men." I shook my weary head and genuinely pitied their ignorance. "You've clearly never been a sixteen-year-old girl in the fall of 1918."

WITH MY HEAD SHROUDED IN BANDAGES AND MY LEGS shaking from lack of use, I wandered with my black bag through the shivering, rasping bodies toward the hospital's exit. The tangy sweet smell of the doctors' celebratory champagne drifted above the fetid stench of fever surrounding me on the cots, and my heart ached to see people still suffering when one half of the nightmare was ending.

"Get better," I told them on my way through the white corridors. "Please get better. The war is over. It's done. Don't miss this. Keep fighting."

I reached the last hallway and came to a stop. I recognized the face of a patient sitting on one of the cots on the right-hand side of the corridor.

She was eating a bowl of soup, her legs nestled beneath a patched-up green blanket, and I would have missed her if she had been facing the opposite direction. Her blond hair had turned pure white.

"Aunt Eva?" I ventured closer to make sure the hazel eyes and bottle-cap lenses were truly hers. "Oh, my goodness. Aunt Eva. It is you!" I threw my arms around her bony shoulders and squeezed her as hard as I could without hurting her. "You didn't die. Your feet weren't black after all. I could have sworn they were black."

"Mary Shelley . . ." She breathed a relieved sigh into my hair and clutched my head against hers. "They told me you were in here, fighting the flu and recovering from a concussion. I've been so worried about you."

"A doctor just released me. Oh, I'm so glad you're not dead."

We held each other close for a good minute or more, sniffing back tears, ensuring neither of us was about to disappear.

"I buried you in onions and nearly went crazy with worry." I dropped to my knees beside her cot. "And I was so certain it had been for nothing. Your face was brown, and some man from down the street helped me get you into an ambulance. He carried you like a hero."

"Which man?"

"Well . . . he's already married."

"Mary Shelley!" A weak blush rose to her cheeks. "I wasn't asking to hunt down a husband. I want to know whom to thank."

"Oh. I'll show you where he lives when we're both home."

I grabbed her cold hand. "You are going to be able to come home, aren't you?"

"Yes." She steadied her soup on her lap. "The fever's gone. I just need to regain some strength. I feel like a train ran me over and left me on the tracks to die."

"I completely understand. I think I must have lost at least ten pounds. Just look at my blouse." I tugged on the loose fabric gapping above my waistline. "I look like a scarecrow."

"But your beautiful hair is still brown." She ran her fingers through my mess of tangled tresses. "Mine's white . . . isn't it?"

I sank my teeth into my bottom lip. "It might be temporary. It's a striking color, actually."

"It might fall out, like Gracie's. I've seen some clumps."

"It might not."

"And to think I was so worried about my chin-length hair before." She clamped her hand over her mouth, and her shoulders shook as if she were either laughing or crying—or both.

"Shh." I helped her stabilize her sloshing bowl. "It doesn't matter. You're beautiful because you're breathing. And you're not purple—I can't believe you're not purple."

Aunt Eva wiped her eyes behind her glasses. "When I heard you had a head injury, I worried you'd gone to save your ghost. I kept dreaming about Julius shaking you in my living room."

"I did save Stephen. And he saved me. He's at peace now." I swallowed. "We let each other go."

"Oh." She gave a small nod. "I'm glad." She directed her

eyes toward her soup with a weighty sigh. "Oh, Mary Shelley. I hope I can be strong enough to take care of you."

"You will be." I rubbed the remnants of her mighty ship-yard biceps. "Soon enough you'll be back at home, putting up with me dissecting your telephone and arguing my way through everything again. You're stronger than you think you are, Aunt Eva. You're my battleship-building aunt, after all."

The corners of her mouth lifted in a smile. "Thank you." She wiped another tear. "Despite everything, I'm glad I've had you by my side these past weeks. You may have driven me to the edge at times, but you excel at fighting to save the people you love."

"So do you."

She nearly argued that point, but she closed her mouth and seemed to accept my words.

"Keep eating and resting for now, OK?" I grabbed the handles of my black bag. "Keep getting better and stronger. I need to go fetch something at the post office, and then I'll put my things away at home and come straight back to be with you again."

"Don't tire yourself out."

"I won't. I promise to take good care of myself."

"Ah . . ." She nodded. "Now *that* sounds like your mother."

"My mother took good care of herself?"

"She did. She really did."

"Then maybe I'll start giving that a try." I kissed her fore-head. "I love you, Aunt Eva. Thank you for living." I squeezed her hand, scooped up my bag, and left the hospital to rejoin the world outside.

MY FINGERS SHOOK AS I SLID THE GOLD KEY INSIDE A lock on the austere brass door of Stephen's safe-deposit box. Inside, I found a black leather case engraved with silver letters that spelled out *SEE*—Stephen Elias Embers's initials. A fitting companion to *LOOK INSIDE*. I slid the case out of the receptacle with care, and right there on the cold post office tiles, I snapped open the latch and met Stephen's treasures.

In sepia-hued and color-tinted images, his view of the world unfolded for me across glossy photographic paper. Golden clouds rolled in from the ocean's horizon at the brink of sunset. Sandpipers waded in foamy seawater that looked as frothy as the top of a lemon meringue pie. California missions stood against a backdrop of clear skies, their adobe walls cracked and crumbling and faded with time. Fields of wild poppies brought beauty and life to the dry desert floor. Biplanes glided over the Pacific, casting wrinkled shadows across blue-tinged waves.

I also found his older photographs from Oregon, which didn't possess the same clarity and skill as his more recent work, but they were beautiful just the same. Mighty Mount Hood with its snow capped triangle of a peak. Portland's Steel Bridge spanning the Willamette River in the heart of the city. My eleven-year-old head, smothered beneath one of my giant white bows, while I perched on the picket fence at the edge of my front yard. Stephen had written one simple word on the back of my photograph—*Shell*—as if I didn't need further explanation. I liked that. It made me feel I wasn't as confusing and complicated as I thought.

He even included a self-portrait in his collection, taken December 1917, before his dad had died. Stephen sat on the boulders of the seawall across the street from his house and held up a sign that read A PORTRAIT OF THE ARTIST AS A YOUNG MAN. Strands of his short brown hair blew across his forehead, and I could practically taste the salt on the breeze rustling around him. He smiled in that way of his that revealed the dimple I enjoyed, and his eyes looked peaceful and free.

Glass negatives also awaited inside the case, nestled in protective sleeves, as fragile as if they were his children. I imagined taking his treasures to his mother, laying them in her lap, and coaxing her back to the world through his work.

"You're not disappearing without a trace," I said to his face in the photograph. "Not if I can help it. Not a chance." I ran my finger down the picture's smooth edge. "I promise to try to stop this world from mucking up everything so badly. And you know I'm good to my word."

I repacked his case and clicked the lid shut.

With one hand clutching the handles of my mother's bag and the other gripping Stephen's treasures, I left the post office and walked home through the swelling celebrations of the war's end. Model Ts puttered down the streets, their squeaky horns honking like ecstatic ducks. Americans of all ages and sizes and colors crept out of their bolted-up houses and re-membered what it was like to smile and laugh and throw their arms around one another for a kiss. Firecrackers popped and shimmered on the sidewalks. "The Star-Spangled Banner" soared out of windows. Drivers tied cans to the backs of cars and wagons, and the air filled with the joyous music of tin clattering against asphalt.

The festivities rose out of the crematorium smoke and the rambling piles of coffins and the black crepes scarring neighborhood doors, which made the bliss of victory all the sweeter. We were all survivors—every last one of us who limped our way out to the sidewalks that afternoon and spit in Death's cold face.

I tightened my hold on Stephen's case of photographs and my own treasures and kept plodding forward to my new home on the edge of a city that had sheltered me during the worst of the storm. The weight of the world lifted from my shoulders enough for me to raise my chin and hold my head higher. A warm breeze whispered through my hair. My own restless soul settled farther inside my bones.

I was ready to live.

Ready to come back fighting.

AUTHOR'S NOTE

I BECAME INTERESTED IN THE BIZARRE AND DEVASTATING year 1918 around the age of twelve, when I saw an episode of a television show called *Ripley's Believe It or Not!* I learned about two girls in England in 1917—sixteen-year-old Elsie Wright and her ten-year-old cousin, Frances Griffiths—who claimed to have photographed fairies. Several investigators, including the novelist Sir Arthur Conan Doyle (Sherlock Holmes's creator) and the photography expert Harold Snelling, deemed the girls' fairy pictures genuine, and the two cousins became famous. The narrator of *Ripley's* explained that people believed in the photographs because World War I was so horrifying. I wondered exactly how atrocious the era had been if grown, educated people were convinced fairies could be caught frolicking in the English countryside.

As an adult, I read "The Man Who Believed in Fairies," by Tom Huntington, an article that appeared in *Smithsonian* magazine, and I again learned about Elsie and Frances and Sir Arthur Conan Doyle and grew further intrigued by their story. The article described the Victorian era's Spiritualism craze, which had spread like wildfire across America and

Europe starting in the 1840s. Spiritualism had gained new popularity during the desperate years of the First World War.

Why was the World War I period so horrifying? For starters, innovations in war technology, such as machine guns, high-explosive shells, and mustard gas, provided new means of terror, injury, and death on the battlefields. Furthermore, the influenza pandemic of 1918 (this particular strain was known as the "Spanish flu" and the "Spanish Lady") killed at least twenty million people worldwide. Some estimates run as high as more than one hundred million people killed. Add to that the fifteen million people who were killed as a result of World War I and you can see why the average life expectancy dropped to thirty-nine years in 1918—and why people craved séances and spirit photography.

The flu hit hard and fast in the fall of 1918, targeting the young and the healthy, including men in the training camps and trenches. The baffling illness then waned shortly after the war's end, on November 11, leaving as mysteriously as it had arrived.

Flu vaccines were crude and scarce, so people resorted to folk remedies to save themselves from the illness. Every preventive flu measure and cure described in this book came from historical accounts of the pandemic.

The contest that Julius Embers tries to win is based upon *Scientific American*'s 1923–24 offer of twenty-five hundred dollars to the first person to produce authentic paranormal phenomena in front of a committee of five. Renowned escape artist and magician Harry Houdini loathed phony mediums and their use of magic tricks in the dark, so he helped judge the entries. No one ended up going home with the prize.

Dr. Duncan MacDougall truly did weigh dying tuberculosis patients on an industrial-sized scale in 1901 to explore the loss of the soul at the moment of death. Most scientists consider his work to possess very little merit due to the many weaknesses in his studies.

For more odd and fascinating forays into psychical research and Spiritualism, explore the wealth of information found in such books as *Spook: Science Tackles the Afterlife*, by Mary Roach (W. W. Norton & Co., 2005); *A Magician Among the Spirits*, by Harry Houdini (Arno Press, 1972; original printing 1924); and *Photography and Spirit*, by John Harvey (Reaktion Books, 2007).

For more information about World War I's devastating effects on the lives of the people who fought and on Americans back home, I recommend *The Last Days of Innocence: America at War, 1917–18*, by Meirion and Susie Harries (Vintage Books, 1998); *Shell Shock*, by Wendy Holden (Channel 4 Books, 2001); and *Bonds of Loyalty: German Americans and World War I*, by Frederick C. Luebke (Northern Illinois University Press, 1974). Be sure to also explore poems and books by such writers as Wilfred Owen, Siegfried Sassoon, Ernest Hemingway, and Katherine Anne Porter: gifted artists who were actually there.

ACKNOWLEDGMENTS

TO MY PATIENT, OPTIMISTIC, HARDWORKING AGENT, Barbara Poelle, who swore we'd get this book published even if it meant she'd have to bruise her knuckles banging down doors: Thank you from the bottom of my heart. We did it!

To my editor, Maggie Lehrman: Thank you for your amazing, insightful, and inspiring notes and for sharing (and improving upon) my vision of this novel. I'm so incredibly grateful you took a chance on my historical tale. To everyone at Abrams who's helped me share this book with the world (Maria T. Middleton, Laura Mihalick, and the rest of the crew): I'm honored to have your talents behind this book.

To my early readers, Carrie Raleigh, Ara Burklund, Kim Murphy, and Francesca Miller: Thank you for your time, feedback, and unwavering encouragement.

To Bill Becker of PhotographyMuseum.com, Sophia Brothers and Sophie Richardson at the Science & Society Picture Library, Holly Reed at the National Archives and Records Administration, David Silver of the International Photographic Historical Organization, and Stephen Greenberg, Crystal Smith, and Douglas Atkins at the U.S. National

Library of Medicine: Thank you for fielding all my historical image questions.

To Mrs. Betsy Martin and Ms. Kathie Deily, formerly of Crown Valley Elementary School: Thank you for making my writing feel special when I was a kid.

To my grandpa, Ward Proeschel, born in 1915: Thanks so much for sharing your memories of the early twentieth century with me.

To my parents, Richard and Jennifer Proeschel: Thank you for my life, and thank you for giving me the gift of the love of reading.

To my sister, Carrie Raleigh: You've been my first reader ever since we were children, and your love, companionship, and enthusiasm mean the world to me. I love you, Bear!

Last, but most certainly not least, thanks to my husband, Adam, and our two kids, for their steadfast patience, love, and support. This one's for you, my loves.